True *Colours*

Book Two of the Soul Song Duology

LOUISE MURCHIE

First Edition, February 2023

Second Edition, March 2024

Book Cover designed by Clare Bentley

Dedication

AND ACKNOWLEDGEMENTS

For my ever-suffering husband and kids. Tina, Nat, Sam (my editor!) my sister, parents, in-laws and friends who I consider family, and other family members who genuinely know me, and have helped me write another romance; thank you!

Contents

Chapter One

Seeing Him Off

Chris

I watch one of the huge TV screens in the mess hall as I wait for my best friend and pilot, Byron Grievson. The names on the screen seem familiar, and I'm sure the woman being featured is my friend's sister, though I've never met her. She'd be damn hard to forget, having the same blue eyes and black hair that my friend does.

The entire mess hall is in silence, and I glance across when I sense movement; Byron is making his way into the mess hall. As he's about to speak, the broadcaster does, and anything my friend was going to say is committed to silence.

"To repeat, reports of a terrorist attack in Edinburgh continue this evening. It is believed to have been thwarted by these three individuals," the newscaster drones on as images of armed police swarming around are lost to the image of the three involved. "It is believed that the lady in red, a former RAF Military Police Officer, has been injured. Police are not confirming that report at this time."

There's live footage from a helicopter above the incident, blue lights flashing all around. I have to weave my way through colleagues as Byron turns on his heel and marches away.

"Wait up!" I shout, needing him to slow down and engage that clever brain of his, not his hot head.

"Can't," he spits out, and I have to increase my pace to catch up.

"You can! Give yourself a minute! You go knocking on the fruits' door like you are…" My words do what I cannot physically do: they make him pause. "And his Mrs answers…" I add, with a strong tone of caution. He glares down at me, knowing I'm right.

"Fuck!" He turns and growls about one hundred paces from the Commander's front door, the veins on his neck showing. He runs his hands through his thick black hair, and his usually cool blue eyes go pale. If the Commander's wife opens the door as I calculate, he needs to be composed and collected. I watch him take a deep breath.

"That's it, and another one, buddy," I coach, trying not to smirk. He nods at me, and I give him a soft grin. I straighten up, and he copies as he takes another breath, making him stand to his full six-foot-three height. He walks confidently to the Commander's front door, knocking firmly three times. Byron takes a step back and waits.

We don't have to wait long, and as I thought might happen, the Commander's wife answers.

"Lieutenant," she greets Byron by his rank with a smile, and he nods in polite reply.

"Sorry to trouble you, ma'am," he begins, sounding calm and collected, "but I need a word with the Commander, please."

"Err…in here," she says and ushers us in. I follow and wait in the hallway, allowing Mrs Robinson to shut the door behind us.

"Grievance," I hear our Wing Commander greet Byron, and I just hope he keeps a lid on his temper long enough to explain what he wants and why.

"Sorry to bother you, sir, but a personal situation has come up." I hear Byron begin his request and a few seconds pass. "Regarding that, sir," I hear him say respectfully, and I peek through the door to see the Commander has the news on, though the TV is now muted. I quietly thank the gods he's keeping his cool; his temper can explode like an Italian volcano.

"The woman in red, sir, is my sister. I'm the only family we both have in the UK." I try not to react to the confirmation of my suspicions.

I hear the Commander reply, and I lose the conversation, though I guess by the fact we're still here that the Commander is granting Byron's emergency leave. Several minutes pass, and I wait, counting the pattern on the Commander's wallpaper; anything to distract myself. Right now, I need to be the one that's focused and calm—something Byron is not always good at.

Byron emerges from the living room, thanks Mrs Robinson, apologising again for the intrusion, before we head out of the door, and back to the barracks.

"I'm gonna need to borrow a car," he says, and I grin.

"You can borrow mine, if you fuel her up as you leave," I reply, letting my laughter show; he's predictable if nothing else.

"Cheers, pal," he thanks me heartily as we walk.

"So, that's your sister?" I ask as my voice uncharacteristically rises. "I've never seen her before," I tell him. *I know I'd like to meet her!*

"You've not met, but you did speak with her a few times when she has called and we've been together," he says as we walk briskly. "She was at Lossie and left the service when we were at Brize." He grins. Byron and I met at Brize over a game of pool, a few beers and the local 'talent' and got along like a house on fire. We've watched each other's backs for nearly six years. In eighteen months, I will leave the RAF, and Byron will be leaving just weeks behind me. "I haven't had a chance to see her much. She went overseas with her new job and hasn't long returned," he continues as we reach the barrack's door.

We make quick work of the stairs and as we reach his door, I ask, "Who were the guys she was with?" He motions for me to come in, and I do, knowing I can help him.

"Her employers. You've heard of Big Mac?" he asks. I ponder; the name is familiar and then I remember.

"One of those guys was Big Mac?" I grin and lean against the desk. "You two did not get on," I state, remembering the stories I've been told. Byron nods.

"Yeah, I know," he sighs. "But, she started working for the McGowan men. She hated retail security." He finishes packing, zips the bag shut, and I watch him put on some shoes, then grab a pair of trainers.

"So you're going to drive to Edinburgh? Where will you go when you get there?" I ask, wondering how he'll find her in such a large, complex city. He pulls his phone out of his pocket and checks a messaging platform most of us use.

"Find her, I've got her new address," he says. "Then I'll make sure she's okay. The news will travel, and I'll bet I get a call from Papa as I head up," he says, not sounding happy about that, but resigned to the fact it would happen.

"Phone," I order, and he hands it over. I check the type of cable he needs and realise it's not one my car has. I go to his desk and hand him a charging cable and a car USB adaptor. My charger is built-in, so he'll need these.

"Cheers, bud!" he says, packing the cable and things into a jacket pocket. Then I give him back his phone and my car keys. "I'll be careful," he tells me; he knows that car is my pride and joy.

"Yeah, don't bloody speed though, okay?" I caution him, knowing he has a lead foot. He inhales deeply, seeming calmer after he does, and then we head down to the car. Byron treats my car as his, tossing his bag onto the back seat and jumping in, so I follow picking the passenger seat. My friend drives us as far as the front gates, then I hop out and have a brief word with the on-duty guardsman, explaining he's got a family emergency. My colleague nods, quickly checks Byron's paperwork and lets him out. I wave him off and begin my walk back to the barracks for some kip when the tail lights have vanished.

The following night, I'm watching the quiet road outside the base; it's a tedious job, but somebody's gotta do it. Grievance told me he'd made it to his sister's place, alive and in one piece.

The assault rifle strap sits over my shoulder with the safety on as I quietly patrol the perimeter of RAF Waddington, which is both a comfort and a deterrent. In the gatehouse, a young colleague observes the same road via perimeter security cameras and we check in via the headsets as required.

This unit has been on rotation since twenty-hundred and slowly, we rotate out for a comfort break, a hot drink and a snack. It's nearly one am when a car comes hurtling onto the driveway and skids to a halt, turning off its lights. Before we can tell them to put their hands up, another car follows suit. The single female in the first car looks petrified, more so when she glances over her shoulder.

"Hostiles," my colleague states and all eyes and guns are trained on the new car that we notice has four men in it. I hear Boomerang next to me reciting something as the second car peels away with a screech of tyres and a dust cloud from the grit.

She repeats it on the radio to the gatehouse and gets an acknowledgement. We switch our focus to the first car; the lone woman.

With red hair, freckles and a nervous smile, she greets us, relief showing on her face, even with these floodlights.

"I'm sorry to drive up like that, but I needed some help." She gulps the air a few times from the wide-open driver's door. "They started following me at the lights and I panicked," she tells us, thumbing to where the second car was. "They were right up my arse too!"

"Who are you?" I demand, not really liking her driving style or that she just assumed we'd help.

"Rosie Mallard, former 47th from Brize." At those words, I feel my blood pressure dropping. "I'm not going to do anything weird, Corporal, I promise, but I am going to get out of the car and touch the ground so I stop panicking, okay?" She waits for my slight nod and then does that, though not with her knees.

Heartlands comes up to us a moment later, his Birmingham accent so different from my London one and Josie's Australian twang; his nickname is because he's from the Heartlands area of Birmingham.

"Called the civvies, they're on their way," he states. "Is she all right?" he asks as he looks across at the red-haired lady. She's not wearing much to be out past midnight, just some shorts and a t-shirt that looks like it's covered in paint.

"Get her inside, into the warm," Josie instructs, and we gape at her. "What? Do you want to have the ambulance here or the medics out to treat her for going into shock too? Move it!" she commands, giving us our orders in no uncertain terms. Without further hesitation, we're helping this lady formerly of the 47th.

An hour later, the civvie police finally decide to show up, and I can hear them give our Sergeant a bunch of excuses. The woman's been in the side gatehouse, wrapped in spare fatigues to keep her warm—well, warmer than her clothes did—for over fifty minutes already. I moved her car after we waited for the civilian police for ten minutes.

I can hear our Sergeant and the normal police talking. So much for being a priority.

"You guys are sure that's the licence plate?" the civilian officer asks. I try not to roll my eyes at his stupid question; of course we're bloody sure. We even have it recorded.

"Yes, we are quite sure. Would you like to see the surveillance footage?" the Sergeant asks, and a few seconds later, I hear the sound of tyres peeling onto the car park as that small incident is replayed. I glance up and see the Wing Commander heading towards us. *Just brilliant.*

"Sarge, fruit is here," I tell him. My Sergeant, Dave "Rum" Hopkins, glances at me, nods, and then turns just as the Wing Commander comes up to the gatehouse.

"Sir," Hopkins salutes the WC, who salutes back.

"What's the latest?" he asks Hopkins.

"Seems the civilian lot don't consider us a priority, sir," Hopkins states. I can hear the civilian copper flounder and flap in a meek protest.

"Let me convey this to you, which has just come via your Commissioner," the WC states to the civilian officer, who is now just as white as the bedsheets we're issued. "You're to find these idiots so that the young lady can go home and this *military* base can go back to normal operations. And if by chance," the WC continues as he begins to leave the gatehouse, "those idiots come back..." He nods to Hopkins who takes his assault rifle safety off.

The civilian officer gulps and heads back to his car as quickly as he can, leaving us to our business.

"Hopkins, you have permission to incapacitate them however you need to, should they return," the WC orders when the civilian copper has driven off the car park.

"Yes, sir!" Hopkins salutes, and we do too. We can only watch as the WC heads back to his home, and we all take our safety off.

It's my turn to check on the lady around three am, but that's because it's my coffee break time. I find her holding a cup of something hot and eating a sandwich that the kitchen sent through.

"You managed to find the chow?" I ask, not caring that she did. The kitchen usually makes enough to last all night, then a little more.

"Yeah, the Aussie lady said to help myself when I got hungry. Wish they'd hurry up and find these gits. I could do with going home," she tells me.

"Did you get any shut-eye?" I ask, and she nods.

"A little. It's a bit like being on deployment, or pre-deployment: too keyed up to sleep being somewhere strange, but the want to sleep is there."

I nod. "We've got a few more hours on duty, and this is the last break. We'll come and get you when we hear from the civilian police."

The woman nods. "Err...you do know your safety is off," she tells me, and I grin.

"Fruit's orders," I reply, and she holds her head up a little straighter and nods in return.

"Oh fuck..." she whispers, then bites a good chunk of the sandwich off and begins to chew it slowly. I quickly grab something from the tray—tuna, mayo—and make quick work of it, downing the cola when necessary.

"You were with the 47th?" I ask, needing to confirm what she said earlier.

"Yes. Rosie Mallard," she replies, and I grin, trying to remember her name, but I'm useless at remembering names. Numbers, I've got. Names? Not so much; not until I know you, or can associate you with someone or something. Mallard. That's a duck. An animal.

"Well, Rosie, try and get a little more shut-eye. We'll be on shift until oh-six," I confirm, and she nods.

"Thank you, Corporal," she tells me. Well, she knows what the marks on my epaulettes mean and how the guns work; very few do.

Just before oh-five-hundred, the civilian officer from earlier comes back and asks to see Rosie. Boomer takes him through, and ten minutes later, they're leaving the side gatehouse, greeted by Hopkins.

I'm trying to focus on my job as well as what's happening in their little huddle. I see the red-haired woman take the fatigue jacket off and hand it to Boomer.

"We can stand down," Hopkin's voice comes over the earpieces. "The men that showed up behind her earlier have crashed their car, all four have been apprehended."

I nod to Rosie as she gets escorted by Boomer to her vehicle and then carefully drives out of the base, a chest of drawers sitting in the back of her medium-sized car. She waves as she carefully leaves, and when I get to the control gatehouse again, I quickly ask about what had happened.

"The four men were drugged up and the car was stolen. They crashed it. They were high, but the civvie cops found several six-inch knives, a converted revolver and a pile of drugs," Boomer tells me, seething as the words fall out.

I can tell I'm catching flies, and I consciously have to close my mouth.

"If she hadn't been quick in thinking and turned up on base..." I start, to which Josie nods.

"Tell me about it, Stevo, she was as lucky as sin that she was one of us in a former life," Josie admits and nods as I take over the camera control for the last time this shift.

I can't wait to tell Grievance.

CHAPTER TWO

The Woman

CHRIS

At oh-six-hundred, we're relieved and debriefed after the evening's event, and I can finally get some sleep.

Grievance has until tomorrow to return and indicates via text he will, though he's not happy about leaving his sister in the state she's in. I don't fully understand what he means, but the tone tells me something else has happened, and he also said 'her men'; I'll find out more when he's back.

I'm on perimeter duty but at the other end of the base tonight. I shrug when Josie laments about it, but there's not much we can do. If Rum says that's our point of interest tonight, then that's our point of interest.

"Have you heard anything about that woman from last night?" Josie asks, and I shake my head.

"Should I have?" I respond, knowing that she didn't give me many details and I didn't give any about myself either.

"No, just wondered if you had, that's all. I hope she got home okay. What a thing to be subjected to!"

"Yeah, wasn't nice for her, but at least they're in custody," I say, not caring one way or the other, but I don't say that part. Josie nods at me and then we're off: watching, listening and patrolling. Grievance texts to say he's heading back to base. I reply on my break that I'll be coming off nights and I'll meet him when he's back.

I get a thumbs up, then it's business as usual until the shift changes.

I grin as I hear my car come around the corner, knowing that Grievance is driving it. He's on the phone when I lay eyes on him, so I hold back until he's finished.

"Doesn't mean I like it," he snips at who he's talking with. They must be Scottish, it's one of the few times that accent of his comes out.

"Cheerio," he mutters, pocketing the phone.

"Did you have a good weekend?" I ask and he tells me of his sister's state, her flight at four am this morning to the airport, and his hopes she's gone to be with their parents.

"Fuck," I reply. "We both had an interesting weekend then!" I grin, filling him in. "The base was on alert Saturday at oh-one-hundred. Some former RAF woman drove onto the base in a panic because she was being followed. Gatehouse called the local police who eventually came. When the woman gave her statement, the police asked if we'd house her. We stood down at oh-five-hundred when the car that was chasing her was found after they'd crashed it into a row of parked cars."

"What the fuck?" he hisses, his eyes wide at my tale.

"Yeah, the police came at oh-five and escorted the lady home. She was ex-47th, like you." Byron's face contorts slightly before he schools his expression.

"What did you say happened to the car that was following her?" he asks.

"They crashed it," I repeat. "Car of four men, drugged up in a stolen vehicle, armed with six-inch knives and a converted revolver. Bottles of booze and some drugs were scattered around the car, the cops said. If the lady hadn't pulled onto the base, goodness knows what would have happened to her."

"She was lucky," he agrees and then he swallows. "What did you say her name was?" He runs his hand through his hair. I hadn't given it out because I am terrible with names until I get to know a person, something Byron knows.

"Rosie something..." Byron stops dead; his eyes are wide and the colour drains from his face.

"Be very clear, Chris," Byron bites through a clenched jaw. *What the hell?* I've never seen him like this over a name. "What was her name?" he repeats slowly as if I'm thick and didn't understand the first time.

"Rosie...she had an animal name..."

"Mallard. Was it Rosie Mallard?" he questions slowly, and I nod.

"Yeah, that was it..." I tilt my head at him, concerned about how he's acting and looking. His knees give way a little before his legs lock to hold him up. "You've gone a bloody funny colour!" I declare, and I can only watch as Byron runs his hands through his hair, over his stubbly jaw and lets out a sigh that deflates him. "You know her?" I ask—that's the only way he'd react as he was. *Who the hell is she?* Byron nods and swallows a lot as if his throat has suddenly stopped working.

"Need to shower and get onto shift," he says. I nod, and we begin walking back to the barracks. I don't push my friend for more information; he'll tell me when he's ready.

Byron is on a week's deployment elsewhere and for a week, I'm itching to know who this woman is to him. He's only ever mentioned that he was with the 47th, that there was someone there, but she moved bases and didn't want to be found, at least not by him.

He texts me to ask if I want to go with him to find the red-haired woman and if so, to pack an overnight bag. If not, can he borrow my car? Well, there's a story I never knew about my best friend, so I agree that I'm along for the ride.

On the day his crew are due back, he knocks on my door. I'm watching some videos on TikTok and YouTube to pass the time.

"Hey, you! Just finished?" I ask, pleased he's back and he nods.

"Yeah, give me fifteen?" he asks and I wave his smelly ass off.

"So," I coax as we walk to the car. "What's the game plan?"

"We find Duckie, I apologise and maybe I recover from whatever the hell she says and does to me."

I turn and gape at him. "And you're just going to take it?" I ask as we pass the gatehouse and I start driving us down to Milton Keynes. This isn't the Byron I know.

"Got to. I was an arse on the last flight we had. I was a total '*deficiente*' during and afterwards. She let me know it, Big Mac let me know it, but Papa made me understand *how*. By the time he'd done that, Duckie had left the base and no one would tell me where she was. I tried to contact her, but the communications came back silent."

So she ghosted him, but it sounds like he deserved it. We're quiet for the rest of the way, me lost in driving and Byron in his head.

"And you're sure it was her that weekend you went to Edinburgh?" I ask, breaking the comfortable silence between us as we reach the edge of Milton Keynes.

"Oh aye, I'm sure," he says. "There aren't many female pilots of the 47th, especially named Mallard," he explains. "I just need to apologise for being a '*deficiente*'," he repeats. I wonder what that word means and so give him a confused look.

He sighs and tells me it means "moron", which for him, is all too apt.

"Moron," I repeat as I slap him on the arm jokingly, as we take another turn into a quiet cul-de-sac and up to a small bungalow that needs a fair bit of work done to the exterior.

Byron knocks firmly on the door of the bungalow. The guttering is partially hanging off and needs replacing, not to mention the grass that needs cutting, the hedges trimmed back and slabs that need demossing. The door creaks open and an old man peeks out from the crack. I notice that he's using the security chain; someone wants him safe.

"Mr Mallard? We're ex-colleagues of Duckie, sorry, Rosie," Byron explains and the old man nods.

"And?" the old man snips, not giving us an inch.

"We wanted to check up on her. I'm Byron, and this is my friend Chris. Is she in?" he asks and the old man shakes his head.

"She's out," he states, not giving us a scrap of information. As wise as he is, his answers begin to frustrate the hell out of me.

"Could we wait for her? Maybe help around the garden while we do?" Byron offers and I refrain from poking him in the ribs. Looking at the slabs and seeing that walking cane leaning against the wall, I see where Byron is going with this and simmer my temper. Beats waiting in the car anyway.

"Rosie was going to start that; she's bringing the new guttering back," he tells us. Okay, so his girl has a task list that's probably as long as the old man's cane. Now I'm keen to help.

"Let us help," I echo Byron's request, adding what I hope will be persuasive power. "We'll stay outside. Here are our military IDs." I pull mine out of my wallet and hand it over. He reads it and hands it back and then Byron does the same.

"You want to help?" he asks again.

"We want to check in with Duckie; I've long since lost her number. I was in the 47th at the same time," Byron explains, and the old man's eyes narrow at Byron's statement.

"Were you? She never mentioned you," the old man says, getting a jab in at Byron.

"I'm sure she has, though the language...I was a moron the last time I saw her and I just wanted to catch up with her and say sorry," he admits in a tone that's almost begging.

Mr Mallard thinks about it for a few seconds, then nods. The door closes and we hear the chain coming off the door.

"I think I know who you are. She'll be a few more hours yet, she's gone to take something to a client of hers, and she'll be picking up the guttering on the way back."

"Where would you like us to start, sir?" I ask, remembering the manners instilled in me. My parents weren't around much and my uncle took me under his wing when I was three, and gave me a home and guidance when Mum and Dad couldn't. Or more to the point, wouldn't.

"Where would you like to begin?" he asks, shuffling about. I spy a walking frame and head over to it, bringing it to him.

The old man chews on his dentures for a second, then sighs and swaps over to the frame.

"I'll get you the keys to the garden shed," he says. "It's the smaller one. Don't go near the big one," He holds Byron's gaze. "That's not a storage shed," he tells us forcefully. We nod, not wishing to pry any further. We don't need to know what goes on in there.

The garden shed is quite well kitted out; a few spades, hard brushes, a power washer that Mr Mallard isn't too sure still works and other gardening tools, including a hedge trimmer and a decent lawn mower.

"Maybe we start out the front?" I suggest. "It'll be the first thing she sees," I hint and Byron nods with the usual mischievous grin I've come to rely on.

Hours later, we're shirtless due to the heat of the day and the physical work. Rosie's not back yet, but we've scraped the moss from the slabs at the front, power-washed them and tidied up. The hedges have been trimmed and we've filled up the two garden recycling bins that Mr Mallard has.

We cut the grass front and back and tidied up the edges. We've even taken down the broken guttering, though we've left the brackets up so I can reuse the holes; I can do that fairly easily with another pair of hands.

We're sitting at the picnic table, which we've also cleaned, enjoying a long, cold drink when we hear the sound of a car pulling up, a door closing close by, and then a few moments later, a boot closing.

"There she is," Mr Mallard says and motions for us to stay sitting. "Best I go see her," he tells us and he shuffles off, but switches to his cane.

We hear voices, a woman's and Mr Mallard's, then they come through the gate and Rosie stops dead when she sees us. The glare she's giving Byron could fell an elephant.

"Grievance." She nods to Byron, her voice clipped.

"Duckie." He smiles, his voice light, as if he's just seen an angel.

"How did...ah..." Her eyes swing to me and I grin. "Hello again," she greets me, giving me a huge smile. Then her gaze switches to Byron.

"What are you doing here?" she asks. The glare is back. "Dad?" she asks a few moments later when Byron helps her dad sit down in the chair he's been using for most of the time we've been here.

"I'm fine," the old man states. "These two young men have been great company today and they've helped with the yard," he explains as he eases himself back into his chair.

"Have they?" she questions, raising her eyes at Byron.

"We have. This is my colleague, Chris," Byron motions to me and I offer my hand.

"Thank you for the help the other week," she says, her voice warm and courteous to me as we shake hands. *What the hell did Byron say or do to her to make her this frosty to him?*

"You're welcome. Did you bring the new guttering back?" I ask as I finish off the large pint of iced squash her father made up. "Your dad said you were going to," I add, more to try and relieve the tension that's now thick in the air.

"Yeah, it's out the front," she tells me in a slightly distracted tone.

"I'll go start on those brackets." I nod to Byron, he needs space to sort this out. "Mr Mallard." I nod to her dad, then I head to the front garden and the job we now need to finish.

While Byron's getting chewed out for whatever the hell he did, I go through what Rosie's brought for the guttering. She's kept it the same shape but changed the colour. I noticed that the guttering at the back looks new and I can't help but wonder who did that.

Grabbing the electric screwdriver and the bits, I get to work replacing the brackets before Byron arrives in whatever state Rosie has left him in.

Byron appears nearly ten minutes later. I've been up and down the ladder fetching this and that; I could use a toolkit belt to hold the small parts. Or Byron.

"Good, you're here," I say to him and he scowls at me. "We could leave?" I suggest, noncommittally, but Byron shakes his head. He won't leave, not yet. I won't until we're finished with this task at least.

"I said we'd finish this," he states and I nod, in understanding.

"Fair enough. Let's get it sorted. Can you pass me these brackets up? I've got two more to do." We're fitting the first line of the black guttering when another car pulls up. We hear the side gate open and a woman climbs out of the car. She's got short brown hair, curvy in all the right ways, so I make sure my mouth is shut. *Dear God, she's gorgeous!*

"You guys are getting that up quickly," she says and I grin.

"It's easy enough," I reply and smile at her, hoping to see one from her.

"Yeah, but you are making good time. Thank you," Rosie says sincerely. I smile and nod at Rosie, who looks much prettier in the daylight than under the orange floodlights of the gatehouse. Byron nods and then turns to the task at hand and we mount the first piece into place.

The women head out into the back garden and Byron sighs.

"Let's do this and leave," I suggest and at that, he nods, though I can tell he's just going through the motions for now. We quickly get the guttering up and connected.

"How do you know how to do this?" Byron asks as we connect another piece and I grin.

"My uncle runs a jack-of-all-trades, doesn't he? Taught me a few things," I remind him, my London accent coming out thicker than usual. He nods and rolls his eyes, but mostly at himself.

"I forgot," he mutters, reaching for the guttering.

We click the last piece into place, corners and all; now we just need to test it. We climb down and the side gate squeaks as it opens.

"Hey, focus," I hiss at him. Her friend bites her bottom lip as she looks me up and down; I have to say, I like what I'm seeing too.

"The guttering is up and all connected. We're just going to grab the hose and test it," Byron informs the girls. The new lady hands me a pint of squash and I down it as if it's my first drink after being in the Sahara. I grab the hose from Byron, winking at her.

"Testing time," I cheerfully declare and begin walking the hose to the front garden. I turn to see Byron standing at the side gate. I give him a thumbs up and he nods to someone else, the new lady I think, as Rosie comes past him to see the test.

I angle the hose head at the joint with the neighbours, which doesn't leak. Then I test the other connection pieces and it all trickles down the guttering smoothly.

"Thanks! You've saved me from an awful job," Rosie gushes, smiling at us both. Her voice is light and normal. Her hands are in her back pockets, shoulders relaxed and she's not glaring at Byron, which is a slight change.

"And you saved me from it too," her friend states. "She'd have dragged me into helping," she declares, a little snark showing.

"Then I'm glad I tagged along with Grievance here," I say, keeping my eyes firmly on the friend. I can see introductions aren't going to be made, so I take it upon myself to do them.

"I'm Chris," I state and her face falls for a brief second before she schools her expression.

"I'm Emma," she responds, extending her hand.

Emma sends Rosie a very strange look, probably girl code for something. Byron grabs the hose reel and takes it back. I don't know who turned it off; Emma's hardly moved.

Rosie follows Byron and Emma lets out a huge sigh.

"He hurt her on an assessment flight," she mutters to me. "I didn't think he'd ever find her." She shivers at that point as if someone's walking over her grave, as my aunt is fond of saying.

"Yeah, he told me that he'd been a moron. I hope she forgives him. It'll mean we can all hang out," I suggest, allowing a small smile to sit on my lips.

"You'd...like that?" she asks, her nostrils flaring a little.

"I would, yeah," I admit. She's damn pretty and she's friends with Grievance's ex-colleague. In another time and place, I'd probably make a cheap pass at her and sleep with her for the night.

"We're working tonight, at a working men's club. Why don't you come and visit? There's darts, pool, beer..." She stops talking. "What's so funny?" she asks, frowning at my smile.

"Pool...American or British?" I ask and she grins.

"British, of course," she replies with a little smirk. "Shall we check in with those two?" she asks, motioning to the house.

"Guess we'd better," I reply, guiding Emma through. I go to touch her back but she flinches and I withdraw my hand. *Why would she do that? And who caused her to react like that?*

As we enter the garden, silence greets us.

"The girls are working at a bar tonight; Em says we should visit," I say, looking at Byron. He turns to look at Rosie.

"Will you be okay if we do that?" he asks and Rosie looks between her friend and me. Emma's making eyes at me and I have to admit, I'm struggling to look elsewhere when there's no conversation.

"Yeah, it'll be good. Come on by around eight?" she answers, and I nod in reply; so does Byron. There's a shuffling sound and we turn to see Mr Mallard coming up to us, using his walker.

"Are you okay, Dad?" Rosie asks, going over to him, reaching her arms out as if to steady him.

"Perhaps the young men need feeding?" he offers and reaches into his cardigan pocket, producing two twenty-pound notes.

"Mr Mallard, that's not necessary," Byron protests and Rosie joins in. At least they finally agree on something.

"Maybe not, but it's been nice having the company of you youngsters today," he says to us. As he looks at Byron, I can see there's an intensity there, as if he's trying to commit him to memory. "And you've worked hard," he continues, which is a statement of fact. I could eat a pizza on my own.

"Mr Mallard," Byron tries again, but the old man raises his hand.

"The pizzas are on their way," he tells us as he looks at his daughter. *Poor Rosie!* I can see her biting her lip to stop herself from expressing her thoughts.

"We can stay for the pizza, but then we have to go to the hotel and clean up, Mr Mallard," Byron explains to him. He's looking between father and daughter, and Rosie's scowl lessens.

"That's fine," he says as he nods at his daughter. I glance at Emma and widen my eyes a little. Talk about being in an awkward position!

Emma winks at me and gives me a quick grin. Maybe this isn't such a bad idea after all.

An hour later and I'm glad we stayed. This would have been too much for Rosie and her dad. Three huge pizzas, two side orders of garlic bread, and a few bottles of cola and we're pleasantly full.

"I'll leave you youngsters, to it," Mr Mallard says as he stands, steadying himself with his cane.

"Do you need a hand up, Dad?" Rosie asks and her father nods. As Rosie heads in with her dad, I begin clearing things away. At least there are no dishes to do. Minutes later, Rosie is back with us.

"Thanks, for sticking around; I had no idea he'd done that," she whispers as she looks at one window of the bungalow.

"It's okay and to be honest, the takeaway pizza was great," Byron enthuses. "It also meant you didn't have the burden of feeding us, and clearing away is easy," he adds. There's a slice left, but it's swiped up by Emma, who grins as she munches it before Byron can collapse the box.

"Are you going to be okay if we head off? I could do with a shower," Byron says. He's not the only one.

"We'll see you at the club later, won't we?" Emma asks as she looks at me intently for a moment. I nod briefly and then she's clearing away the drinks stuff, handing me the empty plastic bottles to put in the recycling bin as we go past.

"Sure thing," I reply with gusto, winking at her in an obvious way. She goes slightly pink and I can see Byron grinning. One glance at Rosie changes that, but he rolls his eyes at us and I see Rosie nodding with a smile on her face. At least she's smiling at Byron now.

"We'll see you later," he says to her, he dumps the boxes into the bin as we depart.

Byron finds details of a nearby Travelodge; everything else seems to be booked for the night. He manages to get us a twin bedroom, we couldn't get two singles, but at least there's breakfast on-site in the morning.

"That wasn't so bad," I state as we head to our room.

"Yeah...but I thought I'd feel..." He pauses and I wait for him to finish what he wants to say, how he wants to say it. "Free?" he suggests. "When she said she'd forgive me, but I kinda don't," he confesses as we head in.

"Breathe, mate, take the time to absorb the words." I dump my bag on the luggage rack and check out the bathroom. "Wanna shower first?" I offer, and Byron shakes his head.

"You carry on. I need to make a call," he tells me. I nod then grab my stuff to take into the bathroom, leaving my friend to call whomever he needs to.

I try to make my shower last twenty minutes, to give Byron time to make his call. When I emerge, he's tossing the phone onto the bed.

"You okay?" I ask. I've never seen my friend with his head as twisted as it is right now.

"Yeah, I was just chatting with Dad," he says as he grabs his shower things and clean clothes.

I nod. "Gotcha," I reply as Byron locks himself in the bathroom.

Chapter Three

The Best of Friends

Emma

When Rosie called to tell me that the pilot guy she's crushed on for years was in her garden, I had to go and see. I remember the drunken nights, the tears she cried.

"You didn't tell me he'd brought a hot friend!" I gush as I help Rosie prepare drinks. It has been a hot day and the guys need fluids.

"You didn't ask," she deadpans back. I nudge her and roll my eyes. "I seriously didn't expect to see him again, or learn he was based at Wadd," she tells me as she erects the sun umbrella. "Or that he'd even find me!" She sits in the chair, sighing as she does so, resting her head in her hands and closing her eyes.

She's not gotten over him and sitting at the garden table now brings those nights we've talked about it all back to me. I remember how drunk we'd get and what she had planned to say to him. I wonder if she has.

"So, how did he?" I ask and watch as Rosie pulls out her phone and begins texting. Her fingers fly across the screen, but I wait. Whoever she's texting is connected to this and there's only one person I know who had her details from those days.

"What did Mac say?" I ask as I carefully sip my drink when she puts her phone down. She only ever texts him when her dad takes a funny turn, or she's been drinking and she thinks about the man that's now here.

"That I need to build a bridge and get over it," she tells me. At least her situation is easier to get over. "Forgive myself, he said," she continues but scoffs as she speaks the words.

"He's right," I tell her with a serious look. "You've blamed *him* for how you reacted; you've chastised yourself regularly. Enough with it already, I agree with Mac! Build that bridge and get over it, girl," I tell her. *Again.*

She looks at the phone screen for a moment, but I continue to stare at Rosie. We've been friends since primary school; her dad was there for me far more than my useless parents ever were.

I give Rosie a stare, daring her to argue back.

"So how are you going to do that?" I prompt. She'd like to not discuss this, but the man is here. So is his hot friend and I don't want Rosie chasing them both away. I'm only just starting to look around after my recent ex.

"Not sure. I've spent so long blaming him," she says, then her mouth stops midway through forming a word. I wait. "But you're both right." She sighs. *Hallelujah!* "Byron's sister is lucky to have Mac in her corner," she adds. So that *is* how Byron found her.

"Shall we take some juice around to them?" I ask, but the guys come through just as I suggest it. *Typical!*

I hand Byron's friend a drink and watch him drink it down like it's the first drink he's had in forever. As his head tilts back, I quietly eye up his form. The t-shirt he has on just about fits him; it hints at the muscles and form underneath and I try not to drool over him. If his legs and everything else are like the top of him...I sigh inwardly. No way am I ever going to be lucky enough to do more than I have; my luck never runs that way.

"I'm Chris," he tells me and my heart sinks. He gives me a weird look and I hide my thoughts; I don't need to be letting him know I'm broken, though I feel my mind and my body are on two different planets on that subject.

When Byron goes to put the hose away, I take my chance to tell this Chris what happened between them, as best I can.

"He hurt her on an assessment flight," I say. "I didn't think he'd ever find her." I shiver at that point, recalling my ex's promise if I ever found someone else.

"Yeah, he told me he'd been a moron," Chris shares. "I hope she forgives him. It'll mean we can all hang out," he suggests and there's a wry little smile on those handsome lips.

"You'd...like that?" I ask, not quite believing this man wants to spend time with little old, useless, broken me.

"I would, yeah," he adds. I can't believe my luck.

"We're working tonight, at a working men's club," I blurt out, not wishing to think about why I'm telling him. "Why don't you come and visit? There's darts, pool, beer..."

and I stop talking as he starts chuckling. "What's so funny?" I ask, confused by the response.

"Pool...American or British?" he questions, and I can only grin.

"British, of course," I reply with a little attitude. "Shall we check in with those two?" I ask, motioning to Rosie and Byron.

"Guess we'd better." He goes to touch my back, but I flinch and he withdraws his hand. That movement...I need to get over my ex. As we enter the garden, silence greets us.

"The girls are working at a bar tonight; Em says we should visit," Chris says, looking at Byron. He turns to look at Rosie.

"Will you be okay if we do that?" he asks and Rosie looks between Byron's friend and me. I'm watching him, trying not to make a thing of it, but he's damn fine!

"Yeah, it'll be good. Come on by around eight?" Rosie suggests, and the guys nod in agreement.

When Dave produces money and tells us pizza is on the way, I can see Rosie fighting between telling her dad off and wanting the guys to stay. I mentally cross my fingers and I get glad when she relents. There's no way she, Dave and I would finish off three extra-large pizzas, two sides of garlic bread and bottles of cola. Though today, I'm beyond my usual level of hunger.

When the guys head off, I watch as their car vanishes, and then I turn to Rosie.

"He's called Chris," I blurt out. "What if he's the same?" I ask, wringing my hands together as my breath quickens.

"Em, there are good men and there are bad men." Rosie holds my hands. "Not all of them are called Chris and a name is just a name. He could have a different name and still be a decent guy. He was nice the night I got into trouble," she tells me. "And he certainly has eyes for you!" she adds.

"Goodness knows why," I state flatly and Rosie glares at me.

"Because you're beautiful, clever, smart and intelligent. How many words are in your latest novel?" she asks. Rosie and her father are the only other ones other than Chris Anderson who know my secret.

"Fifty thousand and I'm nowhere near finished," I tell her.

"Fifty thousand words more than I'm capable of," she says with a huge smile. "You underestimate yourself, Em. And we'd better hustle if we're going to be at work on time," she reminds me, checking her watch.

"See you at the club!" I tell her as I give her a huge hug, then I head off back to mine and grab a shower before I get ready to go to work while trying to rise above my warring emotions.

We arrive at the club just as Charlie is opening the bar section. The function room is starting to fill; there's a wedding anniversary being celebrated. Rosie and I get busy with the event, relieving our younger colleagues who are floundering with the orders. In no time, we have the normal service resumed and thankful customers.

I lose track of time and before I know it, we start rotating the younger girls in. I can see Colleen, Charlie's daughter, playing pool with Lottie, her girlfriend and I see Byron and Chris. I repress the shudder that I have about Chris having the same name as my ex. As Rosie said earlier, there are good men and bad men; names don't reflect their character.

I wave at him, then nudge Rosie to tell her they're here. They prop up the bar for a while, and when I see them next, they're sitting at a small table.

I've switched from the function room to the bar again. When things start to turn south, my stomach lurches and knots. A group of lads walk in, and they gaze around as if they're looking for someone. I don't see gang colours on them, but that's a possibility I'm all too aware of thanks to my ex.

They intentionally nudge Colleen when there's plenty of room to get past. She challenges them and they think she's easy pickings. Then Lottie gets involved and I see Byron and Chris stalk towards the confrontation.

"Rosie, it's kicking off bar side," I hiss at her, dragging the younger ones away to the function end as I pick up my phone. *Do I need to call the police?*

"Don't you even think about it," a voice bellows. Colin, the local copper, drinks here as it's usually quiet and off his beat.

Everyone in the bar is standing, watching, and waiting.

"You're not welcome here, lads," Colin tells them, showing them his ID.

"There's one of you," they taunt him, nudging each other.

"And a few military personnel here," Byron adds. I can see Chris cracking his knuckles, but he's off to Byron's side, like a wingman.

"Call it in," Rosie says and finishes serving her customer before handing off to a newer member of the staff. As I make the call, I can see Colleen put down the pool cue. Oh boy!

"Hello, police, please. Yes, hi. This is the Liberal Working Men's club on Upper Moore Street. We've had a group of lads just come in, causing trouble during a function..."

"Are there lives in danger?" the operator asks.

"Yes," I state and Rosie vanishes barside.

"I've dispatched several units to your location. Hang tight; help is on the way. Stay on the line with me," they say.

Moving the phone away from my mouth, I look at the situation unfolding and my blood runs cold. Charlie suddenly appears and I let out the breath I'd been holding.

"Get out," he orders them as he comes around to the barside from the function room. "Before I get you removed." Charlie's not a small man and he folds his burly arms over his chest.

"The police are on their way," I state as loud and clear as I can. Rosie is there now too.

"Get out," she clearly echoes. I can see the gang thinking about it and I hope they pay attention here. They turn and leave; Rosie, Lottie and Col lead the escort out of the bar, followed by Chris and Byron.

Several minutes pass and I forget to breathe, but then everyone comes back in, not a scratch on them. Charlie tells us that the military lads are to be given free soft drinks for the rest of the night and we nod in understanding.

Byron and Chris start to play pool; a fact Rosie notices but doesn't react well to. I smile at Chris each chance I get and he returns the looks with winks. Rosie catches Byron's eye a few times, though her reception is frostier now than it was earlier.

At the end of the night, the guys offer to walk Charlie, Lottie and Colleen home. Rosie scoffs at the idea, but Colleen is keen to take them up on the offer, telling them that they're wise. We walk with them and then we're heading back to a large car to be driven home. I decide that I can fetch my car in the morning.

At my flat, Chris jumps out and escorts me to my front door.

"Thank you," I tell him, genuinely pleased he's done this.

"Listen, this may be out of line, but I want to understand two things," he says to me.

"Oh?" I ask, going very quiet and still.

"Why do you flinch when I reach out to you? And will you let me kiss you?"

One is slightly related to the other. *Is there any harm in telling him?* There's only one way to find out.

"My ex, his name was Chris. He…" I stop for a moment, pulling up some reserves to tell this Chris about the old Chris. It's getting confusing; my head hurts already. "He hurt me…he grabbed me one time, left bruises. I ended it a few months ago, but he's found a way around me blocking his number."

Chris just nods; his lips are tight and his jaw is ticking. I've pissed him off and now I expect a verbal dressing down.

"Then he's a fucking moron," this Chris spits out in disgust. I blink.

"Wait…What?!" I gasp and Chris pulls his head back. *Is it not my fault?*

"I don't know what shit he's filled your head with, Em, but hell and no." He steps into me, lowering his voice. He's not touching me; he's not reaching out to grab me. "I want to kiss you. Hell, I want to do a lot more. But now is not the time. Let me have your number," he says and I recite it. He pulls his phone out and quickly taps it into the phone, then he rings it, and I can feel it vibrate in my back pocket.

"Save that number, that's me." He looks at me. "I won't ever force you, but I'm hoping that with all the eyes you've been sending my way all night, you're still up for a kiss?"

I nod and pull in a breath. "Yes," I whisper and then his lips are on mine, gently at first. His tongue begs for access, sweeping across my lips and instinct takes over. He pulls me to him and somehow I don't flinch. There's a hand at the back of my neck, a warm arm around my waist. As his tongue dances with mine, my body wakes up. I close my eyes and enjoy his kiss, just because it's intimate.

The kiss is making me forget my own name. How can this man—and this *is* a man—know how to do this? The lights behind my eyes go into various colours, a kaleidoscope and my breath is taken away.

When he stops, it's gradual. That wasn't a kiss; that was a claim. *Oh Lord, I've written about such kisses, but to experience one?* My heart rate has to be off the scale.

"Go in and lock the doors, Emma. I won't leave until I know you're safely inside. Does he have a key to here?" he asks and I shake my head.

"No, but he knows where I am," I state.

Chris makes a guttural sound in his throat that's almost a growl. "Go on, in you go. I'll contact you about tomorrow," he says and backs away. I go in, turning the light on so I can see and then I'm closing the front door, locking and bolting it. Through the living room window of my downstairs flat, I watch as Chris returns to the car and slowly, my friend and the men drive away.

Chapter Four

Learned Behaviours

Chris

Leaving Emma makes my chest hurt a little; something I've never felt before. Knowing that her ex, also a Chris, hurt her? Bruised her? Grabbed her and marked her, making her this skittish and unsure, makes me angry. My parents weren't the best, but they were better than that. My aunt and uncle were the ones who made sure I felt valued, appreciated and taught me how to do that in others. Her ex is already someone I want to meet down a dark alleyway, and I know there are plenty in my old area of London.

Byron drives the car back to Rosie's, and I'm lost in my head. As we pull up, Rosie hisses as she draws in a breath.

"Dad," she whispers harshly as the car stops. She jumps out and heads straight for the front door, though finding the keys thwarts her for a moment or two.

Byron is hot on her heels as they enter and I stand at the door whilst they check the house. I quietly shut the door behind me, but that makes Rosie jump. I give her the customary military nod and she responds with a tight smile that doesn't reach her eyes.

"Everything looks secure," I hear Byron tell Rosie as she enters the front room. I can hear her saying something and crying.

"Rosie?" Byron calls softly to her. I stand in the doorway, checking out what's going on. I can't see anything disturbed or unusual. "You're okay, I got you," Byron tells her, which makes her cry a whole lot harder.

Women and crying just ain't my bag, so I head off to the kitchen and pop the kettle on, ensuring that there's enough water to make three mugs of something hot. I find the caddy of tea bags and instant coffee, grateful for her not having just tea in stock.

I turn as Byron leads Rosie to the kitchen; she's half leaning on him, half walking. Considering she was an ice queen towards him for hours, I'm surprised, but something had changed in that room. I nod to Byron and quietly take my coffee out into the hallway.

I can hear them whispering in the kitchen and just as I come back from checking that there are no broken windows or anything else amiss, I hear what's tripped her off.

"Dad's been...getting sentimental of late." She sighs as if she's got the world's weight on those pretty freckled shoulders. "He's ill. He won't tell me just how ill he is and neither will his doctor. That patient and doctor privilege nonsense." She pauses for a second. "I know Dad has told him not to tell me, which must mean it's bad." I hear her blowing her nose.

They talk for a while and while I hear their conversation, my mind wanders to Emma. It's when I hear Byron saying that we'll pop by in the morning that an idea strikes me.

I enter the kitchen, and Rosie begins locking up as we prepare to leave. Byron stands by the front door until he's sure she's locked it and then we head to the hotel.

Byron commandeers the bathroom first, which doesn't bother me. I send a quick text to Emma, saying I'd like to spend the day with her. I don't expect to hear back and as I fall asleep, the scenarios she's possibly been through invade my dreams.

Over breakfast, I hear back from her.

Emma: I'd like to...What did you have in mind?

Chris: Not been to see the Enigma machine; I'd like to.

Emma: I've been before, but I wouldn't mind going again, let's do that. I'll just check with Rosie that she's okay spending the day with Byron.

I look up at Byron as he comes back from the coffee machine with two mugs of coffee. I already have mine, so they must be for him.

"Two?" I question, suspecting he's got more coffee in his veins than blood.

He shrugs. "Yeah, these mugs aren't big enough and I want to enjoy my breakfast while it's hot," he tells me. "So, what's the plan? I want to spend the day with Rosie..."

"And I want to spend the day with Emma. I've already asked her and she wants to go to Bletchley Park, so we'll head there, if you can persuade Rosie to put up with you for the day," I tease, shovelling some food into my mouth.

He grins and sends a text to Rosie, but it's as we're heading to her house in the car that he gets a response.

"Yep, I'm spending the day at Rosie's. She's going to be replacing her hall carpet." He gasps.

"Does she have the skills to do that?" I ask. She's like a DIY Queen.

Byron taps something on his phone and then he chuckles.

"She's been taught how to lay carpets by a neighbour who hired her for a few weeks this year!" He hmms, thinking about what she's said to him.

"Why does she need to learn all this?" I ask as we near her area.

"I have no idea," he says to me, turning his phone upside down and staring out of the window.

"Well, see if you can find out, 'cause now I'm curious," I tell him, sending him a smile.

"Will do," he tells me as he alights. I wave at them then I drive off, heading to Emma's flat.

When I get there, she's waiting for me out front.

"Hey! You're keen," I tease with laughter after she's climbed in and her face falls.

"Sorry, I got excited," she says very quietly and I kick myself; her quieter response doesn't match her earlier bounce, it's wrong.

"Hey." I idle the engine and turn to her. "Emma, look at me," I command and she does. She looks like she's about to burst into tears and is wringing her hands in her lap.

"I promise you, I'm not going to shout or tell you off. I don't know what your ex did or said to you to make you fearful of a tease, but I ain't him." She nods and I struggle with the words I have in my head. If I say what I think, I'm sure she'll run a mile, as she'll likely take it as me telling her off.

"I wanna start over again, okay?" I say, trying a different tack and she nods.

"I'm sorry," she whispers.

"Why are you sorry?" I ask, knowing already I'm going to dislike the answer, the truth that falls from those cherry-red lips of hers.

"For being too bouncy," she says and purses her lips together. I kick myself because I did it again.

"You weren't too bouncy. I hardly know you and to be honest," I say as I pull the car away from the curb, "I think I like you bouncy." I glance across and throw her a smile, which she returns.

I follow satnav's instructions and see Emma shake her head out of the corner of my eye.

"What do you know that the satnav doesn't?" I ask, picking up her body language. "You're more local, you're bound to know more," I encourage.

"Turn right at the next set of lights," she tells me and I do. I follow her instructions and we're at Bletchley Park about five minutes sooner than the satnav would have got us there.

"This rear car park is known to the locals. It doesn't fill up until last." She grins.

"Smart and pretty," I tell her, which makes her go red. We climb out of the car and I hold my hand out, wondering if she'll take it. She thinks about it for a few moments and then she does.

"Wanna tell me about it?" I ask once I've paid for us.

Emma shakes her head and shrugs. "Not much to tell. He was a part of a local gang. He hurt me, I finished with him, but he's gotten around my phone blocking. I don't answer my phone anymore unless I can see who is calling. If it's an unknown number, I leave it to go to voicemail."

"That's wise," I concur, hoping that the little bit of praise helps her.

"I decided on something recently," she tells me as we take in the front of the building. It's like a mini-stately home—full of architecture—and I'm in awe of the place.

"What did you decide on?" I ask after a moment of silence. I look at her and she's biting her bottom lip.

"To get back out there again. Leave him behind."

I nod and pull my shoulders back.

"And I'm a part of that plan?" I question as we follow the tour ropes through the rooms, which are detailed and intricate, recreating how things would have looked during the Second World War.

"Yes, though I didn't know until we met," she tells me as she stops at one display. She pulls out her notebook and makes notes, then she hides it back in her bag. I'll ask later what she's scribbling notes for and about, but when I know she won't run away from my question.

"You did well last night," I praise her as we come across a 1938 copy of the map of the Atlantic on a wall.

"Oh?"

"Calling the cops when you did. That was brave."

"It was necessary," she responds, and I smile back at her. She's looking at me, but it feels like it's more through me.

"It was also brave, especially when you shouted out that you had," I share; just a little more encouragement and maybe she'll be back to her bouncy first impression.

"I don't like fights," she whispers and I stop.

"No one does, not really. The trick is to end the fight as quickly as possible." She gapes at me. "You know I work with Byron, on the same base?" I ask; she nods.

"I thought you might," she murmurs.

I lean in and quietly explain what I do. "I'm an MP. Military Police." Her eyes go wide.

"Do you have handcuffs?" she asks me as she goes very red. I chuckle and smile.

"I have been known to use them," I admit and she gapes, turning a brighter shade of red. I let her walk away from me, to calm down from whatever thoughts are now going around in her head, but I do smile at her.

We take in more of the exhibitions, the recreation of the past and then we spy one of the surviving Enigma machines.

"It's smaller than I remember," she shares as she admires it. The Germans used it during WW2, and Bletchley Park helped decode it. I didn't know that the French Secret Service and the Polish Cipher Bureau were also a part of the collaboration in breaking the code, but that's what the information sign says. Again, Emma makes notes about it and quickly sketches it out with a few numbers, detailing dimensions.

We get to interact with the exhibits now as we walk around and I see from an information sign that Bletchley Park had over nine thousand people working at it at the height of the Second World War.

"So many people were here," Emma says as we walk around. "This place must've been a hive."

"I can imagine a base, like Wadd, on a bigger scale. Brize is quite big, lots of people there," I tell her, though I can't give her figures or much more detail. "Bases are like mini-cities; they never really sleep. It would have been the same here with that many people. A small town, awake 24/7." She nods in acknowledgement, then she makes more notes in her little book and I have to wonder why.

We walk past the café, and it's nearly lunchtime; the smell of cooked food wafts to greet us. My stomach growls and Emma's follows.

"I think we need refuelling," I tell her and she nods with a grin.

"What would you like?" I offer and she goes wide-eyed at me. I pull us out of the queue and to the side.

"You're...offering?" she asks very quietly and I nod.

"Look, I want to spend the day with you. It was my idea, so yeah, I'm paying." I refrain from asking what kind of nonsense her ex pulled where she thought she wasn't going to share food with whoever she was with or have it bought for her.

"I... Oh!"

"Look, I'm going out on a limb here, but I'm thinking he never bought you food when you were out? Always expected you to pay?" I ask and she nods, the tears threatening to fall. *Again.*

I pull her to me and hold her, then I find her ear and murmur to her, "He's an arsehole. A *man* doesn't ask a woman on a date, or spend time with her, and then not fucking look after her." I kiss her temple and continue to hold her. Her arms are folded up over her chest, between us.

Eventually, she pulls back from me and gives me a weak smile.

"I need to visit the ladies," she tells me and I nod.

"Tell me what you'd like, I'll order while you go and do that," I say. She looks at the board and picks a baked potato with cheese and beans.

"Great! I'll find us a table. What do you want to drink?"

"Some tea?" she requests, and my thoughts become a barrage of swear words as she's now asking for permission, not telling me.

"Tea it is. Sugar?" I confirm, not sure how she drinks it.

"Just the one," she tells me and I smile, "with milk."

"See you in a few minutes," I say and she heads off to the ladies while I rejoin the food queue and order for us.

I perhaps order more than usual; goodness knows the last time she had a proper meal. The more I learn about her, the more I want to show her exactly how she should be treated, show her ex up for the coward and cad I already know he is.

I've placed our food on the table and look around for Emma, when I see her coming toward me. I got worried she'd headed off and tried to walk back home.

"Are you okay?" I ask and she nods, smiling at me.

"There was a queue, that's all," she tells me and I grin.

"Isn't that just normal for the ladies?" I ask with a little snark and she smirks.

"We have to take our time," she replies. I just roll my eyes, which makes her laugh.

On the table, there's Emma's baked potato with a side salad, cakes, a large pot of tea and my lunch, a slice of lasagne with a large side of fries.

"Help yourself to some fries," I tell her and she nods. As she reaches out to grab one, I make her jump. She looks at me and I stare back, then I pull a face and she laughs.

"Sorry..." she says in a low voice.

"No need to be. As you said, you've chosen to leave him behind and I'm more than happy—" I watch as she raises her eyes to meet mine, "—to help you do that. To remind you that life's for laughing." I grab a chip and stuff it into my mouth, then watch as she does the same.

"There are times when we need to be serious, but today? It's about chilling, spending time together." I smile as she nods, smiling back at me.

"I know it'll take some time to undo..." she begins and I reach out for her hand.

"I know," I reply as she takes it and I know I've got research to do.

Things perk up a lot after lunch. Her nerves get parked up and left somewhere else, which is a good thing. We take a walk outside to see the exhibition pieces. The day is warm and though the mansion is magnificent, it is rather cool inside.

"What were your parents like?" she asks and I sigh as the sunshine begins to warm me.

"Useless, for the want of a better word. They left me to fend for myself one weekend and my uncle found me. All hell broke loose. My uncle is my dad's older brother and he tore my parents a new one. He and his wife, my aunt, raised me from that point onwards."

"They left you? How old were you?" Emma seethes quietly. I love that she is getting upset on my behalf.

I shrug, trying not to let it show that it sometimes bothers me. "Around three or four, so my aunt told me. I don't remember my parents being around for much. My aunt and uncle did it all, as well as raise their three."

"You had people who cared," Emma tells me and I nod.

"Lucky, I guess. When I said I was going into the RAF, my uncle asked me if that was what I really wanted to do. He made me weigh up the pros and cons of it before I signed on that line on my twentieth birthday."

We walk around the corner to find some of the classic cars that were used here during the war.

"I've been with them since. My uncle runs a small renovation company, doing up properties. I learned a few tricks from him about maintenance," I share.

"Which is how you were able to do the guttering so effectively yesterday," Emma observes and I nod.

"Yeah. Those kinds of things need doing every so often, so it's best to know how to do them," I say, smiling at her. "What about your parents?" I ask.

She sighs. "More of the same, like yours. They'd get high and forget about me for days. Rosie's dad, Dave, was there for a lot of my growing up once she and I became friends. He couldn't do what your aunt and uncle did, but he made sure I was fed regularly, and had clean clothes. I lived at Rosie's some of the time; I'd just go home to see if they were still alive." I visibly shiver at her statement.

CHAPTER FIVE

More Time

EMMA

Chris asking about my parents sends shivers down him and I want to know why. He seems so strong and capable, but he's also attentive and caring. I've not had a meal that large in a long time, even the pizzas last night.

"They didn't care?" he asks and I shake my head. I've never opened up to anyone like this before; my ex shut me down if I talked about my parents, so I never mentioned them after the first few times.

"Not really. The school trips I went on Dave paid for. The clean uniform, clothes and stuff, Mum would sometimes do, but mostly, it was Dave."

"Mine didn't care because they were too busy having fun. They didn't want me; they made that plain to see," he adds about his own situation.

I nod, sympathising with him. "Mine didn't want me either. It was like I was a burden to them," I confess, not quite sure what his parents thought, or if he knows why his life was similar to mine.

"Kids were too much like hard work," he confirms. We walk on and he offers me his hand. I hesitantly take it, aware that the gang my ex-Chris was a part of still operates around these parts.

"Yeah...little people are, but they're so cute, and sassy and clever," I tell him. My cousin's children fare better. "If it wasn't for Dave, I'd likely be in the fostering system."

"Same here," Chris agrees. "Though, my Uncle Craig and Aunt Jean did a heck of a job raising the four of us. I might have been a cousin, but they treated me as their own.

I got the same trips and hand-me-down uniform, same as the others, but when I needed new stuff, I had it. They were just clever with their money and in a three-bed terrace..." he says, leaving the sentence hanging.

"What was the mix? For the kids..." I continue, prying more into his life.

"Eldest is a lad, Richard. Then there's Maxine and Ruby, almost twins, and then me, the baby cousin. Any siblings?" he asks me and motions for us to sit on a bench with the sun at our backs.

"Just me, which I'm glad about," I share. "It meant I didn't have to think beyond the moment. Dave would buy Rosie some shoes, but then buy me the same size in a different style. Rosie's a shoe size bigger than me now, but at the time, we pretty much had the same growth rate."

"He sounds like a decent man," Chris ventures.

"He is. Rosie hates that he's ill and that he won't tell her what's wrong. She's made guesses; we both have. But..." He nods in understanding, but there's a different look in his eyes now as if something's fallen into place.

"The grounds are lovely, would you like to walk with me down to the lake?" Chris smiles at me and stands, offering me a hand to help me up. I've never been looked after like this, it's a heady thing to grasp and I'm not sure I'm worthy of this attention.

We walk through the restored grounds, which are now part of a conservation project. The whole area was turned into one in the nineties, which was great as it needed to be kept and preserved. The ideas here are informing the novel I'm writing and this place is inspirational for that.

I'm lost in my head as we walk; the birds are singing, the trees are swaying in the gentle breeze and I bring my focus back to the man standing next to me, who has fed me without asking that I pay because I work. I'd made simple ham sandwiches for my lunch, expecting Chris to do what my ex did, but he didn't.

"You're in your head," he tells me with a grin on his face. I smile back.

"I'm just thinking." I don't want to tell him what I'm considering. Planning a paranormal, smutty romance occupies the brain cells and keeps the personal demons at bay.

"Tell me about your job," I prompt, curious about what a military policeman does.

"I keep the base secure. The night Rosie came onto the base, I was at the front gate, on guard duty," he explains.

"She said you all had guns," I whisper and he nods.

"I did that night, and each night I patrol," he tells me. "But I can't tell you much more than that, darlin'." His Cockney accent comes out stronger with the last word.

"I have a good imagination," I tell him and he laughs,

swinging me into his hard chest so I have to stand between his legs. His eyes are like pieces of dark amber and his dirty blond hair is a standard military cut, short all over.

"And what pretty little things are you imagining about us?" he asks and I gasp.

I pull my lips in to keep myself from blurting out what has been going on inside my head since yesterday. My ex was never one for sex. We'd do it maybe once a month in the dark and then he'd roll off me, even if I hadn't been satisfied, which was often, before falling asleep.

"Oh, so you've thought about me like that, have you?" he asks me, his voice all husky.

"How did you...?" I question, my breath escaping in a gush. I can feel that my heart is beating far too fast, or am I imagining that he's doing to me what I write about?

"Because I've had the same thoughts," he whispers into my ear, before kissing me gently on the side of my head. I let out an involuntary moan and Chris chuckles. "Bet I can make you moan louder than that," he tells me. I feel my cheeks warming and my throat doesn't want to work anymore. He chuckles some more, which adds to my discomfort. "Come on, let's carry on our walk." He steps back, holding his hand out for mine.

We follow the path around to the right of the huge duck pond that is at Bletchley Park; it has a lot of benches to sit on if you want to just take in the view and the quietness. Well, maybe not today as there are a lot of people around.

"We're working tonight," I blurt out as we're halfway around the pond.

"We can swing by again. We have to be back on base tomorrow evening, but we've got all day tomorrow to do something, or be together."

I smile at that. I have him for a little longer, like a forbidden secret that I don't have to reveal anytime soon.

Under a willow tree, we stop walking and I turn to look at Bletchley Park Mansion. Taking in a deep breath, I ground myself, wondering what it would be like to kiss him again. *Will it be as good as last night?*

I don't have to wonder long; he's pulled me to him and as the wind gently moves the branches of the trees, I'm experiencing it again. His kiss consumes me and somehow the sleepy Emma within is wide awake and eager for more than just these fire-starter kisses. All I have to wonder about now is when he sees the true me, my true colours, what will he do?

We head back to the car and I remember I brought a small lunch with me.

"What's that?" he asks, pointing to the package in the back footwell.

"It *was* my lunch." My voie drops to a whisper as I answer him.

"Was?" he asks and grabs it before I can. I watch in horror as he opens it and sees the simple ham sandwich on slightly stale bread, the tiny apple and a small bottle of water.

"This is what you were going to eat if I hadn't...?" he asks and stares at me. I want to cry, out of embarrassment, fear, uncertainty... "Oh, Emma," he tells me and then he's holding me. "Let me make something clear," he tells me as he holds me. "When I invite you out anywhere, you'll be looked after. Totally." He pulls back and lifts my face up to his. "Tell me you understand, my twist and twirl?"

I sniff, not quite sure what the last part of his sentence means, but I understand the first part, so I nod. He kisses my forehead and hands me back the lunch bag before helping me into the car.

We drive back in near silence, but it's not uncomfortable. Outside mine, he pauses, turning the engine off before twisting to face me.

"Emma, I'd like you to tell me what kind of things this other Chris did to you, what he said. I don't want to be repeating his mistakes, and it'll help me understand you better if I know how he hurt you," he prods. He's not raised his voice, or called me stupid and fat.

I pause, not sure I want to tell him.

"Can I write them down for you? Give them to you tomorrow?" I ask, wanting to buy myself some time. He nods with a thin smile on his lips.

"That would be great, thank you," he says, his voice gentle and soft.

"I might not get it all," I begin, making excuses, but he holds his hand up.

"Anything is better than me being ignorant right now," he tells me and I sigh.

"I'm sorry," I say, but he silences me with a finger over my mouth.

"Don't be. This isn't your fault, okay?"

"Thank you," I whisper, grateful he's not pushing me for information before I've formed my words.

"I'll see you at the club." Once he's driven away, I head in, toast the sandwich and eat a small amount of food before I get changed for the evening shift. I'll need to walk to the club and if I'm quick, I can just about make it in time.

I make it to the club with a few minutes to spare. I think I'll continue to leave the car here if Chris and Byron come by. Rosie gets dropped off by a taxi and I smile at her.

"You walked it, didn't you?" she asks and I nod sheepishly. "Em," she says, coming up to me to keep her voice low. "You know what we talked about." I nod, sighing.

"I know...but RAF Chris took me home last night." I smile. "And the car was here."

"You need to be safe, so use it, please," she tells me. I've not seen Chris Anderson for a few months, though his contact the other week has unnerved me, and it's affecting how I interact with this Chris.

"Okay," I agree with her, knowing she'll hold me to it the same way I would if it were her in this situation.

"Good, thank you," she responds, dropping the subject, and goes to the cellar, likely to switch out a keg. I sigh and get on with restocking the fridges as the locals slowly come in for their Saturday night entertainment.

Byron and Chris show up later, indulging in games of pool. I see Colleen come and escort her mum home and by midnight, we're stacking the chairs on the clean tables so that the cleaners can get around tomorrow. We lock up, setting the alarms. We all walk Charlie home, then Chris is driving us and I grab the front seat so I can sit next to him.

Chris and Byron swap outside mine and Rosie jumps into the front as Chris comes around to walk me to my door.

He doesn't say a word as he wraps his hand around the back of my head, then angles me into a kiss. His arm is around me, pulling me into him and I wrap my arms around his torso, enjoying the feeling of the muscles and his hard form.

"I'll see you tomorrow?" he asks me as he pulls away, his dark eyes searching mine.

"Yes," I whisper, still unable to believe he's interested in little old, broken me.

Again, he waits until I've bolted the door before he moves off. He turns as he reaches the car and I smile at him from the living room window.

The following morning I awake with a smile on my face, the dreams of RAF Chris receding the more I wake up. Rosie texts me, and an idea forms in my head about spending some of the day together, the four of us. Rosie says she'll ask Byron and I text Chris.

Emma: Would you like Sunday lunch at Rosie's before you have to go back to base?

Chris's reply is pretty instant.

Chris: Yes!

I see the dots flashing and then another text arrives.

Chris: I'm being told the dessert is down to Byron and I.

Emma: Rosie's a decent cook.

Chris: Good to know! We're just getting breakfast.

Emma: Good idea! I'm hungry now.

Chris: Did you eat dinner?

I blink. I've never been asked if I've fed myself, not even my parents did that.

Emma: Yes, I toasted that sandwich and ate the apple.

Chris: I'm glad you ate something. What do you like for pudding? What's your favourite?

Emma: Crumble. Any kind. With ice cream.

I grin. I love crumble and ice cream. No one has ever asked me about my food preferences before either.

Chris: We'll find something the five of us can share. Shall we pick you up? We're just finishing breakfast.

I blink and decide that I'd better get ready and eat something.

Emma: I'd like that! My car is still at the club though and I'll need it for next week.

Chris: I'll help you bring it back at some point today, okay?

I smile. I'm starting to like this level of attention.

Emma: Thank you! My parents may not have instilled manners into me, but Dave certainly did.

Chris: Okay, see you soon.

And with that, I get up, wash, dress and eat something in a record ten minutes. I often faff around and procrastinate about getting out of bed, usually because I'm hungry and my cupboards are empty. Not today. Today, I even remake my bed before the resounding knock at my door tells me that he's there; it's barely twenty minutes later.

I hold my breath when I hear the formidable pounding at my door and I check who it is, even though I know it can't ever be Anderson. He never knocked, not like that.

"Hey!" I open the door once I've checked it's RAF Chris.

"Hey! Ready to go, Miss Keen?" he asks, a playful smile on his lips.

"Nearly," I say, grabbing my keys.

"Rosie's asked us for help in fetching a piece of furniture," Chris explains as I lock my flat. "Where is it going to go?"

I chuckle. "It's best that Rosie explains that one," I reply, not wishing to out my friend and her small business. If he's asking, she hasn't told Byron and that's for her to do.

Chris nods. "Okay, but it's not illegal, is it?" he asks and I shake my head, trying hard not to laugh.

"Not even remotely!" I reply, climbing in the back behind Chris.

At Rosie's, Byron asks the same question and Rosie guides them to the largest shed in her garden, after she tells him she's going to flip this piece. I know how this opens, so I help her pull the doors apart and Rosie slides the canopy cover over to create an outdoor workspace; handy when it's a really hot summer's day, or she's using the paint spray gun.

"Wow!" Chris exclaims and I watch him flex his muscles just daring to touch Rosie's tool collection. His eyes are wide and there's a faint smile on his lips. I have a feeling he's trying to control his excitement.

"What's the plastic sheeting for?" Byron asks as his eyes go wide.

"Spray painting dust sheets," Rosie tells him as we lock the workshop.

Byron suggests we leave now to go and get this piece.

"Why don't I go with Chris?" I ask, sweetly. I want to share with Chris what I wrote down last night before bed.

"Yeah, okay, you two can follow me. I'm hoping that the unit splits in two." She grabs a tape measure as she's leaving her workshop.

We head to Chris's car and I suggest we drop the back seats.

"We'll do that when we're there. Rosie has to pay for it yet," he tells me and I nod then climb in.

"I did as you asked," I quietly announce, afraid still that he'll shout or shut me down. I wish I had never met Chris Anderson.

"You did, huh? Well, pull it out. I'd like to read it while we wait at this place," he says.

"I doubt we'll wait long," I say, knowing how efficient Rosie can be. She likes to get her pieces back to the workshop quickly.

"Will you start reading out the list?" he asks and I go wide-eyed at him. "Please?" His voice isn't pleading, it's just...masculine, deep, sexy, and it makes me quiver hearing him like that.

"Okay," I reply, really not sure I want to say out loud what Anderson did to me.

I unfold the piece of paper from my back pocket and read the first on the list. "It sounds so silly..." I protest, but Chris shakes his head.

"It's not silly, Emma. I'm sensing he controlled you, made you think that you were worthless. Hell, you probably think you're broken." He glances at me, and I can't hide the emotions that his sentence conjures up in me. "You're not," he tells me as he pulls up behind Rosie.

While we wait, he turns to me.

"Listen, what he did to you...was wrong. You're not broken."

I blink at him; I can't form any words.

"He wouldn't listen," I blurt out, telling him the first thing on my list. "I wasn't allowed to tell him no. Ever."

Chris pulls in a breath and then exhales slowly. "Thank you for trusting me with that," he says. He glances up and Byron's calling us over. Chris nods to him.

"Let's drop the back seats and we'll talk more on the way back, okay?" He smiles at me and for the first time in my life, I feel I have someone other than Rosie and Dave who will listen to me.

Chapter Six

Eyes Open

Chris

Emma telling me that her ex wouldn't take no for an answer nearly has me blowing up, but not at her. Thankfully, I keep my temper and Byron's need for help is distraction enough. We get the large base section into my car and the top section into Rosie's, then I follow Rosie back to hers.

"What did you tell him 'no' about, Em?" I ask. I'm now wondering if he forced himself on her.

"Anything, at the start. The 'friends' he made us go and visit. They weren't nice and I didn't like going, but he wouldn't go without me. They were jailed for drug dealing a few years back but they're probably out by now."

I seethe under my breath, but I hold it together, for her sake.

"Anything else?" I ask, surprised that my voice isn't snarly.

"Food...I don't like tuna, but he told me I did, that I'd eaten it before."

I nod and run my tongue behind my teeth, trying not to grind them. That sounds like gaslighting.

"He...called me fat," she whispers, not quietly enough that I don't hear. *Fat? She's not eating properly because of him.*

"What finally made you break up with him?" I ask and I see her shiver. "Sorry, you don't have to tell me," I remind her, her reaction telling me that it's not good. She waits a few minutes—so long that I think she won't tell me what happened. It's something I think I'll have to get used to.

"He got violent while he was taking something, and I hid in the bathroom..." She whispers it at first, then she finds her voice. "He broke down the door to get to me and hauled me up by my arm, bruised it. I managed to run to Rosie's, and her dad shielded me."

There's silence for a few moments, then she carries on. The emotion in her voice has gone; it's like she's reading a passage from a book.

"When he apologised a week later, I'd had the locks changed on the flat as the police suggested. I told him through the door that I didn't want to be with him anymore, that I didn't love him, and I'd blocked him on social media—we were over." She pauses and I glance across to see that her eyes are closed and she's twiddling her fingers.

"He was shouting at me for over an hour, but I put on my headphones to drown him out. The police were called by the neighbours and he was moved on. I haven't spoken with him since and I had to pay for the new bathroom door." She starts crying and I hand her some tissues as best I can. "I did hear him promise that he'd find me if I ever tried dating someone else," she says in a voice so quiet, I nearly miss it.

"Did he now?" I say, my hackles rising and my mind racing.

She nods and dries her eyes on the tissue that's now well-used. I hand her a fresh one. I think I need to put the feelers out for this git.

When we're back, we unload the dresser and I can see that parts of it require repair. But if this is what Rosie does, I'm happy enough to let her get on with it; she won't need my knowledge. We lock up the workshop and head into the house.

Rosie starts preparing the dinner, and I nod to Byron. "Your second favourite hobby," I tell him and indicate towards the kitchen. Byron grins at me and suggests he check on Dave.

"I'll do that with Emma, you help her," I instruct him, nodding to the kitchen. I need him out of the way so I can talk with Emma about what Annie texted Byron this morning.

We go to check on Dave and Emma sees that he has a particular quiz show on the TV.

"Oh, do you ever manage to do the maths questions? I can't do those very well," she tells him.

"You and maths were never a pair. Now, you and English," Dave comments with a smile on his old, withered lips. He seems more tired today than he was yesterday. *Did we wear him out by being here?*

"Yeah, I know," she responds in an accepting voice.

"She's clever with her words when you let her get them out of her head," Dave tells me and he's got a smile on his face as he shares that bit of information about her.

"She's a wordsmith?" I ask, clarifying.

Dave nods. "She'd help Rosie with her English homework and Rosie would help her with her maths. Two different peas but a pair all the same," he says and I grin.

"Do you mind if we sit in the garden for a few moments, Mr Mallard?" I ask, hoping that the old man says yes.

"Sure! You helped tidy it up," he replies, clicking his dentures around his mouth.

"Thank you, sir," I reply and when he has all that he says he needs, I escort Emma outside.

"Listen, I've been doing some homework," I tell her as we sit on a garden bench. I've checked that the neighbours aren't outside.

"Oh? What kind of homework?" Emma asks as we sit on the curved stone bench, her tone curious. Her shoulders are relaxed, which is good.

"About your situation. The coercion, the threats... Have you heard of a non-molestation order?" I ask, using the information Byron's friend sent him this morning. Emma shakes her head.

"They cost," Emma tells me and I shake my head.

"The non-molestation orders are free. The restraining order costs, but I can help you with the money if you need it sooner rather than later."

"What are they?" she asks and we look it up so she can sit and read it. I think about Dave's comments. Sure, Emma can hold a sentence together, but he implies that she's better than that.

"Oh! I didn't know about this," I hear her say as she looks through the website on her phone.

"Will you consider doing that? It doesn't cost anything to do them," I share, remembering what Annie texted Byron.

"They're definitely free?" Emma asks, her voice lifting, and I nod.

"Yes, as free as the air you breathe." Emma gulps in response and then nods.

"I can't do it on my own," she whispers to me.

"You can, but I'll help you, if you feel you need it," I reply without thinking about it. Somehow, for some reason, I need this woman to be safe. "Byron's got a family friend who works with domestic violence victims. Her name is Annie. She told us about it this morning," I say, nodding to her phone. "And Em," I add, waiting for her to look up at me. "If you ever need somewhere to run, drive to Waddington. Tell the gatehouse you're with me; they'll know you when you get there. They'll shelter you until I can get my hands on him if he tries anything," I promise.

Emma nods with a smile and then hugs me.

"Thank you," she whispers, resting her long-fingered hands on my lap. It's the first time she's touched me voluntarily.

We get up and go into the kitchen, walking straight into the middle of a conversation with Rosie and Byron.

"I know how scary you lot are with your guns," I hear Rosie say, and I grin, remembering the night she drove into the base car park.

Emma smiles at Rosie and stands near the kitchen table. "Chris has been persuading me to put a non-molestation order in place," she shares quietly with her friend. She's got her hands folded before her and she's hanging her head as if in shame. Before I can say or do anything, Dave's there.

"Good, it's about time," he says with a smile on his face. Emma looks up and smiles in return, pulling her shoulders back a little. His praise as a father figure does a better job of giving her confidence than I can right now. "What do you need?" he asks as he eases himself down onto a chair.

We sit and plan a way to get this court order in place, researching local law firms from our phones. Byron receives a text and he looks at it in puzzlement, then presses the dial button and switches it to the loudspeaker as it rings so we can all hear.

"How did you know where I was?" he asks and the person he's called laughs heartily in response.

"Who dae ye think?" the Scottish voice booms back, laughing.

"Sis?" he hazards a guess and the laughter deepens.

"Not quite...but in the right ballpark."

"Mac?" He ventures with some hesitation.

"Aye! Has anyone taken your friend through what they'll need?" she asks. It's a Sunday, there's no chance we can get this started today. Byron writes down a name on a scrap piece of an envelope: Annie. I nod in understanding while Emma and Rosie smile.

"No," Emma responds. "I'm the one who needs it," she tells Annie. I can see her starting to shake, so I move in to be closer to her, offering her some physical support.

"Hello, darlin', I'm Annie!" Annie's voice becomes gentle and caring as if she is talking to a small, scared child. "You'll need to sign an affidavit about what he's done to you; if you have examples, a diary of events, take it with you and use it. If anyone else can add one of their own to back you up, it's extra bullets in the gun, okay? *No one* around you right now doubts you. But, you need to sign it in front of a notary or a judge. If the court finds you are in danger of harm, you will first get a Temporary Order of Protection. That shouldn't cost anything where you are; it doesn't up here. Then a hearing will be set. He doesn't have to be around for the first part. Any hearing is *where* you'll maybe face him. Are you up for that?"

I can see Emma swallow a few times and then she turns to look at me. I reach out a hand and she nods. "Yes," she confirms, though her voice is shaky at best.

"I'm not standing next to ye, but I can hear yer a wee bit scared. That's okay." I smile at Emma as Annie continues to talk. Emma catches my eye and gives me a faint smile in return. "Fear is good, but your physical well-being, along with your mental health, are worth being fearful for. Ye cannae let that go as that's what makes you who you are. Use that fear to fight against this, okay? Byron, ye there?"

"I am," he replies and Emma pulls her shoulders back, standing straighter.

"Good. I'm going to send ye some links to help the lady who needs this as I've got your number. There's a new service I've found that deals with DV victims and hides texts and communications from those that support them. We're trialling it up here; I'll send ye the details now."

His phone pings multiple times as links and messages arrive.

"I'm too far away to come help ye, but there's a DV network down there via Women's Aid. Has yer friend spoken with them?"

Emma shakes her head. "She's shaking her head," he replies on her behalf.

"What's yer name?" Annie asks, clearly calling for Emma. I nod, understanding that she's looking for approval, for this to be safe.

"Emma," she says, speaking up.

"Hey, Emma. Okay, here's what I suggest ye do…" Annie goes on about Emma contacting Women's Aid and when she hears Emma is renting, Annie is elated.

"That's good. Ye can move quickly and quietly away from where he knows ye live and once the order is in place, it follows you. The police will mark your next property as linked to the first, so any calls to them should be treated as a high priority. You don't have to be too far, a few miles ought to be enough." I see Emma nod.

"I've already begun packing," she tells us and the look of surprise on Rosie's face tells me that she wasn't aware of that. I can feel the tension and nerves running off Emma and I begin rubbing her back in slow movements.

"Okay, good, that helps," Annie tells us and we go through other things she can do. Annie signs off after permitting Byron to pass her number on.

"You can always do a Rosie," Byron tells her after Annie has hung up. That makes Emma and Rosie's dad laugh, but Rosie purses her lips together.

"If you ever need it," I remind her and Emma nods. That Byron suggested it too, without me asking him, may help convince her.

Rosie and Byron then get into a discussion about what does and doesn't get roasted. To be honest, I'm still alive thanks to the mess hall and Byron's ability to cook.

"We'll go get some ice cream," I state, knowing that Emma likes ice cream with her crumble. Dave shuffles off back to the living room and I can't help but notice he's looking stiffer.

The silence between us both as we walk is comfortable, but I'm keen to hear what Emma is thinking.

"What did you think of what Annie had to say?" I ask as we walk to a nearby mini-supermarket.

"I'm stunned…I knew Rosie would be there when I got brave enough. That there's a whole battalion or whatever you RAF guys call them, to hand, on tap?" She shakes her head. "Who is she?"

I grin. "She's his sister's best friend, as far as I can work out. Not met her yet though," I admit.

"Byron gave me her number already," she tells me and we come across a small park that toddlers might use. There are benches in this small play area and we sit down on one.

"So, why don't you drop her a text? She knows what needs to be done and she has useful information," I suggest. Emma nods and takes a slip of paper out of her back pocket and puts the contact into the phone before sending off a text. I look over her shoulder as she gets a reply.

Annie: Hi Emma! Any friend of Byron's is a friend of mine. I'll send you what I sent him, hang on, yer phone might go a wee bit crazy...

Crazy isn't the word. Link after link arrives, including some software links, and it pings so much that I lose count.

Annie: Now you've got my number. You can call me whenever, for whatever reason. I'm not an official counsellor, but I'll answer you with total honesty, okay? Sorry, I dinnae sugar-coat stuff, wasnae made that way.

Emma laughs and I chuckle at Annie's last text.

Emma: Thank you!

Annie: Yer welcome! Away ye go, be safe!

She sets up the software that protects the likes of Annie, Rosie, Byron and myself so that we can help her. It changes the texts between us to ordering food and fake names. It's all a bit too clever.

"Do you feel better?" I ask and she nods, giving me a confident smile.

"I need to do this." She stands and we carry on walking to the shop. "The thing is I know he'll kick off as soon as I put these orders in."

I ponder what she's saying. "And if you don't, he won't know he's crossed the line and will keep doing it. You could change your number. Annie suggested that too," I tell her and Emma winces.

"There's the cost," she points out, and I smile.

"Not if they understand you're being harassed, that you're putting the molestation order because of it. It's under fifty-quid." She sighs heavily and when we've picked the right ice cream, I feel the need to confirm to her what I meant.

"You did understand that I am offering you that fifty quid, don't you?" I ask as we walk back.

"You are?" she responds, her voice hesitant, tight.

"Yes. It's a thing with Byron and me. We say what we mean and we mean what we say. We don't offer unless we mean it." At the same play park, we stopped at on the way there, I pull her to me.

"I want to do this for you. Please?" I ask. I have never had to beg to help someone and as her eyes widen, the tears begin and I can't help but want to protect this brave girl. I've only kissed her, yet I want more, but there's something beyond that which has me wanting to stand before her and take on all who dare even look at her.

"Thank you. I'd like him to not know."

"Then we'll get it done," I assure her and we head back hand-in-hand, getting the ice cream into the freezer. Byron and Rosie aren't around, and we check the oven timer, which has just over an hour to go. We take the chance to retrieve Emma's car from the club and take it back to her flat, then I drive us back to Rosie's.

"I never even thought you'd need your car, I'm sorry." I genuinely am, I didn't know and I didn't think. "How did you get to work last night?" I ask out of curiosity and she goes red. "Em?" I prod, and she sighs.

"I walked," she answers; her shoulders drop and her voice is low, nearly inaudible.

"Until we get you moved, can you please avoid doing that?" I ask, concerned that if her ex does kick off, she'll be easy to track. She nods.

"Rosie already told me off for walking last night," she confesses, and I pull her to me at the garden gate.

"She's right to be worried. Until we can help get you out of this mess, please do all you can to stay safe. And to repeat what Byron and I said: do a Rosie if you need to, okay?" Emma nods and then wraps her arms around me. "The gatehouse will know to look out for your car, for you. They'll call me, no matter what shift rotation I'm on."

"Thank you," she says as I hold her close. After a few moments, we go inside, to find Rosie's been crying and the table is being laid.

"Where's the ice cream?" Rosie asks and Emma points to the freezer.

"We came back once already. Chris took me to get my car. Are you okay?" Emma questions. I watch as she physically changes her posture from a meek woman to...something else. She'll put up with nonsense in her own life, but hurt her friend? This woman is all sorts of complex and I want to get to know every facet she has.

Why do I want to do that now, when I never have before? I watch as she takes in Rosie's quiet, discreet explanation of her crying—her father's poor health.

Over dinner, Rosie explains what she showed Byron. Now all her DIY knowledge accumulation makes sense.

"All off-grid?" I ask and the girls nod, explaining the cooking, internet, electricity, heating, hot water, collecting rainwater, and toilets…they've not left a thing out. One thing bugs Byron and I'm not surprised: The kitchen. The man wants in on this and he's going to want to cook, which means a decent kitchen.

"And we did the guttering job for you," I tease as I help myself to another spoonful of the mashed potato. "Here was me thinking we were saving you from it." I grin.

"You did," Rosie agrees. "But I did the back section of the house and over the conservatory already, so I know what I'm doing."

I notice that Emma gives her a quick nod in agreement. Byron teases Rosie about the lack of a kitchen and they challenge each other about what the kitchen needs and how it's laid out. I nudge Emma who grins at me, and then we offer more food to Dave. Byron goes on about a proper Aga like his grandmother has back in Italy that his mama swears by. A bedroom gets added on and I can't hide the smirk. These two are meant to be!

Byron stands his ground, his knowledge from the village set up in Italy being a huge benefit right now. Rosie doesn't believe him, but when Byron explains about the Italian storms taking down the feeble power lines, we all get why the village did what they did.

Byron glances at Emma and me. "We should go out the next bank of leave we get," he tells me and I nod.

"The four of us should," I confirm. I'd love to go visit his folks and take Emma with me.

Dave declines the offer and Emma's look becomes sad. Dave's sicker than he's letting on, I'm sure of it.

"I'll walk Emma back, come and get me in about half an hour?" I ask Byron, handing him the keys. Emma's place is a ten-minute walk and I can at least kiss her stupid a few times before I have to leave her. Byron says something to Emma and hands her his hoodie, who darts off and comes back to me minutes later, minus the hoodie he handed to her. *What's he planning?*

"He's sicker than we thought," Emma observes as we get to the end of the road and turn towards her flat.

"Yeah, I worked that out. I wonder why he won't tell her," I ponder.

"Some do, some don't. I looked it up. He's up to something though, the way he keeps pulling out the rings, the photo album. I'm just not sure what," she tells me.

"Listen, I've got Thursday off. Since we've done Bletchley, let's do something else, but I'll let you pick as I don't know the area." I've not spent any time in this town; I usually head to Lincoln and a great pub by the Cathedral, then something local with the lads.

At her front door, she inserts the key and lets me in. There are boxes in the hallway, more packed in the living room and a stack of flat-packed boxes, tape and a tape gun.

"You're doing it all yourself?"

"Yeah. Fancy a quick coffee?" she asks and I shake my head.

"No, I'd rather back you up against that door and kiss you senseless," I reply, watching her reaction as I get to be honest with her.

She bites her lip but nods in an endearing, demure way. Stepping into her, I pull her to me.

"This is how you should be treated, always," I remind her and kiss her, gently on the lips at first, letting her set the pace. She quickly relaxes into me and runs her tongue across my teeth, sparking a fire within me. My breath catches and I run a hand up to the back of her head, angling her so I can devour her. The little minx leans against the wall as if she needs it for support and I move in the half-step, keeping her close to me, my other hand on her arse, pulling her to me.

I feel her pushing against my chest and I slow the kiss, ending it, then I open my eyes to find her looking back at me with hooded eyes and a mischievous grin on her sweet, swollen lips.

"You're a bad boy at heart, aren't you?" she asks and I grin.

"Twirl, you ain't got a clue," I admit.

"You said that to me earlier. What does it mean?"

"Twist and twirl? Girl..." I wait for a second, watching her mouth expand into a soft smile before I kiss her again. "What did you do with Byron's hoodie?" I ask when we break apart again.

"He asked that I hide it in Rosie's room for her to wear when he couldn't be there," she tells me and I grin. I yank my hoodie off and put it on her.

"Do the same," I instruct and the smile I get sets me up for the journey home.

CHAPTER SEVEN

Out of the Darkness

EMMA

I wait until Byron has picked Chris up before I start bouncing around my flat in excitement. When Chris texts me that they're safely back at base, I have a need to talk to Rosie about the guys. I read his message more times than I am sure is necessary. *Would Rosie be up for talking to me about the guys?* I decide there's only one real way to find out.

I send her a text: *I miss the company!*

She calls me an instant later.

"You okay?" she asks and I sigh.

"Yeah, just surprisingly lonely. It was fun this weekend. I didn't expect Stevo to be so hot! Or caring..." Attentive, giving, providing...he's a lot of things.

"I've been telling you for ages, there are good men out there. But I didn't expect them to be someone I knew and actively disliked for so long. Or the other to be his best friend," she replies, not missing a beat.

"No, but that's a good thing, isn't it? You're okay finding out if things with Byron would work out?" I ask her, hoping that she is, as it means I have a few extra reasons to keep seeing Chris.

"Yeah, I am. And you're okay chasing things down with Stevo?" she asks and I notice she's using Chris's military nickname.

"I didn't think I was, but when he texted me to say they were safely back on base, I breathed a sigh of relief. I need to get rid of Chris, permanently. Stevo's shown me I can and that lady in Scotland has given me so much information; I'll be checking it out for days."

"I think she served with Byron's sister; let me ask him," she says, and I can hear her texting him, muttering her sentence to him loud enough for me to hear.

"Yeah, Annie is ex-RAF too," she confirms to me after I hear the text sound. "So you're going to do it?" she asks nervously.

"Yeah, it needs to be done," I confirm. I do need to take a stand, now I have a reason to. "Stevo said he'd help fund the restraining order if I needed one to back up the molestation order." I begin packing a few more things while we talk.

"What are you doing?" she asks.

"Packing up some more things, while I can. I'd like to move and as I was told, renting makes it so much easier. There's a place not that far from you," I share.

"Show me the details," she tells me in a keen, high-pitched voice.

"I'll send it to you when we're finished talking. Thanks for this, Rosie," I say, heading to another small area that I can pack up one-handed.

"You're welcome," she replies. "Send on those details," she reminds me. Promising I will, I end our call, feeling happier and more hopeful than I have in a long time.

It's still early evening so I have time to do a lot of things. I'm keen to get moving, especially after what Annie said; a few miles ought to do it. I feel that being closer to Rosie will do it too.

I spend some time packing up one area, labelling the two boxes and then I send a text to Chris, asking how he is. I haven't taken his hoodie off, and I love the wafts of his scent I get as I move about my flat. I have lived with someone before, my ex, but I suspect that living and being with RAF Chris is going to be very different.

I get a text from him just as I get into bed. Yawning, I place his hoodie next to me on the other pillow, along with my phone and after his goodnight text, I let sleep take me under.

The following morning, I'm keen to get more packed away into the boxes and check I've been paid. I need groceries and I like doing it early when it's quieter. Checking my funds,

I head out to the cheaper supermarkets, going a different route, taking care to park in a different part each time. As I shop for the basics on my list, I begin to wonder what food Chris likes most and so I text him to ask.

Heading to the check-out, I notice he hasn't responded and I leave anything I was going to buy until I hear from him. I re-read his 'goodnight' text from last night, smiling as I do.

At home, I quickly unpack and get something to eat. My phone rings and the number is withheld; I don't reach out to touch it, keeping my arms folded across me. I shiver then send Chris an acceptance for the money to change my number. This has to stop.

It's nearly lunchtime when I hear from Chris but my phone displays a different name each time the texts come up, thanks to the software Annie said would help hide those that support me.

Chris: Sure! Do you need me to put it into your account?

Emma: Yes, please. Let me send you the details.

I quickly send him what he'll need and get a thumbs-up back in response. Ten minutes later, my bank tells me that the money is in my account. I search the internet on how to do the number changes and call my provider.

Sucking in a gulp of air, I steel myself for a difficult conversation, but it turns out to be much easier. As soon as I said I was being harassed, and that I'm putting in molestation orders, they offered to change it for free. I sigh happily as my number change goes through and I quickly text Chris back that my number is changing and I'll be able to give him back the money.

Before my phone number changes, I see a reply from him telling me not to worry about it, to keep it. It takes an hour before I can text him back.

Emma: I can't do that! Oh, this is my new number.

Chris: You can. Put it towards funds for the restraining order or something else that you need.

I look at his message, working out if I can keep it and live with myself for doing it. *Something else I need?* I can get the laptop I've been trying to buy much quicker if I can make three payments early. Deciding that is what I'll do with it, I thank Chris and head to the pawnshop.

"Another two payments and you can take it away with you," the clerk tells me with a smile.

"That'll be good!" I reply cheerfully.

"We'll see you soon," she tells me as I pocket the receipt and payment book. I don't even glance at what else they have on sale; I'm on a budget.

Back at the flat, I text Chris, asking if he's free.

Chris: Until bedtime, yes. Why?

Emma: Can I call you?

Chris: Let me call you, hang on...

My phone is ringing and I know it is him; he's the only one with my new number, so far.

"Hi!" I greet him, my voice higher and more breathy than normal. I am pleased that he's called.

"Hey! Wasn't sure what kind of contract you had and didn't want you using up minutes. I've endless amounts of them on this deal," he explains.

"That's good. I just want to thank you, for the money," I say, needing him to know I'm grateful. "I've put it to good use since the number change was free." I smile as I think about getting the laptop three weeks earlier than planned.

"That's good! Are you able to tell me what kind of good use?" he asks and I hesitate.

"I need a laptop and I'm buying one on a weekly payment scheme." There's silence for a few seconds.

"And you've been able to make a few extra payments?" he asks, not telling me off at all for not spending it on alcohol or anything else.

"Yes, thanks to you," I add as my nerves settle due to the lack of fighting.

"Then I'm glad I was able to help," he says softly to me.

"So am I." *Why is my voice all breathy now?*

"What else have you been doing today?" he questions, and I walk him through my day, the early morning food shop, the number change and Chris cheers.

"I'm so glad you did that! Have you told Rosie?"

"Not yet. She's the next person to tell. Then I guess I'd better tell Annie." I grin.

"That might be an idea. Have you thought about what to do on Thursday?" he asks as I stretch my legs out before me.

"No...I haven't thought about it; I'm sorry!" I kick myself for forgetting to suggest somewhere.

"That's okay, we've got time to decide. Drop me a text when you've made up your mind. I am really not bothered where we go," he says, his voice sounding light and cheerful.

"Have you heard of the Stacey Hill Museum?" I ask, knowing that it has changed its name recently but I cannot remember what to.

"No, I haven't. Let me do a quick search on it," he responds. "I've got you on loudspeaker now, twirl. You still there?" he asks, and I smile bigger.

"Yes, I am." I sigh contentedly at the attention to the small details he gives me.

"It's the Milton Keynes Museum, at an old farm," he states and then I remember.

"Oh, yes! I've heard that's quite good, but the food is expensive," I share.

"That's okay, it's a day out, off base, with a gorgeous twist'n'twirl." I imagine a wide smile on his face if his happy voice is any indication.

"I'm not gorgeous," I say, regretting it almost before I've finished speaking.

"Says who? Your ex? Pah!" he scoffs. "*His* opinion isn't one you want to consider anymore, right?" he reminds me and I lift my head, pulling my shoulders back.

"You're right," I cry out and then I giggle. "Thank you, again."

"I need to go and eat, Em. Make sure you do too, okay?"

"I will, thank you! See you on Thursday?" I ask, checking that we're still on.

"Absolutely! I'll come and pick you up, okay? I'll let you know when," he adds. "See ya, babe!"

I don't get a chance to respond; he's hung up.

I wonder if I did or said something wrong when we talked. I wring my hands and my goblin brain wonders what I did, playing our chat over and over in my head. I'm so absorbed in it that I forget to do what he told me and I keep wondering about it until he texts me back a good while later.

Chris: Sorry about ending our call like that. I needed to eat before they shut the mess hall for the night and I got stale sandwiches for dinner. Byron's away for a few days, so I can't rely on his cooking.

Me: That's okay. I breathe a sigh of relief. He was just hungry and needed to cater for himself and my stomach growls loudly at the thought of eating.

Me: I ought to eat. I had forgotten to.

Chris: That's not good, babe! Let me know when you've eaten. We can chat again then, okay?

Me: Okay!

I look to see what I have in after this morning's shop. I see a tin of vegetable curry, a packet of rice and small pitta bread in the cupboard and now my mouth is salivating. Warming it all up, I am sitting down to eat it in five minutes, taking a picture to show Chris, but I don't enjoy eating it alone.

Chris: That looks decent!

Me: I did the shopping earlier, so I have food in.

Chris: I'm glad!

Me: What is your favourite curry?

Chris: Madras. Love a bit of spice! Though, if you don't, tell Byron if he's making you anything; damn Italian loves hot food!

Me: He's part Italian?

Chris: Yeah...Makes life interesting, him being part Scottish too!

Me: And you?

Chris: Just a simple London boy. Have you finished eating?

Me: Yes.

I don't get a reply, but he calls me.

"That's better! Now we're both free, I can talk with you," he says, his voice sounding light.

"It is! What did you have?" I ask and he laughs.

"Bangers and mash. They rope Byron into helping if it's Italian night. The man makes a damn good pizza," Chris says, his voice light and happy. "Even if it is sometimes spicy." He laughs; I assume he's remembering some of the ones Byron's made.

"What are you good at making?" I ask, wondering if he's inclined to cook as Byron does.

"I'm lucky if I can get a tin open; cooking and me, we just don't get on. My aunt tried teaching me when I was a teenager. I can burn a boiled egg," he snickers; his embarrassment is obvious.

"I can do some things, but living out of a tin isn't so bad. It does mean you don't have to worry about putting all those pesky ingredients together." I laugh at the thought. "I remember cooking classes at school. I was terrible."

"Me too! I burnt the cake we were meant to be cooking in my class; I didn't set the timer and...well, I was heavily supervised from that point onwards," Chris recalls, making me laugh again.

"What are you going to do now?" I ask, aware that it's getting to be quite late.

"I'm in bed already, so when we've finished I'll go to sleep. I need to be up at oh-six," he says.

"Oh-six?" I repeat. "Six am? That time exists?" I ask in disbelief.

He laughs. "Yeah, it exists, babe!" I hear the phone being moved and it beeps. "Oh, darn! You still there?" he asks, his voice suddenly high-pitched.

"Yeah, I am. What happened?" I ask, confused by the beeps.

"I switched ears but pressed some buttons when I nearly dropped the phone." He sighs.

I chuckle. "I do that too! It's like the phone doesn't want to stay in your hand," I agree, and he laughs.

"You're right there! What are your plans for tonight?"

"I've got some more boxes to pack, then I'll go to bed. I'm trying to do it in little bits so that it's not a sprint at the end," I share.

"That's wise of you! I can help you a little on Thursday if you want? That museum doesn't open until half ten."

"Can we be there that early?" I ask. "I am not keen on crowds," I admit.

"Yeah, I figured you didn't when you mentioned the early morning shopping, so that's okay by me. But I wanna have lunch there, okay?" I'm not sure if he's asking or telling me.

"I'd love to," I reply with a little honesty. I would love to, especially as it'll be with him. "I'll let you go to sleep; I'm not ready to go to bed just yet," I explain. Unless it was with him. I can feel my heartbeat increasing a little at the thought of being intimate with Chris, but I keep those thoughts to myself.

"Oh! Now, if I were there?" he asks and I gasp. *How did he know I was thinking that? Was he?* "Haha! You *were* thinking that!" he goads me and I mumble a response. "Haha, twirl, you're killing me!" He laughs and I notice he's not laughing at me the way my ex often would.

"I am?" I gasp.

"Yeah...wait until I pick you up on Thursday morning! I'll give you a good reminder," he says and I hear the tease in his low, husky voice.

"Pushing me against the wall again?" I ask, hoping that's what he wants to do.

"You betcha, babe! I need to get some kip. Sleep well, okay?"

"I'm sure I will," I reply, noticing my voice has gone sultry and low.

"Oh, twirl! Soon, I promise ya! Night, babe!" he says again and I bid him goodnight, letting him go and get some sleep. I carry on packing more of the living room and it's after midnight when I finally head to bed.

The following day, time passes in a haze as I decide that in order to explore things with RAF Chris, my ex can't be allowed to bother me anymore and that means, him knowing where I am.

I apply for the flat near Rosie, crossing my fingers as I send off my enquiry of interest via the agent.

I get a message on social media from an old contact, asking if I've changed my number. I admit I have, but I'm not giving my new number out to anyone but immediate friends. I don't get a response back and after a few hours, I block them. They only have my ex in common with me and that's enough in my mind now to cut ties with them. I go through my friends list and remove the ones whose only link is to my ex.

I then look at putting in the non-molestation order and contacting a law firm locally that, according to their website, specialises in these. They give me their fee for preparing the paperwork and I thank them for their time, wincing at the potential cost.

Turning to a search engine, I find help and useful agencies via the government website, so I contact the local Women's Aid and CAB offices. Both say that they can help me and I like talking with the Women's Aid lady, so I book a time with her on Friday.

Then I text Rosie to bring her up to speed, noticing that I'm running out of time to get myself ready for work.

E: Here's my new number! I'll be at work in about an hour, need to chat. I've started putting the order in...

R: Great news! How do you feel?

E: Tell you when I see you. And I've applied for that flat. Just waiting to hear now.

R: See you soon!

I smile, knowing that a chat as I work with my friend will be helpful. I make it there on time, noting that it's just Rosie and me working at the club tonight as it's a weeknight and it'll be quieter. As we're both experienced barmaids, it doesn't take us long to restock the bar and keep the orders flowing, working at a steady pace.

By half-eleven, we're locking up and Rosie follows me home in her car. I blow her a kiss as I go in and from the living room, I watch her drive away.

Thursday morning comes and I stretch like a cat before I wake up properly. Chris said he'd be here and he was probably up early. I settle on some breakfast and as I'm munching some toast, the door knocks. Chris has made a distinctive pattern, so I know it's him. I still check the peephole though and smile as I unlock the door and let him in.

"Hey, twirl, how ya doin'?" he asks, his cockney accent strong and proud. Before I can respond, he has me backed against the wall. "Ready for your reminder?" I grin, nodding and then his lips are on mine gently. I taste the coffee he's drunk recently and wrap my hands around his neck, pulling him in. I feel his hand behind my head, turning me slightly and as I respond, the kiss deepens. I'm lost in the ocean of emotions that kissing him makes me feel. I want more; more than I want to breathe. Chris slows the kiss and pulls back.

"Mornin', darlin'," he drawls at me with a smirk.

"Hi you," I manage to breathe back.

"Are you ready?" he asks and I shake my head.

"I was just eating breakfast," I say and he backs away. I lock the door and turn towards the kitchen. For a fit man, he can move quietly—I guess that's a trait of his job.

"I'll let you finish up before we go," he says, sitting on a chair in the living room. I only have one breakfast bar stool.

"Thanks," I say, trying to make quick work of the toast.

"Take your time, Em, I'm not in a mad rush." He chuckles at me as I nearly choke; I slow down, nodding.

Chapter Eight

Behaviours

Chris

Emma eats slowly, something I noticed the other day at Bletchley Park. I wonder if that's a trait she's been taught. She tries to rush her breakfast and nearly chokes because I'm here, so I remind her that she can take her time.

She smiles and carries on eating, which is fine by me. I watch as she does so, noticing how tidy she is. Sure, a few things are out of place, but the dishes are done straightaway and left to dry on the side in a rack where the rest of her crockery seems to live.

I look around and see more packed boxes than the other day, but they're all piled neatly and labelled. Her shoes are few and they're all practical ones; she doesn't go for fancy things. My female cousins and aunt could open a shoe shop with the quantity they possess, something my male cousin and uncle moan about every time I visit. This level of tidiness and organisation is usually born in several ways; neither of which I think Emma has been a part of. *Military?* Not a chance. *Raised that way?* I know Rosie's dad did more for her, so it's hardly going to be because of that avenue.

I wait until she says she's ready, watching her check, double-check and then triple-check that windows are secure, and the sockets are off. She smiles at me when she's ready and I stand, offering her my hand.

Watching her told me more about her than I ever thought I'd want to know about someone. Getting her permanently out of this flat is now my top priority.

Her shoulders rise a little as we walk to the car and they don't drop or relax until we're out of the neighbourhood she lives in. Neither does she look out of the car window; she turns her face to me and holds her hand up to hide until we're out of the area.

She's expecting her place to be watched; a visit from me and she's on tenterhooks as a result. I know what he looks like and when I'm driving back to base tonight, I intend on making a call home. She's also very quiet, though in Rosie's company she's quite animated.

"Have you been to this place before?" I ask her as I pull up at a set of lights.

"No. Well, if I have, I've not been for nearly a decade. I'm sure it will have changed," she says, her voice quiet. "Can I...share something with you?" she asks, the hesitation in her voice all too apparent.

"Sure." I glance across and smile at her, buzzing she wants to confide in me.

"I had another unknown number call me yesterday."

I nod in response. "So that's why you changed your number?" I reply as I drive, hoping she didn't take the call.

"Yes. I didn't answer it and then I decided I was going to remove anyone connected with just my ex after an old contact asked me if I'd changed my number."

At another set of lights, I turn to look at her. "That's good. How do you feel?" I ask, aware that her telling me this is her being brave.

"I felt good; now I feel nervous," she shares and I nod in acknowledgement.

"Why do you feel nervous?" I've been reading up on how to help people who have been emotionally abused. I may not be a trained counsellor, but I can ask those questions and get Emma to at least start exploring how she's feeling and why.

"He found a way around me blocking him. It's just a matter of time," she says, shrugging as if it's no big deal, but I can tell it is. She's wringing her hands, biting her lip and not in a sexy way. I reach across and offer her my hand. From the corner of my eye, I see her look at it, then at me, then back to the hand before she takes it.

"Let me put it this way, twirl. I want to be there, okay?"

Eventually she bobs her head, but she doesn't offer up anything else. We drive in companionable silence and the more distance I put between us and 'home', the more relaxed she becomes.

As we approach the museum, she perks up, smiling. "I have been here before. Oh, the food here is good!" She turns to me, beaming and sits forward. This is the Emma I want to see every day and I promise myself that one day, I'll make it happen.

We enter the museum and find ourselves in a huge barn with many small internal shops in the style of the 1800s. Sewing machines that I'm sure my grandmother once used are set in a haberdashery shop, not to mention the traditional sweet shop. The weather can be doing all sorts outside, but inside the huge barn, we're snug and dry.

Emma lights up, turning to smile at me as we come across the old Post Office and I buy her a quarter of sweets from the shop that's manned by a young man in period dress. Then her attention is caught by some machinery that's been restored. For a few hours, we explore what the area would have done, made and been like and talk with the many "*keepers*" that are volunteers with a mine of local information.

Over lunch, with traditional bar food, I check what else we can go and do. I put my phone away and watch Emma as she enjoys her food.

"Do all you military types eat so fast?" she asks and I smirk as I shrug.

"Do you civvie types always eat so slowly?" I tease, remembering to keep my voice light and the smile on my face.

"I…" I lean in as she partly answers, not saying a word. Another trick a website gave me is to give abused people space. If they want to tell you, they'll tell you. "I want to enjoy what I eat," she eventually says, but her eyes aren't on me. They're on a spot on the table; my tease has made her go inwards again and I kick myself for it.

"Em?" I lean in and whisper. "It's okay. I'm not going to take food from you." She lifts her head and I send her a soft smile, noticing how wide her brown eyes are. "You can take as long as you want," I repeat. She relaxes and grasps my hand, before returning to eating her food. When she's finished, we explore the outside exhibits and as we walk around, I reach out to take her hand. She sighs and then takes mine.

"Why the heavy sigh?" I ask as we walk around. Being inside has reset my eyes and they adjust quickly to the bright light of the outdoors.

"I'm still working out your humour," she says, almost shyly.

"There's not much to work out, twirl," I reply, wondering. "I tease, I love, and I laugh." I shrug.

"I'm not used to the teasing," she replies hesitantly, "but I am learning. I want to learn." She quickly adds the last part. I squeeze her hand and pull her close so that our arms bump.

"Then I'll keep on with the lessons," I tell her and the emotion in her eyes wills me to keep trying.

As we take a path around some of the smaller exhibits, Emma glances around. "I've got an appointment tomorrow with Women's Aid," she says, her voice weak.

"That's great! I can't come with you though, twirl; I'm on shift." I wish now I wasn't. If I wasn't so close to the end of my contract, I'd run the risk of a bollocking from the WC, or worse.

"I know. But that's when the woman said she could meet with me," she says, her voice getting stronger.

"That's good. Do you have your evidence collected?" I ask and Emma nods.

"Rosie suggested long ago that I keep a diary. So, when my ex was asleep, or out of it on drugs, I'd note what happened and hide it away. He never found it," she explains, pulling her shoulders back and straightening her neck.

"Rosie's smart," I remind her. "So are you. So, go and do that tomorrow. Let me know if you need anything," I add. She stops and I don't realise until my hands pulls at hers. I stop and take two strides back to her.

"What's the matter, twirl?" I ask, noticing she's trying to form words, but they seem to get stuck.

"I'm..." She sucks in a breath, but I don't push her to say what she's trying to; I know I've got to give her time. "Why is this so hard?" she hisses, stamping her feet.

I feel this frustration is mostly at herself. She looks up at me, near to tears.

"I don't deserve your help," she states and I know my mouth drops open.

"Oh, twirl!" I pull her to me, wrapping my arms around her. I can only suspect what's going on beneath the surface. It takes me a long moment, several in fact, before I can speak. "Of course, you do! I just hope I deserve you," I say to her, my mind working overtime.

I can feel her sobbing, and I kiss her head. "You deserve so damn much! I don't just call every girl my twirl, ya know."

She sniffs as I let her pull back a little. "You know I'm broken, don't you?" she asks and I shrug.

"Show me someone who isn't? Oh wait, a newborn," I say, being serious. "Doesn't mean I don't wanna spend time with you." I watch as she sighs, her shoulders dropping.

"You're not broken," she says defiantly.

"Ain't I?" I chuckle. "Babe, I had good people around me to undo the crap my folks did to me before I knew that what they were doing was bad. You had Dave to guide you. Do I need him to talk to you about what you're thinking? That you're not worth any time I have?"

She shakes her head, shivering slightly. I rub her arms.

"Come on, I feel the need for some fatty goodness," I say and I march back to the car.

Chapter Nine

Kintsugi

Emma

Chris telling me that he's broken too, that only a newborn isn't, slowly gets into my head as he drives us away from the museum and back to Milton Keynes. He's got an earbud in and I can see the satnav on the car display telling him where to go. I have no idea where we're going and I feel like a fool for questioning his help. I expect demands to be made of me like my ex always did. Not that I'd object to giving them to this Chris.

Apart from Rosie and her dad, I've not had that level of help before. It was certainly never something I'd received from a boyfriend. *Is that what RAF Chris has become?*

He pulls into a car park and I realise where we are; Campbell Park. It's pretty flat with good paths and because of the nice weather, there are small street vendors around. I smell fresh doughnuts and burgers, see kids queuing for ice cream and Chris is grinning at me as he sniffs the air.

"Fancy some?" he asks as he helps me from the car and I nod weakly. I've never had someone help me out of a car before. "You are allowed," he reminds me.

"I just feel I'm taking advantage of you," I admit and he laughs.

"Twirl, that simply ain't the case. Come on," he says and he orders a bag of five fresh sugary doughnuts that are still warm.

Sitting on a bench a few minutes later, he offers me one out of the bag and I take it, nibbling small bites, savouring the sugary fresh dough. Chris though opens his mouth and stuffs one straight in.

I gape at him. "Wow!" I mutter, amazed he's eaten an entire doughnut like that in one go.

He laughs eventually when he's chewed the treat. "I'm greedy, don't let that bother you," he jokes. Then, he looks sombre, and my heart sinks. "I know you're not…greedy, that is. Let me tell you a little about me, okay, twirl?" he requests, and I nod as I continue to enjoy the doughnut.

"I'm in my late thirties now. To escape getting deeper into the gang I was kinda with in London, I joined the RAF. I could've joined the navy, but the RAF recruitment officer got to me first and that sealed who I was going to sign up with." He turns to look at me and I watch him as I continue to eat, letting him talk.

"I already told you that Mum and Dad weren't around much, if at all. My aunt and uncle did all that heavy work, including raising my cousins. My uncle managed to keep me away from the deeper part of the gangs and went mad at me when he realised how close I'd come to being right up to my neck with them.

"So when I said I was joining the military, he made me sit down and work out why. The reasons for wanting to be in deep with the gangs were the same as with the military. We talked for days about me joining the RAF, what element, officer rank and all that. At the end of it, I realised that I just wanted a big, extended family.

"My uncle asked me which one I wanted. The military? Or the gangs where he'd likely bury me before *his* time was up? By the end of that long weekend, I'd made my mind up and signed up the following week with his blessing."

"And you met Byron?" I ask, wondering how those two ever met.

"Not right away. I was still troubled, hard to guide, at least for some of the governors I had. But Byron? We got on like a house on fire, cemented our friendship over a game of pool." He laughs half-heartedly and jams his fingers into his short hair. It looks rough and I want to touch it, to feel it. *I've never wanted to do that to anyone before.*

"Couple of the local lads had taken on two younger RAF crewmen who got diddled on a game of pool. Young ones were a tad green around the gills. Byron and I were watching from the bar. He commented, then I commented. We both noticed how the local lads were gleaning money from the gills with the talent, that's the younger pair, yeah?" he asks, and I nod.

"Great! So, we step in. We hadn't played each other before; we both didn't know how good the other was. Byron's a damn demon on the pool table, let me tell you now." He barks out a laugh, hiding a caution about Byron's paying ability in his warning, but I'm attuned to them, so I notice.

"So I break, don't pot anything. Their decent guy gets two down and then Byron comes up to me and whispers to me '*Get ready. It's over.*'" Chris is trying to not laugh, but the memory takes over. "He gets to the table and clears the damn thing. Leaves their five balls on the table, not touching a single one. They start having a go at him, but he's already known in his squadron for his pool skills. Suddenly his lot are there, backing him up. My shift crew are there too and because Byron's getting it in the neck and I'm at his side, they wade in. It was a mess!"

I laugh, mostly because Chris doesn't hold back the laughter anymore; he lets it roll out and I laugh to join in. His deep chuckles turn to howls and last a few moments before he calms down enough to carry on.

"So these local lads get picked up by the police, the bar having called them in. We tell them that they were scamming the new guys and how, including rigging the balls with magnets. The pub was not happy that the balls had been switched out." He goes to continue, but I hold my hand up.

"Wait...the local lads had switched the pool balls for ones with magnets in them?" I ask, my eyes going wide. I forget about eating the second doughnut I've picked up out of the bag for a moment.

"Yeah...Byron saw how they were doing it: ring magnets. The young lads got their money returned; the local lads got banned not just from there but most of the other pubs as the word got out." He grins and wipes his eyes. "We talked about that night for days! We checked a few pubs through the course of a few weeks, making sure they weren't around. Rosie had left by the time he and I had met, but we bonded because of that night." He sighs as if he's happy.

"And here you are," I state, pleased that they met.

"Yep. Here I am," he replies jovially. "With you, which is great," he says, his voice lowering. "To come back to the first point, you're not broken. We all have cuts, bruises, and things we wish we could change. But in doing that, we stop being ourselves. One question my uncle would always ask me was this: who do I want to be in the future?"

I ponder the question, chewing slowly on the doughnut. "What did you reply with?" I ask and Chris shakes his head.

"I'll tell you that when you tell me your answer," he says, which makes me smile.

"What if I don't know?" I ask as he finally helps himself to a second doughnut.

"Then you need to do what my uncle told me to do: decide. And start making steps to it each day, even if you have to crawl," he tells me and finishes off the last doughnut in two huge bites. He's given me so much to think about beyond the immediate situation.

When we have finished the doughnuts, Chris buys us both a bottle of water and we walk around Campbell Park.

"Everyone is a little...what's that Japanese thing where you repair broken things with gold?" he asks, struggling to find the word.

"Kintsugi," I reply, not skipping a beat.

He pulls back, gapes, then resets his mouth and grins at me. "You *are* a wordsmith! Yeah...that word. Everyone is a Kintsugi in progress. We get parts broken off, sometimes we want the part back, other times we don't." He smiles as he swings my hand in the sunshine. The birds are singing, people are wandering around and other couples are holding hands. Families are enjoying the nice weather and kids are on their bikes. The park is busy but not crowded.

"Some parts aren't worth having back and some are worth breaking off, so you can fit a new piece in." He continues to smile at me and I'm content to beam back at him.

"I want to break the old Chris off," I state, following his lead, letting my heart dictate to my head for once. "I've not looked at what I want to be or do beyond that, I've never..." I sigh, deciding now I really need to be brave. "I've never thought much about six months later, or a year later, or even longer than that. You know that interview question that the company asks you at the end; where do you want to be in five years?"

He nods. "Yeah, the RAF recruitment officer asked me that too. I'm still there." He winks at me.

"Well, I never knew the answer to that because I never saw myself staying with any company that I interviewed with. But now...now I get to choose for myself, don't I?" I ask and he nods, beaming at me. He gets blurry and I don't understand why, until he's wiping away the tears that seem to be falling.

"You're able to do things for yourself, twirl. You always have and I'll thump anyone who says that you can't." His voice is sharp, convincing and empowering.

"Thank you," I choke out between sobs.

He rests his head against mine but doesn't say another word.

Chris takes me home and I smile at him in the car. "Have you got time for a coffee, before you go back to the base?" I ask and he nods, checking his watch.

"I have about an hour before I need to leave so I'm back on base in time to change and muster," he says.

"Great!" I motion to the flat. He inclines his head and comes around to help me out, something I would never have had done before. But with Chris, I want him to do it as much as he either wants or needs to.

I let us in and then bolt the door behind us; my need about being safe, not letting my ex in, plays out.

"It's okay, twirl, I get it," he says and I smile.

"Sorry, old habits," I confess and he nods.

"Yeah, I get it," he repeats in a softer tone. Ex Chris would shout at me, and tell me I was stupid. "Will you do something for me?" he asks and I wonder what he's about to demand of me, but I nod. "When you meet with the Women's Aid lady tomorrow, ask about the restraining order as well, please?"

My face must give me away because Chris is before me, his hand is holding onto the side of my face, gently but firmly. There's no pressure like there would be with my ex. He's not forcing me to do anything.

"You were...expecting me to demand something else from you, weren't you?" he questions, and I nod. "Twirl," he says, his voice low and rumbling, "trust me when we do go to bed; it'll be because you want it and you're ready for it. Not because of some expectation that I did something nice for you that needs a favour returning."

His pupils contract and expand as I gaze into his eyes; I pay attention to the warm, spiralling whiskey colour.

"Thank you," I whisper and turn my head to kiss his hand, planting a firm kiss into the strong palm that's firmly holding my head.

Chris nods and motions to the kitchen. "I'd love a coffee before I go," he tells me. "And the bathroom?" he adds with a grin.

"Down there," I say. "Excuse the shitty door, Rosie replaced it but it's gone funny," I admit and he grins.

He stalks down the short hallway and I can't help but admire his arse as he eats up the distance in seconds. My imagination runs riot and I imagine what it would feel like with my hands wrapped around it.

I blink, focusing on the empty kettle and pouring some water into it. Whilst it boils, I make up two mugs: one of instant coffee, the other of tea.

I turn at the sound of the door not quite shutting.

"I can fix that in about thirty seconds if you've some matches and a screwdriver?" Chris says. I nod, going to my tool drawer.

"I have no idea which screwdriver you need," I say and he comes over to rummage through the drawer. He grabs a blue-handled one and the box of matches.

"Come on, I'll show you a trick," he says to me. "Oh, I take my coffee black." He winks and then heads off back to the bathroom. I watch as he lights a few matches, blows them out, and has me hold them a few seconds later. He removes one of the screws and repairs my frame with matches. I gape as he packs each screw hole with dead matches. Ten minutes later, when he's checked every screw-hole for the hinges, he effortlessly swings the door shut.

"How did...wow! Thank you!" I say, appreciative that he's fixed that door for me without charging me a fortune.

"It could still do with a little wood filler, some sanding and a quick lick of paint, but it'll shut now."

"Thank you! It's been like that for months and I thought I'd have to get someone in to fix it again," I confess.

"No need, it was pretty much there; just the holes are shot as a result of him breaking it." He closes the door, checking it again. "The problem you had," he says, opening the door and handing me the rest of the box of matches and the screwdriver, "is that the doorframe got damaged when he broke the door down. The matches will help fill the holes, but I'll sort it properly when I'm here next, if you'd like?"

I nod. "Yes please!" I whisper, then my mouth remembers how to work and my brain can't stop it. "He got angry at me." I wasn't intending on telling him, but now I've begun, the words tumble from my lips. "He...found out what I was doing," I admit.

Chris reacts, but not like I thought he would. He nods and goes to sit on the edge of the bathtub; his hands are placed on his thighs as he waits for me to speak. I lean against the doorframe, using it as support.

"I started writing fantasy stories to pass the time as they kept circulating in my head. He found them," I whisper. "He broke this door down the night he found out and he destroyed the laptop I was trying to protect, thinking it would stop me."

"Has it?" he asks. His jaw is clenched, the muscles tick with effort; I can tell he wants to say more. I shake my head.

"No..."

He stands and comes to me, lifting my chin and looking deep into my eyes, as if he's trying to find my soul. "You keep on writing. Turn him into every bad guy; I'll vanquish every demon you can make him into, whatever you write about." He leans in and kisses me softly on the lips. "Every." He kisses one side of my mouth. "Damn." He moves to the other side. "Time."

When he pulls back, I can just about see him and I pull in a huge gulp of air, then another.

"Thank you, twirl," he whispers against me as he holds me tight. "You've trusted me and I know that was a huge step for you. So, thank you. I'll do my damnedest to never betray that." I feel him kissing my head as he holds me a little tighter.

Chapter Ten

Promises

Chris

I leave Emma's after fixing the bathroom door. She'll need some small repairs done to at least get her deposit back and I vow to do them next time I'm there.

When I get to the dual carriageway, I tell the virtual assistant to call my uncle.

"Chris! How're things?" he asks jovially.

"They're good! I need to chat, see I've met someone..." I admit.

"Kinhell!" he answers back. "Who? Tell me more."

"That's why I'm calling. She's...well, her ex abused her. I'm still working out how, but I need to know more about *him*. He's a bit of a merchant banker." My uncle huffs at my use of the slang.

"Is he now?" A muffled sound echoes down the line and I imagine him covering the phone. I hear him talking to my cousin. "Rich says send him it via whiskey and soda." I grin. You can take the boy out of London...

"On it. Give me a few hours, driving back," I respond, watching the roads.

"We twig! You okay otherwise?"

"Yeah, sound! Just winding down the contract now, not long to go," I remind him.

"Good! Glad to hear it. Do we get to meet this one?" he asks and I laugh.

"Maybe! We'll see how it goes, yeah? Told her about you all," I admit.

"You'll be marrying her next," my uncle teases; only I think he's being somewhat serious.

"Give us a bleedin' chance!" I answer. "Her ex has caused her some grief. She blocked him on social media, but he finds ways around that. She recently changed her number, so I hope she's off his radar. Now she's started getting brave, but I can feel in my bones, she's going to need some help."

"Don't go doing anything stupid *yourself*," he tells me and I read the meaning behind his words.

"I don't propose to," I assure, leaving the intent unsaid. I understand what his statement meant, as I am sure he understood my reply. Don't mess up the end of my term with the RAF. "That's why I called. I needed some sound advice."

He chuckles. "Good lad! Now, tell us more." I go through how I met Emma, her circumstances, the simple repair I just did on her bathroom door and why.

"He sounds like a proper strawberry split," Rich calls out and I laugh.

"Yeah, he's a git, for sure! Hopefully, she'll put in the molestation order tomorrow, or start to. The restraining order? I've offered her the cash for it," I reveal and my uncle whistles.

"So, you're really keen on this one." He's stating the obvious.

"Something about her just makes me want to get her out of harm's way. That's not a bad thing, is it?" I check with him.

"No, son, it ain't." He's called me "son" since he took me in and I've never wanted to correct him.

"Good! We'll see how it goes though, see if she's up for meeting you all."

My uncle and cousin laugh. "I'll chat with you later, gotta get back to this job, yeah?"

"Yeah, laters!" I say, hanging up when they reply with the same. The conversation has lifted my spirits and the drive back is much less tiresome.

Hours later after my shift, I slowly wake and text Emma.

Chris: Hey! Just woke up from the night shift. How are things?

Emma: Things are good. I've met with the Women's Aid lady and she's echoing what you said about the restraining order. She's been able to get me to see a lawyer tomorrow.

C: Let me know when you need the money transferred and to who.

E: You're very kind; thank you!

I notice how her texts are always written out properly, they're hardly ever abbreviated or shortened.

C: You're very welcome, twirl!

E: We're working tonight, not sure if Rosie's told that to Byron.

C: Down to them. I know he's borrowing the car later so he can take her skiing.

E: Rosie, skiing? You're joking?

C: Nope!

E: I'll be very surprised if she goes!

She sends me back a blushing, smiling emoji, nothing else, so I get up, dress and think about going straight to the mess hall for food. Checking the time, I quickly divert into the office and double-check when Byron's crew are due back, noticing that they've been cleared to land. He'll get debriefed, then I know he'll want to find the coffee, so I head to the mess hall.

Grievance finally makes an appearance, and I nudge him as he enters the mess hall, aiming for the coffee machines.

"Hey! How'd it go?" I enquire and he shrugs in response.

"Same old, same old. What about here?" he asks, pouring himself a large, black coffee.

"Quiet; spent time with Em…she's filing that paperwork," I say to him with a smile, trying to hide my concern.

"Great news," he enthuses, gulping some coffee.

"You don't wanna sleep?" I ask, surprised.

"I'm half Italian, coffee doesn't bother me," he quips, which makes me roll my eyes. "I want to see what messages Rosie's sent me first." There's a softer look about him at the mention of Rosie.

"I'm sure she's missed you," I say as I help myself to coffee. I can't help that my face betrays my thoughts.

"What's with the funny look?" he asks and I try to shrug it off. When the look doesn't falter, I lower my voice.

"I'm not sure you and Rosie are going to go skiing." He throws me a look that tells me what he'd really like to do and I can only laugh. I lean across and quietly mutter, "You'd rather take her to bed and get that base outta your system."

The look that comes over his face tells me that I'm right. He shakes it off and quickly drinks the coffee with me as I'm on night duty.

"Oh, they're working tonight. There's not a function on, so they should be home by midnight." I wink, setting his expectations. He thanks me and heads off to do his thing while I head to muster and my shift.

The following morning I spy Byron heading out to do a run and we acknowledge each other. I drop the car keys in his room and then I grab a shower before heading to bed.

It's mid-afternoon when my alarm wakes me and I stretch. I'm on an interim shift today; I blink myself awake. I check my phone and see a message from Emma.

E: Lawyer's encouraging me to file that restraining order. Could you contact me when you're awake?

C: I just woke up. Calling you, okay?

E: Yes!

I hit dial and swing my legs over the edge of my bed, grateful I have a private room. I fling on a t-shirt and it rings twice before she answers.

"Hey, twirl! What's occurrin'?" I ask as I yank on some tracksuit bottoms and move to sit in my chair so if I need to make a video call, I am at least presentable.

"I'm at the lawyer's office that Women's Aid referred me to. They said what you said. But to get the paperwork started, they're asking for payment details," she says, her voice tight, hesitant.

"That's okay. Is there someone there I can speak with?" I ask. A few seconds later, I get to speak with a nice legal clerk who takes my details and five minutes later, I'm talking with Emma again.

"Thank you!" she gushes at me so strongly that I think she's sobbing, though she's doing it quietly.

"You're welcome, twirl," I reply to her. "I'm sorry I missed your message."

"I knew you were on nights, so I didn't want to call," she tells me.

"It was worth being woken up for. It's good," I reassure her.

"Thank you!" she tells me again. "The notary is wanting me to go and sign the paperwork," she adds.

"Well, on you go. I'll call you later when I'm on a break, okay?" I suggest, grabbing my fatigues off the hanger.

"Speak to you later. Thank you," she says, her voice low and whimpering.

"Later, twirl!" I tell her and then I get ready to go on shift.

Later, on my break, I call her; she's at Rosie's with Byron and Rosie's dad, Dave.

"Hey, twirl!" I greet her.

"Hi! How's work?"

"Nothing unusual today. What are you up to?" I ask, pouring myself a coffee.

"I lost out on that flat near Rosie; I found out while I was at the lawyer," she says. "Rosie, Dave and Byron are helping me look for a new place that I can afford," she continues.

"Move up to Waddington," I tell her. *Damn, I want her close and other than the need to protect her, I have no idea why.*

"That would bring me closer to you..." she says, then she adds, very faintly, "That's not a bit too soon?"

"To keep you safe? Hell no, never too soon, twirl."

"I won't have a job up there," she says, putting up a little resistance.

"Jobs come and go. You're a competent barmaid; I'm sure there are lots of places near Wadd that need a woman of your capabilities," I praise her. "It will also mean we can see more of each other," I remind her, looking for positives.

"Okay, I'll look near Wadd too," she says, relenting.

"That's my twirl! I need to go back on duty; I'm getting glares," I say as Boomer comes into the break-out area and scowls at me. "See you on Sunday, yeah?"

"You will. Take care," she says and hangs up.

Boomer stands with her arms folded over her chest and raises her eyebrows at me.

"New girl missed out on a flat, trying to persuade her to move up here."

Josie's expression relaxes, the resting bitch-face fading.

"This the one that you said might just drive onto base?" she asks as she pours herself a coffee.

"Yeah, that's the one," I confirm and Josie nods.

"Gotcha! Now git, before Rum bollocks ya," she tells me and I scarper back out on patrol, joining Heartlands and the others.

Chapter Eleven

Friends

Emma

I smile at Rosie as she drives us to view a flat in the north part of Milton Keynes. It's further from Rosie and work, but it's also much further than I hope my ex would think to look for me.

Byron is following close behind, having been invited by Rosie to come and view the flat with us. It's also closer to Waddington, which for some reason, feels right.

"How did the skiing go?" I ask and she huffs, but there's a huge smile on her face.

"It went well. There are markers around everywhere and I was meant to stay between the black ones." She shrugs, hesitating for a moment. "An instructor had to stop me from falling over after I had wandered into the path of someone trying to come down the slope."

"Did you get hurt?" I ask, surprised.

"No…the instructor stopped me, but it was good. I waddled into the snow area, thinking that I looked like Mr Stay Puff." I nod—we love Ghostbusters—and she continues, "When I was in there, I decided I was a very skinny Mr Stay Puff." Rosie laughs, making me laugh too. We chat about the rest of her day and I tell her what Women's Aid told me, echoing what Annie had said—move.

We find the address and drive around for a few minutes in a circle to see what's where and I note the local shops, the schools and how the grounds of the maisonettes have been cared for.

Already I feel lighter, safer and more at ease. We smile at Byron who pulls up behind us. Then the estate agent is with us and he speaks to Byron, who quickly makes him address me.

We go up to the flat, which I note is on the second floor, the top one. I've not had so much light to live in before—it's amazing! The flat is clean, functional and up to date. The cooker is a lot newer and in better working order than where I am now.

The agent tells me the rent and it's more than the advert says. Before I can say anything, Byron is wading in. Thank goodness for his hug earlier and his presence now.

"That's not what the advert says," Byron tells him, who then shows him the photograph of the advert from the newspaper.

"Ah, that's a misprint," he says to Byron, who glares at him.

"Of one hundred a month? That's not a misprint; you're taking advantage. Rosie, honey, would you get me the number for trading standards, please? I'm sure there's a number for some sort of estate agent ombudsman too." He nods at her, his Scottish accent getting thicker with every word. Rosie winks at me and does as Byron asks. I can only stand with my heart in my throat.

"There is no need for that," the agent says in a shaky voice as Byron raises his eyebrows.

"Really? I know what the rent is; it was advertised and confirmed verbally when we booked the viewing." The agent sighs and then excuses himself; he turns and calls the office. Byron winks at me and my nerves lessen when I realise he knows what he's doing. A few moments later, the estate agent is back and apologises.

"Turns out the landlord reduced the rental amount, but I wasn't made aware," he tells us. Rosie hums at him in a disbelieving tone.

"I'd like to confirm with my friend what her intentions are, in private," Byron says and the agent nods, heading out into the hallway.

Rosie winks at Byron, which makes me smile.

"What do you want to do?" Byron quietly asks me as I work out how to tell him what I want.

"I want the place," I confess. "Do you think they'll hold it until I can show Chris?" I ask hopefully, but Byron shrugs and my hope for that evaporates.

"Let me see if he's free," Byron offers. He pulls his phone out to text. Moments later, Chris is calling me on a video call.

"Hi! Sorry," I whisper and he grins.

"Don't worry, but I do need you to be quick, twirl," he tells me and I began showing him around the place. As I'm talking, I can see Byron and Rosie standing near the hallway.

"Then there are two decent-sized bedrooms," I say and my friends move so I can go show him.

"Twirl, that looks great! I'll get the small repairs done to the old place, yeah? I've gotta get back before Rum realises I'm taking a personal call, but I'll chat with you after my shift, okay?"

He winks at me as I nod and then the chat ends. I'm beaming at Rosie and Byron for several reasons and this flat is one of them.

"My friend would like to rent the flat," Byron states for me to the agent, who smiles at me. Rosie winks at me with a soft smile.

"Let's get the paperwork done in the office." He motions to us and is already on a call as he locks up, telling his office that I'm coming in to sign the lease.

An hour or so later, after a little cajoling on Rosie's part to make up my deposit, I've signed my name.

"It should only take a week for the checks to come through and then we can give you the keys," the estate agent says with a smile. Byron is standing behind me, Rosie to the side, and I'm so grateful my friends are here. Rosie told me as we came to the office that Byron wasn't going to let him try and cajole me into paying more. My friends double-checked the paperwork with me before I signed the lease.

Leaving the office, it's like a weight has been lifted from my shoulders. I smile at Byron, grateful for his and Rosie's help.

"We'll help you move," Byron tells me and I can only smile; I'm not going to argue with him.

He turns to Rosie. "Can you find somewhere to hire us a van? Stevo and I will come down the night before, stay over, help out," he declares, his voice set in determination.

"I can do that; I know just who to ask," she tells him and it's lovely to see Rosie trusting a guy, though it's not hard to trust Byron. Or Chris.

Rosie hugs me as we leave the agent's office and then she's giving Byron a huge hug before he heads off back to the base and we head home.

"So it *did* go well," I praise my best friend and she chuckles.

"Yeah, it did," she agrees with mirth and excitement. I can't help but smile with her.

"I'm glad. You deserve this," I remind her.

"So do you," she tells me. "You like Chris?" she asks and I nod.

"I...told him," I admit to her, fearfully. "I didn't mean to," I begin to defend my actions and Rosie reaches out a hand, asking to hold mine.

"Em, it's okay! The more you can share with this Chris, the better he'll be able to work out how to fit in with you. He's a decent guy." She pulls her hand back after a quick squeeze to use the gear stick. "So is Byron, though to be honest, he's just matured."

"So he's not a total moron? Or a cockwomble?" I ask, recalling the phrases Rosie used back then to label Byron.

"Not anymore. Though I wish I had argued with him at the time, not run away from the humiliation he made me feel."

If she hadn't, I wouldn't be meeting this Chris now. I'm a little grateful for that.

After Rosie drops me off, I text Chris, telling him that Byron stood up for me and that Rosie helped with the deposit until I can get it back from the place I'm currently in.

C: Give me twenty, then it's my proper break and I can call.

E: Ok!

I keep forgetting he's not supposed to be answering his phone while on duty and I feel bad in case he gets caught or worse, punished. Chris calls when he says he's going to.

"Hey, twirl, how's it going?"

"It's going good, thanks to you, Byron, and Rosie," I say to him, happy as I recall what happened and how his friend made me feel safe.

"He's a good one! Your friend and him seem to be hitting it off," he states and I agree.

"I'm glad! He really hurt her, but I hope they can work through it properly." I pause, wondering if I can tell him that I'm grateful for all he's done and is doing. "I'm glad, as it let me meet you," I say, waiting for the boot to fall. But, it doesn't.

"I'm glad too, twirl! Did you have enough for the deposit?"

"I...Uh..." I flounder in my reply. "Rosie bridged the gap until I get the first deposit back," I reveal and Chris's reply throws me.

"That's good, though I would have helped if you asked. She's a true friend," he says. There's no admonishment for taking money from a friend, even if it is understood that it's a loan. My ex did that and there were times I didn't eat because I was made to feel horrible, like a cheat, if I mentioned to Rosie that I needed food or money for the electricity. When Rosie worked out what was happening, she'd do a small food shop for me anyway. Or invite me around to dinner and give me stuff to bring home. My ex disliked her, and she detested him.

"She is," I say, forgetting where I am for a moment. Chris chuckles.

"Where'd you go in your head?" he asks, and I can hear him blowing on something. "I'm just grabbing a coffee, in case you're wondering what I'm doing. It's hotter than usual," he says to me.

"I was just remembering something my ex would do," I confess. "I notice how different you both are. It's taking a little getting used to," I whisper, afraid that'll scare him off. "It's partly why I can't ask you for more," I tell him, sighing.

"Oh, what did he do?" There's a curiosity in his now tight voice.

"It was about money...I don't earn a lot, so what I do earn is always allocated out: electricity, rent and food, etc. He was good at spending the food shopping or the electric money because I'd have it filed in a money pouch." I sigh.

"So you'd end up cold or hungry, or both?" he asks, his voice going tight and deep.

"Yes," I admit, near tears, ashamed I let him do that to me at all, never mind for months. "Rosie found out and she'd get me some groceries, pay the electric meter, or invite me to dinner and send me home with Tupperware. It was one of the things she had a go at him for."

"As I said, a *true* friend," he repeats, though the word true is stronger this time. "I'll bet they didn't get on," he observes and I shake my head, then confirm it for him.

"No...they really didn't." I giggle. "I had to sneak out to meet with her," I admit.

"Never going to happen with me, twirl! If folk are decent to you and you wanna spend time with them, go do it. If they use you, well, you need to either stand up to them or don't see them."

"It's not always that simple," I point out, remembering our childhood.

"No, it's not, but here's a trick; surround yourself with people who do support you, love you, want what's best for you." I can hear him drinking again. "It makes things a lot easier," he chuckles.

"I wish I were that strong," I admit.

"You are, more than you know. I'd like you to remember that," he responds.

"I'll let you know when I am going to get the keys to the new place," I say. "I can't wait to show you." I get excited that he's helped make this happen.

"Looking forward to it!" There's a pause on his side and I hear a cup being put down. "I need to go, twirl, take it easy, okay? Byron's back and I wanna catch up with him. I'll call you later, yeah?"

"Looking forward to it," I whisper and then he's gone.

Chapter Twelve

Vans, Cars & Flats

Chris

The gatehouse let me know Byron is back via text as I'm talking with Emma. I quickly hang up, promising to call her later. My shift ended half an hour ago and I need to touch base with my friend.

"Emma texted me as you were driving back," I say to him as he gets out of the car. "I got to chat with her and she told me what happened with the estate agent." I hold my hand out to thank him, but I pull him into a hug. My brother-from-another-mother has my back. "Cheers, mate!"

"You'd have done the same, if you needed to," he confirms and shrugs in half agreement. "That agent…" Byron growls and I beam at him, wondering which side of him came out. "It was down to incompetence. He didn't like me stepping up, but Mama taught me well," he enthuses, and I'm grateful for his intervention.

"One day I'm going to meet your folks," I promise. "And tell them what a fabulous guy you are."

"You will meet them, but don't tell them what an arse I am right away, okay?" He grins at my teasing. "Next lot of leave, we should all head out to Italy," he suggests, making me smile. I'd love to see Italy. I'd love to take Emma, as was suggested before.

"Emma's going to let me know when she gets the keys," I inform him. We climb the stairs to our floor.

"She was short on the deposit," Byron tells me and I nod, knowingly.

"She wouldn't take it from me, not after…" He raises his eyebrows a little.

"The restraining order," he finishes my sentence and I let my frustration show.

"I wish she'd move up here," I admit, voicing my desire for the first time, even if I hadn't planned to do so. "If anything happens, I can't be there as quickly as I'd like," I share, sighing.

"We could move down, there's a base there," he suggests.

"No openings, I've already checked," I advise as we reach our rooms.

"Fuck," he breathes out.

"Grab a shower so we can head down to the mess hall," I tell him. "We need to figure this out." He gives me an affirmative nod, and I leave him to it.

Ten minutes later, we're enjoying a soft drink in the mess hall.

"She told me what he's capable of, what he's done to her...before..." I tell my friend, quietly. "I would like to see him behind bars. Maybe now she'll press charges." I sigh, running a hand through my hair and over my face. "But, she won't. I know she won't. He's got her so scared." I take a swig of the still hot coffee. "I'm not sure what has to happen before she does."

"Rosie's not said anything about what he did to Em. I've not asked though," Byron offers and I shake my head in response.

"Rosie won't tell you. She'd tell you to ask Em, and it's taken me a lot to get her to tell me the few bits she has. He hasn't raped her, I don't think, but he has hit and left bruises." I ponder about what else he's physically capable of, and it makes me see red. "He's capable of it," I seethed through my teeth.

I notice Byron clench his fists in anger and motion towards them. "I did the same when she told me. She also told me why."

Byron leans in. "I figured you'd tell me when you were ready."

"She started writing fantasy romance stories, with the plan of expanding them into full novels. He found out. Destroyed her laptop, pens, notepads..." I try to keep my temper, but it's hard. "Then he turned on her." I have to remember to breathe. "Every bad guy she writes is going to be an element of him," I spit out.

"And you're going to be the hero, every scenario?" Byron asks; I perk up at that.

"Told her I wanted to be…that I'd vanquish any demon she cares to write about, whatever she writes about." I've never reacted to a woman before, not like this. I'm a love-em-and-leave-em kinda guy. *But guys hitting girls, physically?* I breathe in, willing my temper to reduce; now is not the time.

I can see Byron nodding. "But first, you're going to have to get Little Red away from the Big Bad Wolf."

I chuckle at the reference. "I know. This move will help that, but I wanted her to be up here. He knows that bar; it won't take him long to find her if he wants to," I admit. I'm expecting her ex to have the same gang resources I once had. That way, I can expect the unexpected.

Byron lifts his chin a little. "She's renting it for six months. We've just over a year left. Shall we look up here for a one-bed flat for her?" he asks, but I'm a step ahead of him in that thought.

"Already asked Josie to go looking for me," I admit. She's also good at keeping things quiet; despite her Boomer nickname, she's discreet. "She said to give her a few days." He sighs. "I just hope I don't need it before then."

"I'm thinking I need a car," Byron reveals. "In case," he adds and I agree. We might be needed in two areas at the same time.

"Yeah, that might not be a bad idea. There's a used showroom in town. We can start there, head up to the places in Lincoln itself if we need it." Byron half nods then go glassy-eyed.

"Has to be an Italian car," he grins and I roll my eyes at him.

"Course it bloody does," I laugh and he pulls a face.

I talk with Emma every day, sometimes more than once a day. I'm on rotation for the rest of the week as I've swapped shifts so I have the weekend free to help her move. On the day we're moving Emma, Byron sweeps Rosie out of the room and Emma quietly tells me why.

"She's paid for the vans to move me," she whispers.

"We said we'd do that. We just needed a contact," I say as I stack another sealed box in the pile.

"She's being stubborn about taking the money back," Emma continues, keeping her voice low.

"Byron will give her the money back," I state. "This is on us." I wink at her. She purses her lips together and blushes, then she leans over to me.

"Thank you, again," she says, her tone airy. I pull her to me for a hug.

"You're welcome, twirl." I lift her chin and kiss her on the lips. Byron hollers for me, then there's a knock at the door. I open it cautiously to see Colleen, the girl she was with at the bar, and a whole load of bikers. Some carry themselves as military personnel would and they all shuffle into Emma's small flat.

Someone behind Colleen speaks. "Right, where do we get started then, Col?" Colleen turns to me as if awaiting instructions.

"That pile there is ready to take down. We could use a hand packing some more," I suggest and Colleen gets the men to start loading the boxes, another two to get the bed and another two to do something else. Her small stature doesn't stop her having total control over them; it impresses me.

I turn to find Emma watching me. "You ready, babe?" I ask her and she nods.

"Yeah, let's move on out. You're the best!" she tells me, jumping into my arms and giving me a huge hug. My arms go around her tightly and I hold her to me. She needs this.

Hours later, we're at the new place; boxes and bodies are everywhere. We order pizzas—one for everyone—and Colleen goes around, collecting the fees for the delivery man, who has to bring at least fourteen of them. What doesn't get eaten tonight, we will no doubt eat tomorrow.

Somewhere near eleven, the extra bodies start dispersing, all wishing Emma good fortune in her new place. The bed has been assembled and so has the rest of her bedroom furniture, leaving just Rosie, Byron, Emma and myself in the new flat.

Things are pretty much set in Emma's new bedroom. I notice the temporary curtains in the living room, but it's enough for Emma to have some privacy right now and darkness for Byron and Rosie, who are sleeping over.

Byron dashes out to his car, bringing in the extra bedding we had agreed he'd likely need. We bid our friends goodnight and finally, I can lock Emma in her room.

Emma jumps as I close the bedroom door.

"Hey," I call to her, and she smiles nervously at me. "It's been a long day," I tell her, and she nods. Between doing the minor repairs on her place before we left it behind and moving her to this one, I am beat. "I'm happy to just curl up and hold you, okay?"

I expect a nod of the head, an agreement, but she shakes her head at me.

"I don't want that," she tells me. She turns on the small sidelight and I watch as she moves to the main light switch just behind me and flips it off. The curtains are closed, making the room all about her and me.

"What do you want?" I ask, keeping my voice as neutral as I can. She moves to stand before me and places her small, cold hands on my dirty t-shirt.

"This may be out of line." She bites her lower lip, and her chocolate eyes go wide. "But, you," she whispers and leans up to kiss me. It's soft, gentle and very unsure. So unlike the few kisses we've had before. She pulls back when I don't respond. "I thought…" she utters, faltering and begins to look at the floor.

"Emma," I growl, lifting her chin so I can look at her. "I'm not going to force you. I just want to know; are you sure?" This is probably the first time she's ever told a man she wants him. She nods. "Then do that again, but as you mean it. Like you won't take no for an answer," I command her, and she goes wide-eyed.

"Own it, twirl. Acknowledge it, follow it and let yourself chase that desire. I'll know by your actions." Before I can add any more, she's pounced on me, her arms wrapping around my neck and torso. Her sweet, hot little mouth is on mine. I bite her lower lip a little, just to see how she reacts to a bit of pain and she gasps, pulling back briefly, then she's standing taller, her lips assaulting mine, nipping at my upper lip. My tongue dances with hers and for the first time, she's not acting like she's scared.

She's in control. Finally, she's telling me what she wants. Who she wants. And it's glorious.

Her mouth continues to assault mine, though her hands haven't explored my body yet. I'm desperate to do that to her; to lay her down and worship her, but I also need her to be more sure of herself, to accept what I can give her, to own herself.

She pulls back, her teeth threatening to puncture her lip, and she's biting so hard. Gently, she tugs at the t-shirt, and I smirk then remove it for her and throw it to where the basket is. Emma visibly loses balance for a second, as if her knees gave out, and then she's holding onto me, her eyes wide.

"Own it, twirl," I remind her and she nods. She finds her gumption and pulls me to her, her confidence returning. Her fingers dig into my shoulders as our tongues dance. I turn us and ease us down onto the bed, her on top, which sends her wide-eyed again.

"Never been on top?" I ask her, keeping my voice low and she shakes her head. I grin and tuck my hands behind my head. "Feel free to explore, do what you will," I offer.

"You're sure?" she asks and I nod briefly.

"Yeah, I trust you." A long moment later, I feel her fingertips gently explore my torso, the ridges I've worked on over and above the military standard. I lie back as I feel her gently trace my pecs, graze a nipple and then up to my arms. I flex slightly which makes her jump and then she's giggling quietly, just enough so I can hear her.

"Chris," she breathes at me and I open my eyes.

"Yeah, twirl?" I ask and see she's biting her lip.

"Am I allowed to do more?" I groan and she pulls back, but I quickly grab her.

"Em, you can do whatever you like. I know you won't harm me," I begin.

"Harm you?" She gasps. "Someone did? Who?" she demands and I chuckle at her change of attitude.

"No one has, twirl. No one else has been allowed to do what you're doing to me right now." That truth both scares and excites me in equal measure. She makes an 'O' with her mouth.

"I want to kiss you," she tells me and I nod. Only, it's not my mouth she wants to kiss. Her sweet little mouth kisses one part of my abs, then another and another, slowly working her way up to my pectorals.

"Such a tease," I whisper. "So good," I add, encouraging her. She straddles me at my words, taking more control and makes me jump when she licks an erect nipple. Her mouth is at my chest, my throat and then, it's on my lips. I can taste my sweat on her sweet lips and decide it's my turn for a taste.

Chapter Thirteen

Taking Control

Emma

Never before have I been allowed to explore a man; my ex...no, I can't think about him right now. As I kiss Chris, after exploring most of his fit torso with my mouth, I've run dry of ideas of what to do to him. *Am I allowed to undress him? See him naked?* The light is on and before I can summon up yet more courage to ask, he flips us over.

"There's no right or wrong here, twirl. Just us, enjoying each other, yeah?" I nod and he pulls me up, removing my top to reveal the grey sports bra I have on for today.

Chris doesn't say a word as he lifts his eyebrows, a smile curling his lips before he pushes me back onto the bed, resting on top of me, and kissing me. I wrap my arms around him, holding him close, hiding under him and as his kisses move, so do my hands.

My jaw gets the attention, as does my throat, my neckline and then he pushes the sports bra out of the way to get access to a breast. I wiggle, remove it, and throw it to where the other clothes have been tossed.

"So bloody gorgeous, twirl," he tells me as he takes a mouthful of my breast and sucks. I'm not a small girl, never have been, but he's making me feel like I am beautiful, desirable—wanted. That I'm not broken or a freak.

He moves to the other breast with his mouth while his hand tweaks the already erect nipple of the first. Rolling it between his fingers, he tugs gently, then squeezes it and I arch up, moaning at the sensations he's creating in me.

His kisses move under my breast, over my ribs, across and down my stomach.

"Oh, God!" I moan, arching backwards, unsure of what to do with these sensations he's creating in me. *Am I on fire?* Then he's not just tugging at my jeans and knickers; he's removed them. As one, together. *Shit!* I didn't shave. I don't get a chance to complain as he kisses one hip, then the other. I try to close my legs, stop him from seeing, but he rests between them and calls my name softly.

"Em," he says, and I look at him, almost ashamed. "You're beautiful, did you know that?" I shake my head slowly. "Let me show you; I'll stop if you want me to, okay?" I give him a slight nod

"Do you want me to stop?" he clarifies and I shake my head. He smiles. "Trust me?" he asks and holds a hand out. I take it and nod. "Thank you," he whispers to me as he comes up to kiss me fully on the mouth. "Just feel," he reminds me as he breaks our kiss. I'm blissed out with the many sensations he's making me feel and as his mouth licks my sex, I groan in delight.

Slowly, fast, sucking, long, deep licks...his magical tongue dances on my epicentre in various rhythms, and I can't control myself. I arch up, clamping my legs together, or I try to as a kaleidoscope of colours erupts behind my eyes. As I look at him, I see warmth, swirls of reds, oranges and pinks before my eyes adjust properly.

"Dear God," I whisper, and he winks at me. He offers a hand and helps me sit. I hadn't noticed he is now naked too and his member is long, thin, veiny and proud.

I go to reach out to touch it, then I pull back. Chris takes my hand and guides me in how to touch him. I follow his lead and wrap my hand around him, stroking his length. I look at him; his head is back, his eyes are closed and his neck is taut.

"Am I hurting you?" I ask, and he opens his eyes and then shakes his head once.

"Not a chance, twirl...fuck me!" he growls. "Your touch...so damn good." I move to kneel before him. Placing a hand on his chest as I stroke him, he brings his head to me, his hands wrap around my head and he pulls me in for a kiss that leaves me breathless. I can taste myself on him and I find it strangely satisfying that this man, this caring man, is turned on by me.

One hand vanishes and then it's between my legs, playing, tweaking, making me gasp as one sensation after another fills me.

"Tell me what you want, twirl," he whispers into my jaw as his kisses move.

"You...please," I beg.

"You want me?" he asks and I nod.

"Yes..." I breathe out.

"You want me to make you squeal?" he growls in a low voice that's almost cracking. He has a wonderfully dirty mouth.

"Yes," I whimper, then repeat it but stronger, "Yes." He nods and pushes me down onto the mattress. He leans across and pulls a condom from somewhere and quickly wraps himself up.

He kisses me as he leans into me and I can feel him at my entrance. With one hand supporting him, the other reaches between us and guides himself into me.

Inch by delicious inch, he fills so deeply that I can't think. Slowly, he withdraws and as he pushes back in, he kisses me. I entwine my arms around him.

"Wrap your legs, twirl," he tells me. "I'm going to love you, long and slow, then hard and fast." I nod as he does exactly that, sliding home so deeply and intensely, that I have my first-ever intercourse-induced orgasm. I arch against him, throwing my head back and he kisses my throat.

I come back to earth with him still deep inside me, and he claims my mouth as if he hasn't just kissed me in places I've never been kissed. As his hips find their second and third gears, I bite on his shoulder to stifle my screams, burying my nails in his back. As I do so, it triggers his climax, and he shudders deep; long and for moments, the world is just him and I. Still.

I wake confused in the dead of night. The lamp is off and Chris is holding me, an arm and leg draped over mine. I turn to him and instinctively, he pulls me to him, murmurs something but doesn't let me go.

I snuggle down in his warmth and it doesn't take me long to go back to sleep.

When I wake up again, Chris is coming into the bedroom in fresh boxers and smelling great.

"Hi," I breathe, pulling the quilt over my naked chest.

"Good morning." He smiles at me as he brings me tea. "I'll cook us breakfast in a bit, but I thought you might need one of these," he says, motioning to the cup. I smile, grateful for his care.

"Thank you," I whisper, taking an appreciative sip. "What is that?" I ask, motioning to his mug.

"Coffee. There is a coffee machine," he says.

"I don't own one." He smiles at me as he climbs back into bed. "So, how?"

"Me. I need decent coffee, twirl." He winks as he pulls the quilt up over his legs. "That instant ain't great."

"Thank you," I reply, then I sigh contentedly. "You didn't have to," I share, but he chortles.

"Twirl, I fully intend on being here between my crazy shifts," he says to me as he puts his coffee mug down on the bedside table. "And you deserve decent coffee too," he whispers to me as he leans across, cupping my head and kissing me deeply, making me clench.

"I don't like coffee," I admit and he chuckles.

"Noted," he replies with a smile.

"About yesterday," I begin, and he pulls back, an unsure look on his face. I reach out and place my palm on his jaw. "You let me do things to you I've never..." I bite my lip, which is sore. "And did things to me that no one else has done," I say, looking into his amber eyes. His pupils contract and I wonder if I should just shut up when he pulls me into him and kisses me. I move so that I'm straddling him.

"Twirl, that was just the start, yeah? I promise you," he says as he brings his lips closer to mine, "there's a hell of a lot more to come."

"I've never...come like that, not during sex," I admit and then his lips are on mine, devouring. His strong arms are around me and he pulls me up like I weigh nothing.

"It ain't going to be the last time, twirl," he says when he stops and rests his forehead against mine.

Chris is cooking breakfast for us all when Rosie and Byron come into the kitchen holding hands. I smile sheepishly at Rosie; she always seems to know what I get up to before I can tell her.

"Morning," Byron calls out as he enters. "So, what else needs doing today?" he asks us. I look at Chris, unsure of when he and Byron have to be back on the base.

"Unpack a few more things, sort out food and other stuff, no doubt. Return that van, but first, we eat!" he commands with a grin.

We talk over breakfast and make plans and when we're done, Chris and I get on with unpacking more of the boxes for the kitchen while Rosie and Byron get on with sorting out the living room. Rosie knows how I live, so I'm sure it'll be fine.

I get a call from the solicitors, advising me that a judge has granted me the 'Temporary Protection Order.' I sigh in relief. It takes about twenty minutes before the anxiety begins.

"He doesn't know where you are now, twirl. And keep parking the car in sight of the flat, but not right outside, okay?"

I nod at his instruction. Something I can run to if I need to, the direction set to get out onto the main road and to Waddington.

We finished unpacking the few boxes for the kitchen and then we start on the bathroom. Chris hangs the cabinet so I can keep things tidy.

"I don't get how someone who isn't military is so damn tidy," he tells me as I unpack another small box.

"My ex," I explain and Chris nods. "He wasn't a slob, it was the only redeeming feature he had, but he was OCD with it," I clarify.

"The military are too; everything has its place and everything in its place. Nothing unnecessary," he adds and I grin.

"Not a bad motto to live by," I offer and Chris acknowledges me.

"On that, I agree," he says. He steps back and puts down the drill, then he's pulling me to him and kissing me senseless.

"Our friends," I protest, but Chris shrugs.

"Might be doing the very same. Don't worry, nothing more than this until the next time, in two days," he promises and I shiver in anticipation.

Byron and Chris drive away at tea time. My car is down at the next block of maisonettes but over the road; Rosie's car is behind it. If my ex were to come past, it'll look like I live at the other block, not here.

Rosie smiles at me as she hands me a squash. She's taking some time before she has to head back to her dad.

"Are you pleased with the new place?" she asks and I nod then sigh happily.

"Yes," I state, confident in that knowledge.

"And Chris...?" Rosie asks, making me blush.

"Showed me just how much he cares," I share, hoping she picks up on that. "I've ticked off some of my private list," I reveal, knowing that she'll understand.

"You have?" She goes wide-eyed at me. "Byron wants to take me away for a few days, so we can..." She goes red, which makes me chuckle.

"Yeah, well, I don't have your dad to consider in my equation, and now I'm out of that place I shared with my ex, I'm so much happier." Rosie smiles at me. "I feel better," I add. "How can a place drag you down so much?"

"Memories," Rosie carefully replies. "Not all of them are good," she tells me.

Chris is on rotation for a few days, so while we talk, I quietly get on with making this flat my new home. I saunter around the local charity shops in this small part of Milton Keynes getting the basics of what I need. While Colleen's men had put up the curtain rail in the front room, I need some curtains that go with the colours to shut out the world when I need to. I browse the cheaper household shops and find something that will work without breaking my budget and then I head back to hang them. I check my account to find that the deposit has been returned from the original flat, so I pay Rosie back, sending her a message to let her know.

I sit down for half an hour, working out what bills I need to cater for and also work out if there's enough for the final payments. A round bus trip and a few hours later, I have my laptop.

I thought I was just getting the machine and the power cable. I wasn't. It came with a carry case full of extra things. The pawnshop also offered me a new memory flash drive and I agreed to it, knowing I can back up my files and give them to Rosie to look after. Then, I headed home and for a few days, with my muse riding high, I write.

On the second evening, Chris texts me and I realise I forgot to reply to his text from early yesterday. Oh, hell!

C: Finished my shifts! I've got a few days off. Would you like some company?

E: Sure! Are you on the way now, or will you leave in the morning?

C: I can be there for twenty-one.

E: I'll be in.

I call Charlie, asking what shifts I am on for the bar for the next few weeks and ask him for a few extra if that's at all possible. He puts me down for two extra that he's going to be short for.

I look around the flat, which is still quite tidy. I make sure everything is in its place and nearer the time Chris says he's going to be here, I unchain and unlock the front door. Until he locks the door and it's chained shut, I'm on tenterhooks.

Chapter Fourteen

The Muse Crashes

Emma

Chris smiles at me as he enters and locks the door the way he knows I need. He seems nervous and I don't know why.

"Coffee?" I ask, folding my arms over me. Looking at the floor, my actions echo his nervousness. He shakes his head and walks to the sofa. Just as I think he's going to sit, he turns to me. His eyes are narrow and his lips are thin. "What's wrong?" I ask, standing behind the sofa.

"You've been too quiet these last few days, twirl. You've got me worried. What's going on?"

I blink at him. "I've…" I glance at the laptop on the kitchen bar and he follows my gaze.

"You've been writing?" he asks. I nod, the bile in my stomach threatening to rise. "Is that why you've been ignoring me?" he asks, his voice just audible, looking between me and the laptop.

"I didn't mean to," I begin and I let my hands drop. "I'm sorry! I got into the zone." I lick my dry lips and inhale a few times.

"Hey," he says, suddenly appearing before me, lifting my chin so my eyes meet his. "I ain't angry; I just don't want you pushing me away." He goes to say something else, but refrains. After a moment, he continues. "You've hardly had a conversation with me these last few days; I've been doing most of the talking."

"I'm sorry," I whisper and reach out for him, hoping he won't push me away. "My muse came back when I paid off the laptop," I explain. Suddenly my stomach growls. Loudly.

"When did you last eat, twirl?" he questions. I mumble a response because I think I ate yesterday; until he asked, I was sure of that. "Em?" he asks as the world becomes bright and colourful, then goes black.

When I can take note of my surroundings again, I'm lying on the floor, one hand above my head, the other to my side, and my legs in a running position. This is the recovery position; that much I know. Chris is rubbing my back and there's a blanket over my legs.

"What..." I go to ask as I begin to push myself up, but Chris pushes me back down.

"Don't try and get up, twirl, not until I've checked that you've not broken something from your fall. You fainted. Seriously, *when* did you last eat?" His voice rises intensely. "And I mean a meal, not a snack or just some bread and butter, or a bit of fruit." His hands are checking me over, but not in a sexual way. They go from my legs to my back, my arms then my head.

"I don't remember," I say, being honest. "I had to get the thoughts out of my head. I wrote pages! Nearly fifteen-thousand words, though it's probably all gobbledygook," I explain as I defend my actions. From this vantage point, I realise that it was silly of me.

"I'm going to help you sit on the sofa, okay?" he asks, though his tone is far from a casual question. I nod and then he's hoisting me up to sit on the sofa. He looks into my eyes and moves his finger about at the front of my face.

"Follow my finger, twirl, I got you," he assures me. I do and then he smiles. "You..." he says sternly, "didn't look after yourself. You've gotta promise me you'll do that when I'm not here," he demands. "No more scaring me. I wish I had bloody come down last night now," he mutters loud enough for me to hear as he stands. I go to stand too. "No! You stay there. I'm going to cook you something and you're going to eat it before you explain in detail what you've been doing." I simply nod, his anger evident.

I watch as he goes and digs around my cupboards, then pulls out a saucepan and boils up some water from the kettle. In minutes, he has a packet of pasta going, some sauce waiting to be warmed up, and he's toasting bread and making up garlic butter. How can he make garlic butter? Fifteen minutes later, I'm eating what he's prepared from a tray in my lap. He's eating too, but he's watching me quietly as I eat. As usual, he's finished before I am, but he doesn't rush me.

When I do finish, he gives me something sweet—a chocolate ice cream, which I eat. After another glass of water, he finally smiles.

"Do you feel better?" he asks, gentler than he did earlier when he arrived. I nod.

"I'm sorry," I whisper. He comes over to the sofa and kneels before me, taking my hands in his huge, calloused ones. I want to let out the emotions that are swirling inside of me, but I daren't.

"Twirl, don't ever scare me like that again. Please," he says, his tone still containing strains of worry.

"I won't," I promise. He didn't shout at me, he didn't need to, but he has made it clear he's not happy with my actions.

"Good. Now, what the hell got you so distracted that you forgot to look after yourself? You can't write if you're in the hospital," he reminds me and I nod.

"It's all on the laptop," I tell him. He looks around and sees where it's set up at the breakfast bar. As he goes to fetch it, I moan as I move my neck.

"Your neck hurts?" he asks in alarm and I nod.

"Neck strain...I've been sat there writing." I point to where he's currently stood. I stretch my neck the other way and some vertebrae make a wonderful popping noise. His eyes go wide at the sound.

He looks around and shakes his head. "Twirl, we need to get you a decent working area. That's not great for long-term sitting and working," he states. He's right, it's not.

"I just moved," I say and he raises his eyebrows at me. I can just about afford a desk, but looking for one wasn't on my agenda.

"And? We'll get it sorted tomorrow, okay?" he says and I sigh. I don't want to argue. "Em," he chastises, his tone demanding.

"You're getting bossy," I observe and he laughs.

"Twirl, you scared me—you bet I'm being bossy. You also fainted from a lack of food and water. What you did was daft and irresponsible." He sighs and my heart sinks. "But it's fixable, yeah?" He strokes my hands as I clamp them together. Then he's smiling and heads off to the sink to start doing the dishes.

"Oh, Chris, you don't need to," I say, standing. The kaleidoscope comes back and I fall back onto the sofa. Chris is there in seconds, ensuring that I am okay.

"Rest. I'm going to do the dishes, then we'll get you into bed, alright?" Now he's asking, but it's not in the usual, pleading way. It's in the: *'I'm going to do this and you'll agree'* kind of way. A dominant way. So I do all I can do: nod in agreement.

I watch as Chris does the dishes and stacks them how I usually have them, tidying everything away as I would. The way my ex would demand it of me.

"You put it all away," I observe in awe and he nods.

"I figured you want to continue doing it that way. It's efficient," he points out. "But, Em, you can change how it all gets organised if you want. This is *your* place. Not his. Not even mine."

"I...can?" I ask. I've never thought of changing how *he* made me do things. I ponder for a moment, a livable mess like at Rosie's. "I like it this tidy," I confess, and Chris nods.

"Then we can carry on doing it that way, twirl, that's fine." He holds his hand out and I take it. He helps me up and to the bathroom, and then he turns off the lights.

"Did you check the door?" I ask; and he nods.

"Yeah. Do you want to check it too?" he questions, and I nod in agreement. He watches as I make sure that the door is chained and that both locks are deadlocked.

"Thank you." I smile at him as he helps me walk to the bedroom. He helps me into pyjamas, then into bed, before turning off the lamp and joining me. He spoons me, pulling me close and it's the last I remember.

The sunlight is coming in around the curtains the following morning. Chris isn't in bed with me, but I can hear and smell food being cooked. I smile and go to sit up, but again, I get dizzy. *How?*

I groan and lay back on the headboard, closing my eyes until the dizziness wears off.

"Hey! You okay?" Chris's voice comes from the doorway, concern evident.

"Yeah, I just tried to move and got dizzy," I moan.

"That's probably because you're dehydrated. Here," he says and I hear the clanking of a tray being put down.

A moment later I have a glass in my hands.

"Drink it, but not all at once, twirl, I got you," he encourages. And for the next hour, he's fussing over me, helping me. Once I've had that glass of water, eaten and tended to my own needs in the bathroom, he's got me another glass of water.

"Feel better?" he asks me, nearly an hour later.

I nod, smiling at him. "Yes, thank you. I hadn't realised I had done that," I admit. Now I feel foolish.

"It's fixable. Just, be kind to yourself. Set reminders if you have to, but please don't do this again." I find it strange that he looks into the loo again after I've used it.

"That's...are you being weird?" I ask. His head snaps up; he shakes his head.

"Just checking the colour. I can tell how dehydrated you are by the colour." He smiles.

"Oh, you're a medic now?" I enquire snarkily and he grins.

"Babe, we've all got basic first aid for combat situations. We're all taught it," he clarifies. I simply smile and accept the next glass of water he gives me, knowing that I'll feel better when I've had a drink.

When he checks in with me later, I do feel a heck of a lot better, so I guess he knows what he's doing.

Under watchful eyes, Chris takes me to a second-hand furniture warehouse on the hunt for a desk. While I sat slowly drinking my third glass of weak squash, Chris had cleared one wall in the spare bedroom, collapsing the empty boxes and stacking the ones that still need emptying to the other side, making half of the room useable. He also put up the curtain pole and measured up what size curtains I may need.

I'm feeling rather ashamed of my actions and he's been checking regularly whether I want a drink, food, or a snack.

"Chris, I'm okay." I smile at him when he asks again for what feels like the hundredth time.

"Twirl, you collapsed. I'm keeping an eye," he tells me.

"I know, but I ate that huge, cooked breakfast, so I'm not hungry and if I drink any more, I will be living on the toilet," I tease; he goes to respond, then he notices the grin I'm trying very badly to smother.

He pulls me to him and laughs at me. "Twirl, I'm with you, right here, right now." He smiles as he points out a simple desk and as I look at him, he's crowned in a rainbow, as if sunlight is coming through a stained window or a window crystal has caught the light, fracturing it. Over him.

I blink and it vanishes, making me both sad that it's gone but amazed that it was focusing on him. I look up into the ceiling, which is made of industrial roof material. There are no windows that high up nor can I see anything that would cause that.

Chris hones in on the desk and pulls out a tape measure that I didn't realise he brought with him. He measures it three times, checking things and then he looks at me expectantly.

"Would this work for you?" he asks. It's white on top, clean with metal legs that detach. I look around for a chair to use and we find one, then we match the two together. The chair looks like it would be a sofa chair, but it's on wheels. As we're checking things out, one of the sales assistants comes over and in three minutes, I have a price for both items and they're within my budget. The table isn't long, about a metre and a half, but long enough to fit the space.

On the way out, Chris spies some cube shelving about my height.

"That'll go well in the corner by the desk, and it'll give you a place to put some of the books you've not unpacked yet," he states.

"I've spent enough," I say and then he pulls me to him, kisses me.

"It's my treat." He goes to pay for it before I can stop him. I check out the tag and sigh; it's the price of two coffees from a high-street chain, so I don't moan at him because he's right—it will look brilliant in that corner.

Hours later, the items have been delivered by the second-hand shop, and Chris is cooking up some spicy lamb steaks, new potatoes and fresh veggies from a local market stall. All the new furniture items are in the spare room, waiting to be assembled.

"The market's not the same as in Brixton, but the intention is the same," he says to me.

"I thought you couldn't cook?" I ask, aware that he's looking after me again and he shrugs.

"This isn't really cooking; it's warming things up and frying things. I don't consider that as cooking. What Byron does—that's cooking. Making a sauce from scratch, using milk and whatever else? Fresh pasta through a rolling machine? Everything from scratch?" He grins. "My aunt did the same; a roast dinner every Sunday. Usually, chicken with everything. I never worked out how, at Christmas, she timed it all to feed the six of us at one pm so we would be done in time to watch the Queen's Speech at three." I gape at the order of his aunt, the woman that raised him and that he watches the Queen on Christmas Day.

"People watch that?" I ask. He blinks.

"Twirl, she's my Commander In Chief. Hell yeah." I can't help but grin. "One tells her troops to jump, we ask how high." He grins as he casts me a look. "I've got a lot of respect for the Royals. When I introduce you to the family, I hope you'll be aware of that," he says, caution in his voice.

"Wait, what? Introduce me?" I say, my eyes becoming large. My heart begins thumping in my chest as the air gets thin.

"Yeah, eventually, in a few months," he says as he plates up the lamb steaks, potatoes and fresh vegetables.

"Oh...so, not right now." I sigh, relieved. I thought for a moment he'd invited them here. He chuckles as my body relaxes from the sudden tension.

"No, twirl, not right this second, but soon, yeah? I've got a week of leave to take; the question is when." He makes me sit down at the breakfast bar that he's cleared of my laptop and notes.

We eat and he asks where I want the desk and how I want the room set up. Without realising it, I've finished my dinner; every scrap.

"That was delicious," I compliment him, pushing away the plate.

"Do you feel better?" he asks and I nod as my cheeks warm up.

"Yes, thank you."

"Good! Then let's get this desk set up, yeah?" He doesn't berate me anymore or continue to tell me off. That's a change I can get used to quite quickly.

Hours later, the desk is in place and most of the other boxes have been unpacked. The cube space in the corner works brilliantly in this spare room and Chris hangs up the extra curtains that were in a box. I had forgotten those had come with me.

Chris turns on the desk lamp, then turns off the overhead light and smiles. I beam at him; this is perfect.

"Would this work for you?" he asks, his eyes wide and I go giddy, clapping. This is amazing! Chris is supporting me, not making me hide what I want to do and I feel better about it.

He chuckles at me and I suddenly want to kiss him, hold him and as he reaches out to steady me, I plant my lips firmly on his.

CHAPTER FIFTEEN

The Passion Rises

CHRIS

Emma's soft mouth lands on my lips and I am shocked for a very short moment until I get with the programme and pull her closer to me. I turn the chair and sit on it, making her straddle me, pulling her down. This chair suddenly isn't big enough for the both of us.

I don't need words; this is a moment for action. Wrapping an arm around her, I pin her soft curves to my hard chest while my other hand goes to her head, angling her just how I need her. And by God, do I need her. She scared the living shit out of me when she collapsed. Using what basic medical knowledge I had kept me calm and when I worked out what had made her faint, I was fuming.

This though? She's taking charge, showing me that she's keen and interested *in me*. Her hips begin to move, rubbing against me so that the friction builds. Frustration and pleasure course through me at the same time. I shift us forward a little and widen my legs so hers do the same, and now I wish she wasn't wearing jeans.

From her ample breast, my hand travels down her ribs and I cup her in her most sensitive part, my palm grinding against her clit. She inhales sharply and pulls back a little. As I open my eyes, she does too and smiles softly.

She doesn't say anything; she doesn't need to. Biting her lower lip, she moves to climb off me and tugs at me, making me stand. I do, but I refuse to take a step anywhere else. We're doing this right here.

I walk her back until her arse is at the desk and move between her legs. Opening her again, I grind against her, building the friction once more. Her arms are around me and her fingers explore my back with gentle strokes, so I remove the t-shirt I've been wearing.

"Did it hurt?" Her hands come to the front to trace the few tattoos I have on display. As her fingers touch me, my pecs flex from her feather-light touch.

"Yes and no...depends on what you can take," I tell her.

"I've always wanted one," she says, going red.

"And you haven't yet because?" I ask, already suspecting her shitty ex had a huge say in it.

"Him," she confirms and I lift her gaze to meet mine.

"There's a brilliant place in London where I got these done. When we go down, we can get you one then," I offer and she grins.

"Thank you." She continues to trace the jet-black abstract art over my left pec. "I can't feel it," she breathes, fascinated by it.

I make an agreeing sound. Her touch is so light, it's almost not there. "Emma," I moan. If she weren't sitting before me, I'd think I was dreaming.

I must have zoned out as her fingers were tracing my throat, her soft hand brushing against my stubble. I unbutton her jeans and slide a hand down inside as my mouth assaults hers, my fingers finding her wet, slick core. I cup her head, angling her so I can devour her. One finger goes in and then another joins it as I begin slowly thrusting my hand in and out. The heel of my palm brushes her clit as our tongues dance.

The kissing stops; her gasps increase and one hand drops to brace herself against the desk as the other clings to my shoulder. Her convulsions hit and she clamps down on my hand, stopping me from fucking her.

"Dear God," she hisses when she can catch her breath. I pull her forward and then I drop to my knees, taking her jeans and knickers down to her ankles, making her step out of them.

"That was one," I state. I walk her back the half-step and make her perch on the desk again as my mouth finds her hot, wet core. I lick, and she ripples at my touch, trying to close her legs.

"Ah-ah," I chastise, holding her wide open to devour her. She's soaking wet; her juice is trickling down her inner thigh and I chase it with my tongue. "You're so wet," I moan at her, watching her. One hand is on my shoulder again, the other is clamped to the desk, bracing herself against it.

She moans as my tongue continues to drink her juices and I suck on her clit. Her fingers dig in—nails sharp—and I swear she draws blood as she comes into my mouth, filling me with the sweetest honey I've ever tasted.

"I want you over the desk, babe. I want you to remember me fucking you here when you write," I tell her, pulling back to drop my jeans and boxers.

Without a word, she turns and bends over the desk, trusting me. She presents her perfect arse and her swollen sex to me, watching me over a shoulder. If I die now, I'll be happy. Pulling a silver packet out of my jeans, I wrap up then I play with her arse, feeling the globes, squeezing their perfect shape.

"You have a fine arse, woman," I growl as I move into position. I run my hands up under her top, unhooking her bra, and then I play with her tits, tweaking and feeling how damn perfect and full they are.

"Chris…" she moans, need and desire evident in her begging tone. "Please," she pleads, thrusting her arse into me. I'm tempted to slap her for doing that, but I don't, not yet. When she trusts me more, perhaps, but not now.

"Patience…I'm enjoying the view," I tease as I squeeze her arse with one hand and lean in to play with a tit, pulling and tweaking.

She can't decide which she likes more as she tries to chase both sensations at the same time. I pull back and grab her hips as I line myself up before I push home. Grabbing her shoulder, I use it to brace my weight as I pull back and drive into her again and again. The sound of flesh slapping against flesh fills the room, as do her moans and my groans.

"So fucking good, twirl!" I growl out as I slam myself home time and time again. My balls begin to tingle, but I need to hold back; I need her to come either before me or with me. My free hand finds her clit and so has hers. She's feeling me fucking her hard and begins to beg.

"Please…oh yes, please!" she cries out. Her head is bowed as I continue my assault, hair hiding her face as our fingers work her clit. "Yes!" she screams. "Oh, Chris, yes! Yes!" She clamps down on me, her body shaking as she comes, triggering my climax. I fire into her a few more times and roar as I pump everything I have into her, grabbing her hips to steady her as her legs give out and the desk takes our weight.

When I come to my senses, I push up and kiss her from her spine up to her neck, moving her hair. She turns to me, demanding a kiss. Her mouth fuses to mine, and her arms wrap around me as best they can.

"Bloody hell," she whispers and I grin.

"Write about that," I tease and she blushes.

"I might just do that," she replies between kisses.

Her hand glides down my sweaty chest to my abs and hesitates at the V. Her fingers are just brushing my pubic hair.

"It's okay, you can touch me." She bites her lips before taking me in her hand.

"I've always wanted to be on top," she tells me and I grin.

"We'll need a bed for that. This bedroom floor isn't the best to be kneeling on." She nods and I pull her in for a kiss, my hands wrapping themselves around her head.

Somewhere in the last few moments, my heart decides she's it. She's the one; the only one I'll ever need. *Now I just have to convince her of it.*

Hours later, we're in bed, but we haven't gone for round two; not yet. Emma's lack of taking care of herself meant she fell asleep cuddling into me. Some of our clothes are still in the office space, but I don't pay them any mind as I hold her and let sleep take me under.

The following morning, I smile as I wake up; Emma is still curled up, but her back is to me. I reach out and spoon her, wrapping an arm across her torso, my legs behind hers and my cock decides it wants her arse. I tell myself I can bide my time as I nuzzle into her, breathing her in.

I close my eyes, though I'm not asleep. I just enjoy the time I have curled up with this gorgeous, brave, clever woman, thanking my stars I landed in her orbit.

I can tell when she begins to wake up. She goes to move and can't, which nudges me to be fully awake, ready to give her whatever she wants.

"Good morning," I whisper into the shell of her ear quietly. I kiss her ear and her neck, planting soft, loud kisses and I let her turn to me.

"I need to pee," she tells me, almost embarrassed.

"Don't be too long," I tell her as I let her get up. She throws me a look and darts out of the bedroom to the bathroom. I hear the toilet flush and grin. Grabbing another condom from the bedside table, I wrap up, my mind already playing out how she will look and feel above me. It makes me slightly harder.

I rearrange the pillows and throw the cover back so she can see everything on display. I've never waited for a woman to come to me before; I've never had to. When she comes back, she stops at the doorway. She looks at my fully erect cock, then my face.

"You wanted to be on top," I remind her, holding out a hand and she nods.

"Did I not tire you out?" she asks as she steps back to the bed, and I shake my head.

"Not even a little," I tell her as she takes my hand. I pull her up onto the bed and she goes to straddle me. "Wait…" I say and she freezes as she is. I wiggle down and get beneath her, then I wrap my arms around her waist and begin sucking on her sex. My tongue delves deeply into her, and she shivers slightly. Her moans of pleasure and little squeals of surprise keep me as hard as iron while I fuck her with my mouth. Her body vibrates as she comes, shivering and rippling with cries of surprise.

I grin as I move up from under her so that my cock is next to her sex and before she can ask me anything, I ease her down onto me, taking every inch of warm wetness I can.

"Hands on my chest, babe," I tell her when she can't seem to decide where to put them. I grip her hips and ease her up and down, showing her what to do. *How can she not have been on top before?* Her beautiful tits bounce, their warm caramel peaks pucker in the cooler bedroom air and I play with one, then the other, while guiding her up and down.

The way she's moving, she's hitting her clit against me, which makes her bite her lip and dig her fingers into my chest. I don't care, I'll take every inch of pain she gives me and enjoy it. My hand comes to play with her clit and then she comes, clamping me like a vice so I can't move. Convulsions ripple through her again, making everything shudder. The aftershocks happen and her grip loosens up, but I can see she's still riding the effects.

I grin and turn us so I'm on top. I reach down and kiss her, making her arms wrap around me. I grab a breast and kiss it, biting it to love it as I slowly withdraw from her and push into her deeply again and again.

She can't stop making those cute sounds; the moans, the begging. Her legs pin me to her and they hold her at just that angle so I can hit her clit. In moments, I feel her tighten around me again as she comes, and so do I with another roar.

Panting, I brace myself over her and wait until she's at least responsive to me.

"Good morning, twirl." I grin, grabbing a kiss.

"It sure is," she agrees, pulling me down into her embrace again. "You're a beast," she says with a playful smirk on her mouth.

I kiss her neck and withdraw my half-limp cock, discarding the condom into the bedroom bin. Then I pull her to me so I can stroke her, kiss her and continue to touch her.

"You're a starving kitten," I tell her and she playfully meows at me, making me chuckle. Our stomachs rumble and gurgle in unison, driving home their emptiness, so I kiss her quickly, get up and go to fling on my boxers. Of course, they're not here.

"Office," Emma tells me, giggling when I'm looking around. I'd forgotten that.

"I'll cook," I tell her.

"I can do that," she says, "but, if you're insisting." A smile plays across her face. I wink at her and set about finding my clothes from the office and getting dressed into fresh stuff before I begin the task of cooking us both food.

CHAPTER SIXTEEN

Contentment

EMMA

Chris looking after me, indulging me in my sexual fantasies as well as tending to his, gives me warm, fuzzy feelings all over. I try to recall the last time I had a fantasy about any guy only to fail at doing so. I gently remove myself from the bed and grab a shower as I hear something hit the frying pan, which makes me clean up quickly.

Dressing in baggy clothing that hides everything, I venture out into the living room and kitchen area and my mouth begins to water at the smell of food being fried.

"I still think you're a secret cook," I tell Chris as I sit at the breakfast bar. He turns to me and grins like the cat that got the cream.

"I'll make sure we don't starve, but I am going to have to get lessons from my family. You'll love Jean," he tells me as he busies himself at the hob once again. Moments later, everything is ready.

Sausages, bacon, beans, tomatoes, fried egg and a toasted muffin make up the feast before me. I wait until he's sitting with me before I begin, even though he'll finish way before me. The coffee machine gurgles and pours out a fresh coffee.

"I notice you don't drink coffee," he says as I eat. I shake my head in reply whilst I chew.

"No, I keep it in for guests." I take a sip of the tea he's made me. God, that's hit the spot! "I much prefer tea," I state and he grins.

"Just like Jean," he says.

"That's your aunt?" I confirm and he nods.

"Yeah, Craig and Jean. I don't use their titles though; haven't since I was a teenager."

"And you don't call them Mum and Dad either?" I need to get it straight in my head who is who and how he refers to them. Not having much family stability when I was growing up, I'm respectful to those that have it.

He shakes his head as he empties his fork before getting up to retrieve his coffee.

"No," he pauses as he cuts up some bacon. "It never felt right. I tried it a few times, but in the end, they said I could use their names. So I did and that," he says as he stabs his food, "was that." He grins right before he shoves the forkful into his mouth, winking at me.

Grinning, I carry on eating until my plate is cleared and Chris has had his second coffee.

We're watching a movie, or at least, I'm trying to, a little later on. My mind is running story scenarios and scenes in my head and I get out a notebook and pen, scribbling down the ideas as they come one right after the other.

"Need to get them out of your head?" he asks as I turn another page. I nod, focusing on the thought until it's down on paper. As I turn to him and grin, I realise he's paused the movie.

"Sorry," I mumble and go to put the notepad and pen away. He stops me and grins.

"Go and write it up. I'm good chilling here," he says, his feet up on the storage ottoman that doesn't match anything else I own. I love it, though, as I can store things in it and use it as a footstool.

"You're...sure?" My ex never got it and I found my muse left when he was around. This time, she's dancing around in my head and it feels like she's doing the tango.

Chris nods at me and I grab my notepad, dashing to the office to begin transferring the scenes to my manuscript, one at a time.

Chris appears later, making me get up to use the bathroom. When I return, he's left a tea and some fruit snacks on the desk. I head back out to thank him and he grins as I come up to him, planting a kiss on his lips.

"Go on, Doyle, on you go," he tells me.

"Doyle?" I ask, confused.

"As in Conan Doyle."

"I doubt Sir Doyle wrote smutty fantasy shifter stories." I smile as he laughs.

"One of my cousins loves those kinds of romances. Paranormal she calls them?" he asks and I nod, confirming. "If I ask her, I'm sure she'll give your manuscript a clean-up with its English. She did damn well at school with it, got her A-Levels in that subject too," he says. I notice how his chest puffs out a little as he talks about this cousin, or any of the family that helped raise him.

"How much would that cost?" I ask, knowing that most editors want a small fortune for copy, development edits and proofreading services; rightly so. But it was and is, way beyond my budget.

"I doubt she'll want anything if I ask her as a favour. Want me to?" he offers and I nod.

"I have a few already finished..." I pause. "Well, they're finished in my head and on paper, bar any editing."

"I'll ask her. Now, go and do your thing, twirl, I'm good." I give him one more kiss and then I head to my desk and get back into the zone.

Hours later, I stretch; my mind is finally at peace. Everything I had churning around is either down in the manuscript or on the notepad to build on when my muse wakes back up.

I check my word count for the day; it's at nearly five thousand. I stretch again to release the last bit of tension and jump as firm hands begin to massage my neck.

"I was thinking I was going to have to pry that keyboard out of your hands, twirl," Chris tells me as he leans down to my ear. His breath is on my neck and his touch is perfect, loosening up muscles I can't reach.

"I'm done!" I declare, right before he makes me moan in relief as he loosens my muscles.

"You are?" he asks as he spins the chair around, leaning over me. I nod and he pulls me up, guiding me away from the office room. "Good, come on," he tells me and I follow him to the living area to find that he's tidied up the cooking from breakfast and has made...is it dinner? It's three pm.

The smell of pasta bake with garlic pizza bread fills the flat and my mouth waters.

"You're amazing," I tell him, hugging him tightly.

"So are you," he responds, and I grin. "Did you get much written?" he asks; I nod.

"Over five thousand words and I have three more plot points to work on," I share as I dance to the bathroom. When I've taken care of myself, I head back and join Chris.

"You know I've gotta head back to the base tonight, yeah?" he asks as he serves up a small mountain of pasta.

I sulk. "Damn!" He comes over and kisses me deeply. "Wish you'd reminded me." Now I wish I hadn't spent the time writing.

"I ain't going quite yet, twirl," he says and rests his head against me. "Let's eat,"

An hour later, I'm helping clear down the kitchen area again. He's washed up, despite having cooked and wouldn't let me do more than dry the pots and put them away.

"You are bossy," I remind him. He shrugs, but he's grinning at me as he does so.

"You scared me, twirl. I get that you've gotta get that stuff out of your head," he says as he passes me a utensil to dry, "but, not eating? Not even drinking water? That's just mad." He holds the next item to be dried until I look at him. "So yeah, I'm bossy." He looks like he's about to say something else, but he throws me a wink and turns back to the sink.

"I shouldn't have got so focused," I admit and he drops the cutlery he was washing back into the basin, dries his hands and comes over to hold me.

"Twirl, you've gotta do you, yeah? Would those ideas have come out as they had if you'd waited?" he doesn't wait for my reply. "Probably not. We'll never know, but—" he lifts my head to look at me, "know this: I've got you, okay? I *want* you to know that."

His face goes slightly flushed as his eyes widen and he wraps a hand behind my head, gently holding me as he leans in to kiss me. I put the items I was drying down on the counter, not caring where or how they land.

He walks me backwards until my back hits the fridge freezer and pushes my legs apart to stand between them. My hands grip his solid biceps, and I close my eyes as he kisses me, grinding into me, building some friction; I'm enjoying the feelings that come with being kissed so thoroughly, and my only thoughts are of him.

We don't stop kissing, even walking to the bedroom where we fall onto the bed. Chris is above me, his arms by my head as he continues to kiss and grind into me.

When he stops, it's to remove some of his clothing, but he prevents me as I go to remove mine. He teases each piece from me as if it were made of delicate, expensive fabric, which is far from the truth.

"You know," he gets me down to my bra and knickers, "you hide yourself too much, twirl. You're fucking gorgeous," he says as he unclips my bra and takes hold of my ample cleavage. "So damn perfect." He nibbles a nipple, then sucks on it as his hand grabs my inner thigh. Chris pinches it making me wince and groan as both pleasure and pain cascade through me.

"Do you like that?" he asks and I nod, surprised that I do. The grin on his face is wolfish and he continues his assault on my mouth. I wrap my arms around him, desperate to feel every inch of him that he can give me.

His mouth trails kisses back to my breasts and he focuses on one with his mouth, the other with his hand. The sensations have me twisting and turning, both to make more of it and more because it's too much.

"Which position now, twirl?" he asks as his kisses come up to my throat and jaw.

"Any," I breathe. I don't care as long as he's inside me. Desperation makes me grab him and rub my hand along his entire length.

"On your knees. All fours," he commands and I scramble to comply. As soon as I am in the position, he pushes into me, his hand on my shoulder, just like he did when he took me over my new desk.

The sound of us, the feel of his hands on my hips sends fire through me that I can't control.

"Chris," I moan, "Oh...yes!" I cry out, the first climax taking me over the edge. He eases back and rides me through it, his thrusting matching my body's convulsions. Then he's pounding into me again and I dig my hands into the covers as best I can, holding onto anything and nothing as he makes me climb to another climax.

"Yes! Fuck, yes...Emma!" he screams as he shudders into me and my inner walls clamp down on him, my knees finally giving way.

Sometime later, he's kissing my back, shoulder and neck from behind, his weight over me, pinning me to the bed.

"You're a beast," I say to him, chuckling.

"Your beast," he clarifies and I turn to face him as he flops next to me after he's discarded the latest condom.

"Yes," I whisper and cuddle up to him, kissing him and touching him. I doubt I'll ever tire of feeling him.

His phone pings and he curses. Retrieving it, he smiles.

"Byron's heading back. Suggested I meet him at a petrol station for a coffee." He looks at me and sighs. "Please," he says as he crawls to me on the bed, "look after yourself for me, yeah?" His pupils go wide and then narrow as he searches mine for answers. I nod softly.

"I will, I promise," I reply and we dress. He doesn't take a coffee to go but does clean the coffee machine out.

"I know you won't use it until I'm back," he says and I admire his attention to detail.

"Drive safely," I whisper as we kiss at the front door. With one last searing hot kiss, Chris makes his way down to his car. From the living room window, I watch him drive away with a piece of my heart that I hadn't realised I'd given to him.

For a few weeks, we spend time at the flat together when he's not on rotation. If he's on a short or quick rotation, we speak. Anything more than twelve hours gap, he's at the flat and we develop a routine.

Hot, blinding, screaming sex, then we chill out and eat. He tries a few new recipes with me that he says Jean sent him. We learn how to cook chicken in the oven, potato fritters in a pan and more than just basic canned meals.

"I need to tell you about one of my cousins," he says to me one evening as we're curled up in bed. He's been here for a few hours, so I've eaten well and we've had mad sex that didn't quite get to the bedroom.

"Oh?" I ask, wondering what he's going to share with me. Over the last few weeks, he's shared snippets of his cousins, Richard and Maxine. Richard has a steady girlfriend, and Maxine has two kids with the same guy, but not much has been forthcoming about Ruby.

"Yeah. Ruby's a bit special, but for God's sake, don't tell her that. She'll have your head," he chuckles as he pulls me tight. "Craig and Jean found out when she was a few months old that her vocal cords weren't developing. They wondered how she hardly ever cried and just thought for a time she was a quiet baby. Until she accidentally got hurt one day by Rich. She was crying, tears coming down her little face, but no sound."

I pull back and cover my mouth with my hand, astonished. "Oh, yikes," I reply, unsure of what to say in response.

"Yikes is one word for it. She went to a different school for deaf and mute kids so she could learn sign language. She's the one with the A level in English," he admits.

"Oh! But, can she hear?" I ask and he nods in the semi-darkness.

"Yeah. She's mute by definition, but she's damn bright. When you talk with her, she'll need to answer you in BSL or text."

"How good are you at sign language?" I ask, amazed that Chris knows it.

"Rusty as hell!" he chuckles. "But thought you might want to know," he says. "She asked if I told you yet and I said I hadn't. She wants your number so she can talk to you about the books," he says, his voice tight.

"Oh!" I hadn't expected her to get in touch, but he did say he would ask her. "How long has she been asking?" I ask.

"Only a few days," he admits and I poke him.

"Chris!" I admonish, "that's not fair."

"She told me you were a figment of my imagination and that she is surprised I have one that detailed," he chortles.

"I can text her in the morning," I offer, snuggling into his warmth.

"Great! I'll tell you more about her then, okay?" he says as he pulls me to him, kissing my forehead.

I agree with noises as sleep takes me under.

The following morning over breakfast he tells me more about Ruby. For some unknown reason, her vocal cords just didn't develop. There was no reason for it, given her two older siblings were loud and boisterous. As she was growing, she learned British sign language and Chris shows me a few words. Hello, I'm sorry, goodbye, tea, food, wine...I chuckle at the wine bit, but he tells me with all seriousness that it's a word I'm going to need to know with her.

For an hour, he coaches me on a few phrases as he recounts stories of how she learned that word, phrase or sentence.

"Rich and I got good at protecting her from guys who thought she was dumb because she's mute," he growled. "We got into so much shit at school to start with. When she told Craig and Jean, they went mad. I think Jean marched up to the school one afternoon and had it out with the head teacher and his staff. Then Jean moved Ruby to a mute school and she thrived."

"She sounds tough," I say, sipping my tea. Chris has insisted on buying decent tea bags, which I have to admit, do taste a whole lot better than the cheap ones I'd gotten used to drinking.

"She is! She still gets douche-bags for boyfriends, same as anyone else. On that," he says as he takes his mug to the sink, "she ain't no different."

"So don't treat her any differently?" I confirm, hearing the advice in his statement and recalling his comments from yesterday. He nods in agreement.

"Exactly that. So, are you ready to text her?" he asks and I nod. He holds his hand out and types her number in, sending a quick message to the woman who is like a sister.

Emma: Hi! I'm Chris's girlfriend. He says you've been asking after me?

Ruby: Don't believe you! Video call me, otherwise, I think it's Chris being an arse.

I laugh and hit the video call button and a girl with dark brown hair, a little nose and similar eyes pops up on the screen.

I sign hello to her and she gapes, and then she texts Chris. He shows me the screen.

Ruby: You weren't lying? She's your twirl?

I look at the screen and reply. "Yes, I am. Hi, I'm Emma." Ruby signs back, making Chris laugh.

"Rubes, that's rude!" he laughs and I wonder what she said. Then he shows me his phone.

Ruby: How the hell did you manage to get with a gorgeous girl? She's too pretty for you! And she wrote these stories you think I'll like?

I look at Chris's phone, then the screen. "I did! I appreciate any help you can offer in polishing them up. Shall we continue over text?" I ask and Ruby nods, gives me the thumbs up and the video call ends.

I sigh, my nerves lessening.

Ruby: Seriously, how the hell did he find you? You're so pretty!

Emma: His best friend Byron is dating my best friend.

Ruby: Byron's with someone too? Wow!

Emma: Yeah...they met when they were both in the 47th, but Byron was a bit of a cockwomble with my friend.

Ruby: Cockwomble! I love that word!

Emma: I do too! Can I text you later?

Ruby: Yes! Now I know the books are yours, I just need access so I can get stuck in. What exactly do you need?

Emma: I can understand how the English language is written, but I've been over them a few times now and I can't see the errors in there anymore; unless I leave them for weeks. Can you take a look? I'm happy to give you drive access.

Ruby sends me her email address; I give her access to the three stories I have finished so far. Combined, they make a decent-sized book.

"There, she's got access," I say a few moments later. I open the first book up and can see that Ruby's in there already.

Ruby: Okay, I'm in. I'll make suggestions; it's up to you to either accept them or reject them, okay? Everything I do is a suggestion, not a demand or final. It's your work, your call. I look forward to meeting you in person though! Please tell me you'll come with him to meet us?

Emma: I have been told I will be, but I'm not sure when.

Ruby: I look forward to it! I'll make sure he takes care of you. Let me know if he buggers it up.

Emma: Thank you!

Now, it feels like I have more family than I know what to do with.

Chapter Seventeen

The Reprisal

Emma

Mid-October brings with it howling wind and rain—typical British autumn weather. Chris and I have had days out here and there visiting different areas. On days when the weather was unkind (which was regularly), we stayed indoors. I've been trawling second-hand and charity shops for used but complete board games.

We've also been reading and editing my stories. Ruby has been amazing and she's helped me understand more about the structure of English, suggesting changes here and there that just polish my work.

I've got an extra shift at the bar, so I get ready to head to work, focusing on wearing decent clothing in this wet, cold weather. I want to carry on editing, but earning money is taking priority; I don't want to rely on Chris for everything, though he's made it clear he will provide.

As I dress, I take stock of how he makes me feel: safe, seen, appreciated, supported. All the things my ex never made me feel. With Chris, I feel I can do *anything* or be anyone. I never feel frumpy, fat or disgusting. He makes me feel the total opposite and thinking about our lovemaking—for that's what it's been—brings a smile to my face.

I finish getting ready. I look in the mirror and see a woman dressed in low-heeled boots, black jeans, the club's polo shirt and a waterproof coat. She's smiling. *When did I start smiling?* Never before have I been pleased with the image that stares back at me. Mirrors and I never got on...until now. Smiling some more, I jump in the car and head off, running into the bar after parking to avoid getting soaked.

It's just a few regulars in tonight and Charlie lets me go early. The new member of staff seems to be rather capable and learns things on the first go. He promises to pay me for a full shift and waves to me as I leave. When I get to the car, it won't start; it is dead. Nothing comes on, no control panel lights, no headlights, nothing. I sigh, frustrated that this is another thing I'll have to get fixed, another thing that's going to cost me money I don't have. But that's now a problem for another time. Grabbing my umbrella and zipping my jacket up high, I march to the bus terminus head down with my collar and hood up, determined to get back home so I can write for a few hours.

I get to the bus station and find where my bus leaves from. I walk to the stop, relieved I am now sheltered from the rain and shake my umbrella.

Suddenly, my head is yanked back and I fight whoever has a hold on me. From the shaky reflection that I can see on the plastic windows, I know it's my ex. *Shit!*

I scream, trying to find purchase, grabbing at what I can as he hauls me away from the bus stop towards an exit. But there's nothing to grip onto here, all the surfaces are smooth. I won't go down without a fight.

"Fucking bitch," my ex seethes and he twists me, making me drop to my knees. I see him lift a leg and then I feel his boot in my ribs. The air is gone from my lungs and I'm unable to stand, crumpling to the floor. "Told you, you're fucking mine!"

"No!" I manage to cough. I now know that I don't belong to anyone unless I say I do. Chris has shown me that.

"Yes!" he roars and I see his fist come towards me. I hold my breath until I feel the blow, which forces the air from me. "You're going to be my ticket in!"

I don't understand what he means and have no wish to demand answers right now. Another blow lands on my ribs and I try to move my arms to shield myself.

"Let's see if he fucks you when you're broken and bruised!" he snarls. More sharp pains shoot through me; the blows feel like fire and I raise my hands to protect my face. I can't see properly—it's like someone turned the lights off on one side as sharp pain and the smell of copper and rain fuse together. I feel a shooting pain in my arm and I scream. I hear voices, the blows stop and there are footsteps, some running towards me, some away. I focus on what little I can do, which is breathe. I can't see, and I cough up something; the taste tells me its blood.

"Hey, Miss? The ambulance is on its way. Stay with us! Mike, give me your jacket," the woman's voice commands. It's the last thing I remember.

I have weird dreams of bright white lights zooming past above me, beeping machines, flashes of light, deep throbbing hums of machinery, and many people talking in hushed, desperate voices. There's another bout of shooting pain from my arm that makes me scream, and then, blissful, welcome calm and warmth. I'm comfortable and dry, but I can't make out where I am.

"Emma? You're safe, sweetie." The voice is soft, warm with a Norfolk twang. "You're in Milton Keynes General, on a secure ward. We've found out how to gain access to your phone. I'm Doctor Bentley and we have your friends coming to be with you. Hang in there for me, okay?" the gentle female voice tells me. A doctor. Friends. I try to mumble something, Rosie's name, but I fail. "Yes, we called Rosie. She's on her way. The police want a word, but only when you're able and your friend is here. They're standing guard outside, okay? Whoever did this won't be able to get in here," she assures me.

"Chris," I manage. I want Chris, but I can't really talk.

"Ssshh, we'll talk when you're able. Rest until then, lovely," she tells me and I let the darkness sweep over me.

"Emma?" Rosie's voice cries out my name. My best friend is here, and she's sobbing. I cry too, mostly because I hurt if I move anything on my right side, but I know where I am now that I'm slightly more awake. I've replayed the doctor's opening words in my head so many times. I managed to get a glimpse of my reflection in a mirror and I cried before she turned up. I'm exactly what my ex said I would be.

Broken.

Bruised.

Beaten.

No one is going to want me now, least of all Chris.

"Oh, hell!" she seethes. I can hear the air going through her teeth. "Emma, will you look at me?" I shake my head and can't hold back the pain from the sobs. I don't want to look at anyone because then it means they have to look at me. To see me. To look at this broken, bruised, worthless woman. *How the hell did I think I could get away from that monster?*

"Em, come on. It's just me. The cops are outside, and Byron's waiting for Chris. We called him; he's on his way already." I feel her hand holding my good one, the one not laying heavily across my stomach that feels like it's on fire. "Come on, bestie, please?" she begs and I turn to look at her. I can't see out of my right eye, but I can with my left.

"There you are," she tells me, her voice soft. "Hey."

"Hi," I whimper, then I cry, or I do the best I can to cry. Jesus, it hurts. My phone vibrates and Rosie answers it. It's Annie.

"Hey, Emma! I'd ask how ye are, but I ken yer not doing too well and where ye are. Is anyone sat with ye?" she asks, her broad Scots voice a strange comfort, even from the distance she is.

"I am. I'm Rosie," my best friend shares.

"Byron's Rosie?" Annie questions, and I can just see Rosie grin.

"Yep!"

"Aye, right, that makes sense." There's an intake of breath on Annie's side. "Okay, the police are going to want you to go through what happened. Emma, you may not want to do this, darling, but give them as much detail as you can, including details on the restraining and molestation orders. And do yourself a favour: get out of Milton Keynes."

"My job," I protest and Rosie shakes her head.

"We can always find ye a new one. I've not seen the police report yet and I really shouldn't, but I'll find a way to read it. I dinnae know how he found ye," she states.

"Bus terminus. I had to catch the bus to go home," I tell her, and Annie swears colourfully. I knew military people sometimes had a potty mouth, but...

"Right, please will ye get out of Milton Keynes? We can do what we need to once we find him. I've got Byron sending me details and I'm gonna call in a few favours," she explains to me.

"There's no need," I begin weakly, but both Annie and Rosie scoff.

"There's every damn need," Annie bites back. "Will ye, please? For yerself, if you willnae for Rosie or Byron's sake?" Annie's guilt-tripping me. Rosie nods and holds her hands in a prayer position, asking me. Begging me. I sigh.

"Okay," I relent, totally unsure of where I'd go or what I'd do.

"Good! Rosie, hen, watch yer six. If he found Emma via the bus terminus, he'll likely come hunting again and may use you," she cautions. I hadn't thought of that. I'd take another beating like this to make her avoid him.

"I'll tell Byron too," my best friend states. "We'll be watching for him."

"Right, I'm getting details coming through from Byron. I'm away to go make things happen, but keep me posted, aye?"

"We will," Rosie confirms and Annie hangs up.

I sigh and swallow a lot, my mind a blank as to what needs to happen now, other than getting a drink in me.

"Need some water," I say and Rosie helps me drink from a plastic cup. They're not giving me a straw as my jaw took a beating, and sucking is going to hurt.

There's a knock at the door and it opens. Rosie turns and stands before whoever has entered, then she relaxes and sits back down. This new person isn't going to hurt me.

"Miss Blackthorn, I'm DI Jameson." I turn my head to see another woman with her hair tied back in a ponytail, a dark pair of jeans and a thick coat that's dripping water. She steps forward as I try to focus on her. "We have the CCTV from the bus terminus, but can you tell me what happened?" Her voice is soft and gentle, and Rosie is here, holding my good hand. I go through what happened, explaining about wanting the extra shift at the bar, the car not starting, and then walking to the terminus. I have to pause often; it hurts like hell to talk.

"I didn't know he was there. I feared he would kick-off. I should've changed jobs," I blurt out and then I cry again, silently this time. I can hear someone else crying; Rosie. She's crying with me or at me.

"Miss Blackthorn, you're doing really well. What you're doing is brave," the officer tells me. I tell the DI my ex's name, Chris Jordan Anderson, about the non-molestation and restraining orders. The DI just nods and writes it all down in her notebook. Rosie tells me that my right arm is broken in two places and my right eye is swollen shut, but they don't think it's dislodged, or worse. She also shares that they put me through a CT scan and that I've deep bruising on my legs and thigh as well as quite a few cracked ribs on my right side. My arm, face and bruised leg are the main injuries. The DI notes it all down, then tells me again that I'm brave and that they'll find him as she leaves.

"I'm so sorry! You said he'd escalate. I wish I understood that," my best friend tells me, her scowl evident. I sob quietly, unable to speak and ask the one question I need an answer to: *What will Chris say when he sees me?*

I find out sooner than I would like when I hear raised voices outside.

"That's Chris," Rosie states.

"He can't..." I begin, unable to continue.

"He will be fuming, but not at you. For you," Rosie tells me. "Either he gets to him first, or Byron and I do. Either way, he's dead," she vehemently tells me, quietly enough that the DI still standing outside the door doesn't hear.

Chris takes his time to come in to see me, and Rosie peeks out of the door.

"He's getting questioned," she tells me and I quietly sob.

"Why?" I ask, wishing this wasn't happening. I turn to the window, wanting to not be here, to run away, to not see Chris.

"Same first name? Goodness knows," she says as she sits. There's a gentle knock at the door a little while later and Chris's voice calls out softly.

"Twirl? I'm coming in, okay?" he asks and Rosie turns to nod. He enters the room, closing the door but not tightly behind him. Rosie gets up and gives him the seat that she's occupied since I woke up.

"Oh, fuck, twirl!" His voice is quiet, soft—raspy but not at all sexy. I've never made a man cry before and I can only imagine the tears he's shedding if he can. He takes my hand and goes to reach out, but I turn away, ashamed of how I look. "Hey, twirl, this ain't down to you." He strokes my good hand in small, soft circles. The door clicks shut as Rosie leaves us alone.

Chris leans in and gently strokes the good side of my face with the back of his hand. He lightly cups the broken, busted side of my face, holding me, calling to me softly. I turn to look at him, though I don't want to. I can't help but do as he asks and look at him.

"I promise you, twirl, if I ever come across him, I'll kill him."

I nod, unable to speak as he vanishes behind my tears.

I drift in and out of consciousness; sometimes I see nurses, and other times I just think I feel them checking on me. The chair has been replaced with a fold-away bed and there's light coming in through the hospital blinds.

"Hey, you're awake," Chris says softly when I shift positions. I don't jump when I hear him. Goodness gracious, my arse is numb and I need to pee.

"Bathroom," I mumble and then he's there, helping me out of bed with my good side, the side I must've protected somehow. Chris helps me do what I need to, the humiliation of needing help to even pee is now high on my list of most embarrassing situations, but Chris doesn't say a thing.

He helps me back into the bed and then he's sitting on my good side, asking if I want something soft to eat. I sob at his questions, unable to ask him the one thing I want to know—why? I'm so far from brave right now. I close my eyes after ordering scrambled eggs and some porridge, things I don't have to chew too much.

"Em?" Chris calls out after a nap. I have no idea what the time is and I dare not ask. I turn to look at him and he smiles at me, touching my good hand. I flinch and pull back. "They got him; he's in custody, twirl. You're safe, okay?" I nod and sob some more, aware that they have my ex in custody. *This Chris didn't do this to me; did he?* I take the painkillers that the nurses give me and for a few hours, I no longer care.

Charlie calls at some point, asking how I am. Colleen told him I'd been attacked and he was outraged. He also tells me that the police have removed my car as evidence.

"It wouldn't start after my shift," I explain and Chris's eyes go wide. *Why does he care?* "I can't continue to work at the bar, Charlie, I'm sorry. I've gotta move. Further away."

"I understand, Emma. I wish we'd realised about the car; you could have stayed with us," he tells me.

"It is what it is. It's not your fault," I say, but how I wish I'd gone back into the bar and told them about the car. I just didn't think. I was so focused on getting back so I could get the latest ideas and good feelings out of my head, I didn't consider it might have been messed with.

"Did the police say what they wanted her car for?" Chris asks and I cast him a weird look. *Why is he still here and interested in this?*

"No, they didn't. But, they did come heavy-handed. They had the keys too," he tells me, and I sigh. They must've searched my bag for them, or been handed them by someone.

"Okay, thanks, Charlie," I reply.

"It was Col," Charlie says sharply and I can't reply. My mouth is dry. Chris answers for me.

"What was Col?" he asks, looking at me confused as he strokes my good hand.

"It was Col that found him. When Rosie texted last night, she went out into the pouring rain. I didn't know why until she came back, soaked but damn happy, in the small hours. She went around his haunts, hunting for him, and called the cops when she found him. She was there, under a tree watching when they got him."

"Tell her thanks," Chris says. "Emma's a bit unable to talk right now," he says and I begin to sob. Charlie hears and wishes me well, then ends the call.

I heave in some air a few times, trying to calm my breathing, and then I sigh, exhausted. Chris tries to hold my hand again and I pull back as if his touch was an electric shock.

"Em?" Chris calls out to me and I turn my head to look at him, too tired to speak. "You know that your ex is the one to blame here, don't you?" he asks. I snort my response; I've had enough of talking today.

"Hey, twirl..." he says as I close my eyes. I open them again to see him. *He's not my ex.* I have to remind myself of that fact. *He didn't do this to me.* "You know I'm Stevo, right?"

I nod, seeing him for the first time. "RAF Chris," I mumble, making him grin.

"Yeah, that's me. The one who took you to Bletchley, bought you doughnuts at the park." He leans in and lowers his voice, "Fucked you over your desk, helped you move." He stalls on that and I twitch my good hand, wanting to hold his hand but afraid to. My confusion adds to my already shitty situation. I try not to let the tears that are building fall, but as usual, I fail.

"I fail at everything," I whisper, forgetting to keep my thoughts in my head.

"No! You bloody don't. This isn't on you, twirl. This is on him. He's a… shit, I can't even come up with fancy words for calling him a dickhead," he says, spitting out the words with venom.

"Cockwomble," I begin and he gives me a small laugh. Then he comes in closer to me.

"He's a dead cockwomble if I meet him. But, he's in custody," he confirms, his voice dripping in promise. "And he ain't me."

Chris swaps out for Rosie later in the morning and she greets me gently. I open one good eye and smile at her as best I can. My broken arm is in a sling and cast. I'm resting on my back, dozing while gazing at the ceiling panels.

"Can I get you anything?" she asks and I grumble about talking, then remember that this is my friend. She didn't ask for this to happen to me or for my bad attitude, so I try to make a joke.

"A new life?" I ask as I try not to cry again. I feel so empty and as if I don't deserve anyone's time right now. *Why didn't I go back into the bar and tell them about the car?*

"That's a given, we'll get you there. I went to identify him; they made me do two line-ups, to be sure I got him twice. I did, even though they made him change clothes."

I close my eyes and call him an arsehole, which makes Rosie chuckle. She reaches out and touches my good hand, which makes me flinch, then I remember it's only us in the room.

"Sorry," I whisper to her. I wish I could be as confident as she is.

"Em, I'm just sorry I didn't know to pick you up; I wish I had."

"Don't," I tell her as I wiggle myself to sit up. "Damn bum's numb," I moan. "But don't you start feeling guilty. Stevo is right, the only guilty one here is Chris Jordan Anderson. He was told to stay away, even though I knew this would kick him off. I told Annie it would. She told me to change jobs as well as move, but I didn't. I can't go back now. Charlie knows I quit."

"How does he know?" she asks, her brow frowning slightly.

"I told him when he called. Do you know it was Colleen that called the cops to his location? She found him, followed him, and called the cops. She didn't lay a finger on him but stood and watched him get arrested."

"So that's how he was found so quickly," Rosie breathes out. "We did wonder."

I nod, slowly. "Charlie told us when we spoke. Col's texted to say she'll organise the guys again to move me. All I need is somewhere away from here." I smile as best I can with a busted lip, sore jaw and a closed eye. The fact that Stevo is already arranging it grates me.

I continue, "I don't care that they see me like this, but Col says my ex won't be breathing if her guys see me." I chuckle, wondering who will get to him first. "Which makes meeting them all again in this state very tempting." I lie back on the pillows and heave a sigh. "So tired," I whisper as sleep takes me under.

Stevo is with me when I awake and so is the DI.

"Sorry," I mumble as I try to adjust myself. The DI smiles and I look at Chris, the warm pinks and oranges I'm so used to seeing around him are back, not the nothingness I have been seeing when I've looked at him recently. "Bathroom?" I beg softly and he nods, helping me out of bed. The DI walks to the window and looks out at the lashing rain as I slowly make my way to and from the bathroom with Chris's help.

When I'm back in bed, the DI turns to me and speaks.

"Miss Blackthorn, I'll be quick so you can continue to rest. He's in custody. We've made it clear to the magistrates in our paperwork that we think he's a flight risk, given that he's violated a molestation and restraining order. If it all goes well, he'll stay where he is on remand. If not..." She winces but not as much as my heart sinks. This is a caution; he could come after me again. I expect him to if he gets half a chance.

"Thanks," Chris says and the DI nods, and then she turns to leave.

"We're also adding '*damage to a motor vehicle*' to the list of charges against you. He tampered with your car. The club CCTV didn't pick it up, but one of the neighbour's systems did."

Stevo swears and the DI nods.

"I thought you'd want to know," she says and wishes me well. I'm to stay in touch, she says and Stevo makes sure she has his number as well as mine. Stevo sighs and looks at me after she's gone.

"He's gotta find you first, twirl," he says to me.

"He doesn't know my new place," I say and close my eyes.

"I'm moving you from there," he tells me, but I close my eyes in response. "Don't try to ignore me, twirl." He waits, but I don't respond. "He's put you in this state and if it were down to me, he'd have taken his last breath already." I open my eyes at that statement. "Good. You're still listening. I'm moving you so that you're safe. You'll be a five-minute jog from the base, two minutes at a flat run. Byron's going to check the place out for us and video call me so you can see, okay?"

"I don't want to move!" I protest though I know it's the only viable option open to me at this point.

"I know you don't, twirl, but I need you well out of this bastard's range and into mine. He comes near you, I'll know about it. He tries anything..." Stevo doesn't finish the statement, but he doesn't have to.

I nod and hold my hand out for him, squeezing it slightly when I feel his huge hand in mine.

"I've got another forty-eight with you, then I need to be back on base. My sarge says you're to get well soon," he says and kisses my hand. "Now, you rest because I can tell that's what you want. Ruby has been texting you; she's ready to rip him apart too. And she's deadly silent," he says. Given Ruby's muteness, I find that statement ironic.

Chapter Eighteen

The Best of Friends

Chris

Byron calls me as expected and he's walking us through the place. I'm watching how Emma reacts and she smiles softly, nodding in places.

"Boomer, you there?" I call out, expecting Josie to be around.

I can see Josie rolling her eyes. "Yes, Stevo. Do you want it?"

"Yes, please!" My reply is enthusiastic and Emma scowls.

Josie nods. "I have the keys. The owner said they'd get the rent sorted from when Emma moves in."

"You're taking charge again," Emma whispers at me and I place my hand over the speaker.

"I need you safe, twirl. We can talk about the rest of it after that, okay? But, you know what Annie and Colleen have said; get out of Milton Keynes."

"My things?" she asks.

"We'll get it sorted, babe," I reply quietly to Emma. "Josie, let me know the details please." Emma shakes her head, but I don't care that she wants a say in this right now. Her last choice didn't ensure her safety.

"Will do! See you when you're back on base," she says and we hang up.

"Always so bossy," Emma says and I touch her hand.

"I wasn't there to stop him. You were too far away, twirl. This way is closer to me; I can be with you every night standing guard if I have to. Or right next to you. We can't guarantee the justice system will keep him on remand," I remind her. That makes her sigh heavily and tears begin to fall. *Fuck.*

"I know," she sobs. "But a job? Paying the bills?" she asks and I smile.

"I can cover the rent. Hell, I'll stop renting my room on the base and kip on your damn sofa; they're keen to get me used to civvie street. But. I. Need. You. Safe."

She's in no state now to hear that I'm in love with her, that I have been for weeks, that she is my forever. I want to tell her, but would she believe me, given the state she's in? Rosie told me some of what the bastard said to her. I can't risk that she won't believe me after what he declared, so actions are needed more than words.

"And you need to get better, yeah?" I add. "You can't do that if you're watching your back in this town." I watch as she concedes my point, as painful as that is to make *and* receive right now. She sighs and wipes away yet more tears. I pour her some water and she drinks it.

"You rest up, twirl. I've got this little bed; I'm right here. And Byron gave me a change of clothes." I smile. "So I don't quite stink anymore." That makes her chuckle slightly. Thank the Lord he keeps spares in the car; a trick he said his sister told him. One I'll copy when I get my arse back to base. The man even offered to wash them for me and the hospital got me some soap and a clean towel, so I've showered.

Emma sighs, nods and turns her head, favouring her battered side, partly because I think it's furthest away from the door. In moments, her breathing is even.

I get a text from Byron about five minutes later. I've taken off his jogging bottoms, trying to keep them decent for tomorrow and sleep in just the boxers and the t-shirt. The hospital staff have given me a toothbrush and some toothpaste, the same for Emma, though brushing her teeth right now is painful. Mostly everything she does at the moment must hurt like hell.

B: So, what was happening during that call?

S: Em doesn't want me taking control.

B: She needs our help though.

S: I know. Told her I was getting her out of the area and when I know she's safe, she can breathe and live and heal. But until then, I'm organising her safety.

B: Don't tread too heavily here, my friend.

S: I'm trying not to. Annie also said she needs to get right off his radar and away from MK. That's the only thing that's made Em listen and concede: Colleen & Annie telling her to get out of Milton Keynes.

B: Plus, she can be here and heal away from him.

S: That's what I said too. She agrees, though she's reluctant. I'll be happier knowing I'm a five-minute walk away, or a two-minute run from the front gates.

B: You and me both!

I realise he's the only one who hasn't seen Emma in the state she's in; then I remember Ruby and my family haven't either, though I've had a splurge of texts from them about it. I snap a few photographs and send two to Byron.

S: This is what he did to her, physically. She's going to need therapy. Annie suggested one of the base therapists. What are your thoughts?

My screen goes black before Byron replies.

B: Being honest, not sure who I'd trust on base with this...maybe Johnson? Let me think about it. Josie might have a good feeling too...

S: Yeah, sorry, mate. I'm running on adrenaline. You get some kip. Thanks for everything. She's sleeping and they've set me up a camp-bed, so I'll grab some shut-eye too. Cheers!

B: Good idea. Catch you tomorrow!

The following morning, I'm woken by Emma nearly falling into me as she tries to leave the bed. One of the nurses must've moved it during the night as it's higher than I recall. Damn! Some guard dog I turned out to be. I kick myself for my lack of attention.

I help Emma to the bathroom and clean her up, the same as I have every time so far.

"You need to let me do it," she tells me later on after some food. They've been feeding her soft foods as best they can: porridge, mashed potato, beans and eggs; things that don't take a lot of chewing or biting.

"I like helping," I tell her.

"You don't have to do it out of guilt," she tells me. "And I know you've got to get back to base at some point," she adds.

"I am not doing this out of guilt," I tell her, keeping a lid on the next line that's on the tip of my tongue. *'I love you'* can't be said quite yet, though I'm bursting to tell her.

She gives me a funny look that tells me she doesn't believe me, but I school my thoughts, or at least I think I do.

I spend the day finding chargers for Emma's phone, going to her flat and getting what she needs—a change of clothes, soft stuff that isn't going to dig into her bruised body.

I forgo the bra, none of what she has would be comfortable right now, but grab fresh knickers and everything else, including a wash bag. I look around the place, regretful that she has to leave here, but this town needs to be left behind. I just hope she likes the new place as much.

Back at the hospital, the nurses buzz me into the secure area for trauma patients. One of the nurses smiles at me and brings me up to date on Emma's condition. They've confirmed with her that the eye isn't dislodged, which is great news. The swelling is going down and the bruising will get more colourful as her body heals.

The arm needs to be in a cast and sling for weeks more yet and I can only nod at that news. I'm expecting for it to be in a cast for a few months; they had to pin it because of where and how he'd broken it.

The doctor comes in as I'm helping Emma with her lunch, cutting her food up into smaller chunks.

"Hi, Emma. I'm Doctor Bentley. How are you feeling?"

Emma looks up at the doctor and shrugs, offering no words.

"That good, eh?" The doctor smiles and reads the chart from the bottom of the bed. "Well, here's some good news, I'm considering letting you out of here. I'm pleased to see your eye isn't dislodged." The doctor goes through what I already know.

"So, I should be able to see out of it soon?" Emma asks. The doctor nods.

"I want to see how much you can see out of it now. Can you close the good eye for a few moments?" she asks and Emma complies with a quick examination. After a few checks with a bright light, the doctor pulls back. "That's great. Your pupil is contracting and expanding with the light, so it's reacting as it should. That's a very encouraging sign. Once the swelling around that area starts to recede, you should start seeing things, though it may be blurry for a while as your eye slowly works its way back to full strength."

Doctor Bentley explains about her arm, the rest of the bruising and the ribs, which she also checks.

"You're recovering well. I'd like to do an MRI again before we discharge you to go home. Have you somewhere safe to go?" she asks and Emma nods.

"It's being organised now," she replies. She doesn't look at me or reach across for any reassurance from me. The doctor nods and smiles.

"That's good. Where are you moving to?"

Now, Emma looks at me and nods slightly. "Near RAF Waddington, where I'm stationed," I reply and the doctor notes it down.

"Then I'll transfer all your extra care to Lincoln General. I assume you don't want to come back here for anything?"

Emma shakes her head. "Not if I can help it," she responds, her voice strained.

"Very understandable," the doctor replies softly. "In the meantime, I'm going to suggest they start adding in some better protein for you to help in your recovery." She notes things down on the chart. "Lots of rest and hydration, okay?" Emma nods and the doctor smiles at us both then leaves.

Emma sighs as the door clicks softly shut. I have to be on rotation at twenty-hundred and I'm leaving it as long as I can to depart. The doctor comes back a few moments later.

"You've been here for days. Where did you park?" she asks and I tell her. "Leave it with me, I'll get the parking charges lifted for you." I thank her, but paying the small fortune for a few days of hospital parking was something I was expecting to get hit with.

"Hey, twirl," I call to Emma as she sighs again.

"Yeah?" she answers, turning to look at me.

"I've gotta be back on base tonight," I explain and she nods, her mouth turning downwards. She looks beyond me, to the floor by the door and the tears begin to fall.

"This ain't your fault, twirl. If I thought he'd do this, I would have moved you well away from here the first time."

"It was my job. He was able to find me because of it. Now, I can't work," she sobs, defeat evident in her voice.

"Not right away, no. But, we'll find you something, twirl, I promise."

"Why?" she asks, wiping away her tears. "Why are you being so nice, when…" She stops.

"I'm Stevo," I jump in, figuring that she was getting confused by our first names; the doctor hinted that the painkillers might confuse her. "Not the Chris that did this to you. I'm Christopher Michael "Stevo" Stevenson. *Your* Stevo," I reiterate to her. "And you're my swirl-and-twirl because you want to be." I hold her hand, stroking it softly.

"I know. I'll be safe here. He's in custody now," she replies, putting a brave face on her situation.

"Where else would you feel safe, twirl?" I ask, wondering what else I can do to help her here.

"On the base?" she says, her voice light and snarky. I chuckle slightly.

"Yeah, that would work too! Do you want to live on the base?" I ask, but she shakes her head; I concede the point. I figured she wouldn't. "Okay, so I won't aim for that then, twirl." I look at her and she's trying to close her eyes. "You go to sleep. I might not be here when you wake up though," I say, taking her hand and stroking it, forcing back those three little words for a little while longer.

My alarm goes off at five pm. I groan, not wanting to leave, but I have to. I have to drive back to the base, I'm on duty in three hours. Quietly, I leave Emma's hospital room, kissing her softly on the cheek. Finding her notepad, I write her a quick message. Though my writing isn't terrible, it's not as neat as hers. I snap a photo of it and send it to her on messenger. A nurse grabs me and gives me a free pass to leave the car park; she's the same one that's been around for days.

I thank her, then I grab a coffee and pastry from the canteen and hightail my arse back to base, though it's the last place I want to be.

The shift goes as slowly as rush hour traffic around the M25. There's simply not enough coffee or snacks to eat. I see from my message that Emma's read my note, at least digitally, but she's not done anything else.

Byron comes up to the gatehouse where I'm on the cameras and asks me if I have Colleen's number. I tell him I don't, so he sends a text to Rosie, who texts it back. Grabbing the number from him, I text Colleen.

Chris: Col, it's Stevo. Rosie gave me your number. How quickly can you and the lads help me move Emma?

Col: Give me a time and date & it'll be done.

Chris: This weekend, please.

Col: Going to need the keys.

I look up at Byron. "Did Boomer give you the flat keys?" I ask and he holds them out to me with a grin.

Chris: I have them here. I'll show you where it is if you're able to fetch them from me.

Col: Will be there. When is good?

Chris: My shift ends at oh-six. There's a coffee shop on the high street. I can meet you there?

Col: Send me the details. I'll be there around ten?

Chris: I'll grab a few hours shut-eye then. Cheers!

Col: Can make it later if that helps.

Chris: 13:00?

Col: Done!

I smile at Byron and pocket the keys.

"Colleen is going to be up here at thirteen-hundred to fetch the keys. I'll show her where the flat is."

"I'll get some vans organised," he says and heads off after I thank him. Then I focus on work. None of my colleagues gives me stick for taking an extra ten minutes on my break.

"Stevo!" Rum's voice grabs me when I swing past the gatehouse and I head up to my commanding officer, expecting a telling-off for my chat with Byron earlier. "Need to advise you of something," he says and I nod, heading into the side gatehouse with him.

"What's up?" I ask, unsure of what's happened now.

"Civvie police asked us for your whereabouts on the night your girl got attacked. Thought you'd want to know," he tells me. "Wanna help me figure out why?" he asks and I sigh, going through how her ex is also called Chris and the number of questions they asked me.

"Then I think they were verifying that you were here," he states. I nod, grateful as all hell I was but wishing I hadn't been in equal measure. I share that with him; he's one to appreciate my brutal honesty. "Well, you were. That gun sign-out and CCTV shows it was you. No way could you have gotten down to MK and back in ten minutes and I doubt even Superman could've." He grins.

"Cheers, Rum! What did the fruit say?" I ask, aware that this enquiry would have gone up the chain of command.

"I told him what I knew had happened to your girl and that they're probably asking to eliminate you from their enquiries over it. Being honest," Rum says, glancing around, "they're not the brightest. Kept trying to imply it wasn't you on duty when Grievance called you." He rolls his eyes. "Grievance backed it up with a call to the gatehouse, which is also logged."

I nod. "He's smart," I state and Rum nods. He looks as tired as I feel; it's been a long night.

"He is. Anyway, I've put it in front of HR, so that they know."

"Why?" I ask, confused. I stand, wanting this over with.

"If you need to get legal on your side," he reminds me and I sigh.

"Fucking civvies," I seethe and Rum nods again.

"Yeah. Keep your wits about you, your nose clean and stick to regs, okay?" he advises. I salute and Rum dismisses me. *If they want to pin anything to me, they'd better make sure I've bloody done it to start with.*

Chapter Nineteen

Getting My Head On Straight

Emma

Rosie texts me, asking how I am. I can't put into words how I'm feeling. She's got her new guy; she won't want to hear about how empty my life is yet again.

R: How are you today? Shall I call?

E: No...text is good. My eye is healing, and the doctors told me it's not dislodged. But they want to do another MRI soon to check as more of the swelling goes down.

R: Is Chris back on base?

E: Yeah...he wasn't happy, but I told him that with security here at the hospital and my ex in custody, I'm safer here than anywhere apart from his base.

Moving onto the base has its appeal, but still, no thanks. *What will I do when he decides he doesn't want me?*

R: Don't tell him that! He'll get you onto the base and never let you leave! :P

E: At least I know Chris won't ever be able to get to me again!

Not if he wants to live, anyway. That thought brightens my mood very slightly. Rosie said that the guards on the base have guns. I'd pay to see him fight anyone of their calibre. Or try.

R: Stevo likes you. You know that, right?

E: I know, but why would he? He's stopped himself from using the L-word with me. I'm no good, probably never was. Sorry, I'm useless at this.

Honestly, why the hell is he still around? I just don't get it.

R: Just because he's not said it yet, doesn't mean he's not feeling it. You're recovering from a brutal beating at the hands of another "man." Give him time to show you that he means it too, you're not in the right mindset to hear it. He's found you a new place near Waddington, he's been there the entire 48 hours he was able to AND grabbed extended leave to be at YOUR side. Not mine. Yours.

I read that message several times before I can reply to Rosie, replaying his actions over the last few days. Is she right?

E: And how the heck will I be able to pay for it? That new flat I mean. I'm falling behind in rent as it is...

R: We'll work on that! Let me call...please?

E: It's getting late, and they gave me something to help me sleep ten minutes ago, I need to rest. I lie and then see the dots vanish, then reappear.

R: It's too early for one of those. I'm calling!

She knows I'm lying, but I don't answer. I can't. *Shit!* I breathe quickly, wondering what to say so I take my time to reply to her, re-reading our conversation so far over and over again.

E: Okay, fine. I just don't wanna talk verbally. I eventually admit when my breathing seems to even out. Two men named Chris in my life are confusing me.

R: Because I'd call you out, as you would do me? I love you, but you deserve better than Chris. Chris PUT you in the hospital. Stevo stayed with you at the worst time. Stevo stayed. Doesn't that tell you more than I ever can?

The text gets blurry and I swipe away the reason for it. Yeah, he stayed. I notice that Rosie uses Chris's RAF nickname. Stevo. Stevo was here for me, not Chris.

E: And what have I done with him? Spent some time with him, let him sleep with me. I know that sounds bitter, but it's the truth. I just don't get why he'd want to spend time with me, especially now.

R: And was it good? Did he look after you? Make you come before he did?

E: Yes... Damn, now I have to admit it to myself.

R: Does he hug you and kiss you? Has he ever shouted at you? This isn't fair; Rosie knows me and what my ex did to me too well. I replay the statement: Stevo stayed. Chris put me here. They're not the same person.

They're.

Not.

The.

Same.

Person.

E: Yes to the hugs and kisses. No to the shouting… He's even taken to talking to me when he enters the room, telling me where he's going and when he'll be back. That's the Stevo I know.

R: And has he ever NOT been back when he said he would?

I try to phrase what I want to say; that Stevo has never broken his word, never made me question or doubt him and that I am confused about what I remember. But, I retract all that for a simple reply.

E: No.

Rosie doesn't respond and I breathe out, thinking we've ended our conversation; until she enters my room nearly twenty minutes later. Then, I realise I cannot escape her support and love, as much as I want to.

"No avoiding me now," she says as she smiles at me. She doesn't look at me with horror or compassion. She just looks at me as she always has.

"Yeah, I noticed," I reply, snarkily.

"Oh, you did, huh? Good!" She flops down into the big chair that seems to be far from comfortable. Everyone wiggles into it when they sit down in it. "Now, I'm happy to be here until they kick me out."

"He's moving me," I blurt out, my mind needing to get this out there and my tongue trusting her.

"Who is?" Rosie asks, her face neutral.

"Chris," I state and she shakes her head.

"No. *Stevo* is moving you so you're well out of your ex *Chris's* reach if he doesn't get detained on remand," she tells me in a very matter-of-fact way.

She wiggles forward on the chair, taking a hold of my good hand.

"*We are* your family. Me, Byron *and Stevo.* We're the ones helping you move, determined to keep you safe. Stevo more than anyone," she says to me gently.

She goes blurry and her hand is holding mine again.

"Stevo *isn't* your ex. He's in love with you," she reminds me.

"He's not said that. Why would he love me? Look at me!" I exclaim, pulling my hand back and motioning to my battered, bruised and broken self.

"Why wouldn't he?" she counters, making my thoughts stop in their spiral. "He loved you before, when you were just as broken mentally, which is sometimes a lot worse than physical stuff." Rosie sighs and I hear the chair moving. "I wish I knew what to say to make you understand. We love you. *Stevo* loves you; I've seen it in his eyes. I'm sure you've felt it, maybe even wondered if you dare love him back." Rosie dries some of my tears. "He's organising your move. A move away from Milton Keynes, away from your ex's range. If that's not love, Em, damned if I know what the hell is."

My hand is suddenly full of tissue, which is a good job because I now need it.

Rosie stays with me for a while longer until the nurses kick her out, though they do so gently. I can hear her talking with them outside, then she's back to hug me; the first one since my ex grabbed me. Not even Stevo has done that.

The door clicks closed behind her and I let my head flop down onto the pillow. I turn to look at the rain that once again has chosen to lash down, and my head hurts come the morning.

The nurses bustle about me the following morning, then Doctor Bentley is with me.

"Are you ready?" she asks and I go as wide-eyed as I can at her.

"Ready for what?" I ask, letting the alarm sound in my voice. She looks at me strangely.

"Did no one tell you that we're taking you down for the MRI?" she asks and I shake my head. "Someone should have," she says, then she sits on the chair next to the bed and smiles at me. "Do you want to go down now? Or later? If we do it now, you can get out of here," she coaxes, and I swallow. Leaving this room is all I've wanted to do, but now that I am—even for a little while—the prospect makes me stall. Leaving the hospital? I hadn't considered that.

"You won't be leaving the hospital just yet and we'll make sure you won't be alone. I'll be there all the way and Jessie will be too." She gestures to the nurse that's been bustling about me most of today and the last few days.

I nod and the doctor pulls the nurse aside. Jessie's shoulders drop. They continue their chat in private, ending when the doctor nods and stalks off somewhere. The nurse is smiling when she comes back to me though.

"So, I'm taking you off on a little adventure," she says, coaxing me out of bed. "Someone should have told you earlier; I'm sorry no one did. Do you need the bathroom before you come to sit in here?" she asks, pointing to a padded wheelchair.

"Please," I say, then she's helping me to the bathroom, leaving me to do what I need to on my own, but hovering at the door.

An hour later, I'm back in my room and Stevo is there waiting for me. He's got more clothes; it'll feel good to wash, though how I'm going to manage it, I do not know.

"Hey, twirl," he greets me with a soft smile, his eyes dancing.

"Hey," I whisper back, trying to hide from him. He's seen me semi-naked before and with all this bruising, yet he's here? Rosie's words about him play in my head: *"He's in love with you."* Is he?

"Where'd you go?" he asks and I choose to sit on the chair, rather than the bed, which feels a bit better on my bum. They've added a second chair to the room.

"They took me for an MRI. Doc should be back in a while," I state, then I sniff the air. Then I sniff my clothes. I realise I stink.

Chris smiles at me. "Need a shower, twirl?" he asks and I nod. He vanishes and comes back with Jessie a few moments later, who smiles at me.

"I thought you might need to shower," she says, handing me something. "I'll help you get this waterproof cover on so your cast doesn't get damp. It's yours to keep, okay?"

Stevo sits in the chair, watching us as I nod to Jessie. "I'll be right here, twirl," he says gently as the nurse puts on a waterproof apron. I blink at her.

"I'll come in to help you, make sure you don't lose your footing," she says with a smile. Then she leans in. "Don't worry, he won't peek," she promises. That's not quite what concerns me.

Twenty minutes later and I breathe a sigh of relief. Jessie was professional and helped me wash the bruised side very gently, letting me use her as a balancing aid so I didn't fall. She didn't tsk or make me feel bad about the state I was in either, which did worry me. I feel so much better and the fresh clothes help. Chris has the smelly stuff in a bag that's waiting by the door.

I again choose to sit in a chair and he takes the other one; he turns them both so that they're facing each other.

"So, Rosie and the others are already in full force moving you out," he says and I sigh, blinking back yet more tears. I stare at his hands, noting the veins on his forearms and how they pop. I want them around me, holding me. But I daren't voice my wishes. "You know he's never going to look for you there, don't you?" he asks and I shake my head.

"Can't trust that," I declare and he sighs.

"I can," he says and I lift my head, looking straight into his eyes. They're wide, caring and soft. "Your name isn't on the lease. Mine is. I've filled in a form for the post office to redirect your mail for six weeks, until we're sure we're getting all the mail you should be getting."

I look up at him. I hadn't thought of that at all. "Oh!"

"Twirl, did you do that for the last place?" he asks and I shake my head slowly. He sighs and rubs his hands over his face. I let my head sink to my chest and try to hide more in this chair. "It's okay. I'll get the mail picked up from the old place," he assures me.

"I told the bank and things, but most of my stuff comes through digitally," I quietly share which makes him smile. I updated the banking app with my new number, for verification.

"The beauty of the modern age, for sure!" he agrees with vigour.

Only, that's not why I did it; it was to keep my ex from being a nosy swine.

"I'm ready to listen, twirl," Stevo says quietly, a curious look on his brow. I suck in a breath and let it out, then I begin to explain.

"Chris was nosy. Said I had good organisational skills when we first started dating, but that he hated my ability to do that at the end, that he couldn't find anything." I let my shoulder slump as my motor mouth kicks in before my goblin brain can stop it. "There were many other things too; my boobs." I look up at him and for the first time since my ex grabbed me, I see Stevo.

Not. My. Ex.

How the hell had I gotten them so confused in my head?

I blink and shake my head and then Stevo is there, holding my hands, the one in the cast as well as the one that isn't.

"Narcissist. That's what he is; a bloody narcissist. You," he says as one hand moves to my bruised jaw, "are clever, beautiful, and a fighter. Sure, you're down, but you'll get back up. I'll be there all the way to help with that." His eyes are still soft and I see tears in them.

"Please," I reply, begging. Oh, hell yes. Please.

He nods and helps me up and then he sits under me, making me sit on his lap. We find a way for me to cuddle into him that doesn't hurt and I breathe him in, sobbing that he's holding me.

Waking up later, I am a little disorientated until I realise I'm still on Stevo's lap. I blink and look around, seeing Doctor Bentley smiling at me from the other chair.

"Hello, Emma. I have some good news. Would you like to hear it?" she asks softly and I nod, swallowing a lot. Stevo must hear me as he asks the doctor to pour me some water, which she does and hands to me. As I drink, she begins talking.

"Your MRI shows that the pins are helping your arm bones heal. I want to keep them in for another month at least before they're removed and your arm is allowed to heal on its own."

"How do you plan to do that?" I ask, afraid I'm going to have to spend more time in this hospital.

"Lincoln General will schedule you in as a day patient and a colleague of mine will get them out for you when the time comes. It'll take him about ninety minutes to undo the stainless steel rods and remove them. Then it'll just be a case of letting your arm continue to heal in a soft cast."

I move so I can look at Stevo; I don't want to do that alone. "You'll come with me?" I ask him, and he nods.

"Sure thing, twirl," he confirms while giving me that slight nod Rosie has on occasion.

I look at Doctor Bentley. "When?" I ask.

"Your partner here has given me your new address, so I'll forward all your paperwork to my colleague, and his secretary will schedule you in. You'll hear from him in a few weeks' time, but it shouldn't be more than a month away from now."

"Thank you," I say, snuggling into Stevo's arms again. Doctor Bentley stands and smiles at me.

"Thank me by going home, getting better and going to the trial that's going to happen to the bastard that did this. I've already given my statement to the police. When it goes to trial, I intend on being there in your corner." I snap my head up and have to blink lots of times to see her.

"I can go?" I clarify and she nods at me with a soft smile.

"Yes. Free as a bird," she says with a huge smile on her face. "I'll let you pack, but I've signed the discharge papers. Go when you're ready; Jessie will let you out." Her voice is too high and I realise she's trying not to cry.

"Thank you," I whimper, and Doctor Bentley nods then stands and heads out. I let out a huge sigh as the door clicks shut.

"Want to go and see what the new place looks like?" Stevo asks. I bite my lip slightly and nod.

"What time is it?" I ask, and he grins.

"Nearly five," he says as his stomach rumbles, then mine copies. "And yeah, I'm hungry. What do you fancy as your first meal after this place?" he asks.

I grin. "Nuggets and a huge chocolate milkshake, please!"

He laughs. "Sure thing, twirl, we can do that," he says, helping me stand. Fifteen minutes later, I'm packed and ready to go.

In the drive-through, Stevo orders for me and we sit in the car in the drizzling rain. I'm enjoying my nuggets and chocolate milkshake when we get a knock on the window, making me squeal as I jump. Through the rain-streaked window, we see four police officers in high-vis jackets and Stevo curses. Sighing, he gets out of the car into the rain and an officer pops his head into the car.

"Are you okay, Miss?" he asks and I shake my head.

"I was until you all scared me!"

"We got a report that a beaten-up woman was in this car. I ask again, are you okay?"

I nod. "My boyfriend didn't do this to me, my *ex* did. Check out the assault case on Emma Blackthorne; DI Jameson will verify that he," I say, pointing to Stevo, "isn't the one she has in custody or has on CCTV putting me in this state. He's taking me to a new location, away from the reach of my ex, who is on remand."

He nods and speaks into his radio, then he's back and apologising, wishing me a good recovery.

Stevo comes back into the car moments later, soaking wet and fuming, but not at me.

"Staff at the drive-through called it in," he says, his jaw clicking. I want to reach across, but I'll knock my food over myself if I do.

"Stevo?" I call out, making him look at me. "They weren't to know. I'm glad they were vigilant," I say. He'd eaten most of his food, thankfully. I can't tell him what I'm thinking; that if this were real, if he *had* done this to me, I'd have been saved.

He lets me finish my nuggets and milkshake before getting wet again to bin our rubbish, waving at the one cop car that's still opposite us.

"ANPR," he says as he gets back in.

"What's that?" I ask, putting my seat belt back on, not quite understanding.

"Automatic Number Plate Recognition; they've run my plates, verified who owns the car and likely everything else about me." We watch as the police car turns on its lights and pulls away.

"Clearly, they're happy with what you and I told them," I add, watching them drive away. He nods, but his lips are thin.

"Stevo?" I say, reaching across with my good hand. "Thank you." Though I can't help but feel guilty that the cops were willing to bust him about something he didn't have a hand in doing.

Stevo drives us to Waddington. The Milton Keynes constabulary still has my car, not that I can drive at the moment with a broken arm. It's dark by the time we get to the new flat and Stevo parks behind a row of shops. I see a metal staircase leading up to a flat above one of the convenience shops. It's the only way in or out of the place and there's a secure gate at the bottom with a buzzer on it. I sigh, my nerves building. There are no other cars about, nor any vans. Did they manage it? The lights are on.

"Who is in the flat?" I ask, wondering how many bodies are there and who else I have to face.

Stevo shrugs. "Let me check, twirl," he says and makes a call, putting it on the loudspeaker as it rings.

"Hey, mate, how's it going?" I hear Byron's voice, tight and cautious.

"It's going okay! How're things there?" Stevo asks, giving no indication we're in the parking area.

"Going good. We had to give one of the single chairs away, we just can't get it into the flat. The sofa, one of the chairs, bed, desk and other items are in."

"You want to see this, Em. It's brilliant!" Rosie enthuses and I can't help but grin.

"I'll see it soon. That's why we're calling," I say, still nervous. "Who else is there?" I ask, looking at Stevo.

"Just us," Rosie confirms. "Col and the others left about an hour ago; the vans have been returned. We can head back to mine if you don't want us to be here when you get here; we understand." I begin to cry in relief. It's just my best friend and her boyfriend, my boyfriend's best friend.

"Thank you! We'll be up in two minutes," Stevo tells them and I nod.

"You're outside?" Rosie asks in surprise.

"Yeah...I couldn't stay in anymore," I explain faintly, not wishing to tell them they've discharged me.

"Pop the kettle on though, mate, yeah? I'm gasping for a coffee!" Stevo demands though I know he doesn't drink tea.

"On it!" Rosie replies and Stevo hangs up. The rain has eased off and Stevo helps me out of the car. I realise that it must've rained here, but it has moved on. I can smell things burning, bonfires probably—it's nearly that time of year—mixing with the petrichor smell I love so much. With a nod, Stevo helps me up the stairs and into my new flat.

The front door opens directly into the sitting area, which is arranged to look straight at the front door. There's no need to turn around to see who is there; I can see it all from every seat. I can hear Rosie and Byron in the kitchen; the sound of a teaspoon stirring against a mug is a familiar and welcome sound.

Stevo locks the door and I notice the deadbolts he slings shut on it. I nod, thanking him with a soft smile, my shoulders dropping their tension.

Off to the left of the room are my writing desk and the chair. The desk has my laptop and notebooks arranged and ready for me to use. Vivid memories of Stevo bending me over it, rendering me senseless, playback in my memory, and I jump slightly when he touches my good hand. That was Stevo wanting me. I hold back the tears, the shame of thinking about how I have been.

"Memories?" he whispers to me and I nod.

"Good ones," I tell him so he doesn't worry, making him smile.

"We'll make more," he whispers as Byron and Rosie come out of the kitchen area. Stevo has found the sofa and sits down, waiting for me to decide where to sit. There's a single chair, but I don't want to sit there. I find my place next to Stevo as Byron comes into the room.

"How are you doing?" Byron asks as he sees me. He doesn't flinch or treat me any differently than he had before I was attacked.

"I can see," I quip, which causes Byron and Rosie to smile at my humour.

"That's good! I hope you like the place. Col and the team did wonders, especially Rosie here," Byron praises. I throw my best friend a 'thank you' look, grateful that she's put my furniture into the flat as I most likely would have.

"Did you see the little office area?" Rosie asks as she sips her tea; her shoulders are pulled back, and I think she did that area personally. My plants are there.

"I did. You all did great, thank you," I tell them, trying once again not to cry. Stevo reaches out and offers his hand. I slowly take it and he squeezes mine, reminding me he's here.

"Is there anything else you need?" Rosie asks softly as I look around. "I managed to get you some basic items from the shop: beans, bread, milk…"

Slowly my eyes close and the tears fall; their love, their effort for me…I can't hold it in and I lean into Stevo, who wraps an arm around my head to block my field of vision. I feel a kiss on my temple from him.

"What did I ever do to deserve each of you?" I ask, unsure what I did in a previous life to deserve this now. Stevo's arm drops as Rosie comes to take my good hand.

"You're our friend; our chosen *family*," she says and I can just see her through another waterfall. "Do you remember what I told you when we were seven?" I nod, recalling that promise one night when I turned up at hers in the dark. She carries on, but not for my benefit. "We should have been sisters. This is what families do," she explains gently. "We take care of each other." She kisses me on the head and I suck in a breath, nerves pounding me, then remember it's Rosie, and she'd never hurt me; not physically, not ever.

"We'll let you get on with your evening. I need to drive us back," Byron states, shifting forward in his seat. "But Rosie's right, Em; you're family."

They say their goodbyes, but I stay on the sofa, exhausted by everything that's happened since I left the hospital. Stevo deadbolts the door as they leave, and the smell of bonfires wafts in briefly through the open door.

Stevo clears the cups away when we've finished and I'm dozing on the sofa.

"Do you want to chill in bed?" he asks as he shuts off the main light, closes the curtains and turns on a side lamp. I nod, though I'm quite comfortable here. He helps me up and I visit the bathroom, doing what I need to do one-armed. I huff in frustration when I can't even pull my knickers up to sit comfortably on me, and he helps. Not once does he moan, chastise or make a joke.

The bed has been made with fresh sheets—Rosie style—and I laugh nervously at the half-dozen extra cushions and the throw draped onto the bed. Then I chuckle a little as I look at Stevo, who has no idea where to start.

"If you can move some of the cushions to the sofa, they can live there. This is Rosie being Rosie," I say, still smiling. He nods and moves four of them, leaving two behind.

He helps me into an oversized nightshirt and I get into bed.

"You don't usually sleep on that side," he tells me as I settle down. "Will it help if you do?" he asks and I nod. I usually sleep on the right side as you look at the head of the bed.

"It might be best this way," I suggest and he nods. If he chooses to share the bed, I don't want him worrying he'll knock me.

"That makes sense. Do you need it adjusted for nighttime? Loosened off or anything?" he asks, nodding to my slung arm. His hands are by his sides, casual, but I sense a lot of uncertainty there.

"I don't know. I was told I can take the sling off at night." With his help, it's removed. He helps me get settled in bed and goes to leave me.

"No! Don't..." I begin and he looks at me, his mouth dropping open. "Please, don't go," I clarify, wanting him to stay. He nods, heads out to the living room and turns off the lights, leaving one on in the hallway to the bathroom.

"In case you need it," he explains when I motion to the lamp. "New place," he clarifies and I just nod.

I'm getting warm and sleepy, and I half notice him strip down to his boxers, close the door over and climb into bed on the other side.

"I'll try not to knock your arm, twirl," he tells me. He turns to me, and I reach out with my good hand. We find a comfortable position and him just being near, touching my hand, is the last thing I remember.

Chapter Twenty

Baby Steps

Chris

I watch Emma close her eyes and finally rest. With the MRI, the visit to McDonald's, and then the police knocking on the car window, today has been unintentionally long.

I play back the police intervention in my head, remembering when they got a hold of DI Jameson and their uneasiness when I showed them my military ID. She verified that they had the culprit in custody and I wasn't a suspect.

Them running my plates must've confirmed who I was and I suspect I'll get a visit from them shortly, even though they've been sniffing around already. I need to advise Rum of what happened on the way home when I see him. I also need to tell Emma what shifts I'm on and I'm half tempted to put in for garden leave duty now, get put on a regular, boring as fuck rotation, rather than do it in March, but I can't decide on that yet. I feel the need to continue being unpredictable to outsiders.

When I know Emma's asleep, I grab my phone and quietly head back to the living room, turning on the lamp. Sitting back on the sofa, I bring up the chat app with my family.

Chris: Got her to the new place.

Rich: Good! You're not going to like what I found out today though.

I sigh, dreading to know what Rich has found out, but I swallow my fear, needing to know. *Chris: Hit me with it...*

There's a pause and I see the dots start up, then vanish, and then start up again. I can imagine that they're mostly together. Rich has a girl, but they're not living together that I know of, so he's likely at the family home, along with Ruby, Craig and Jean. Maxine will be with her fella and kids, probably in bed already.

Rich: He's got connections.

That I didn't expect, now I want to know which crew.

Chris: To which lot? Ours?

Rich: No...our rivals.

I curse quietly under my breath.

Chris: They ain't gonna put up with what he's done.

Rich: They booted him out a few months ago though for bragging that he had hurt her.

That doesn't surprise me either. I know of their leader, Adam, we've met a few times before I enlisted; it's why we butted heads. We're too much alike. *Chris: Who kicked him out?*

Rich: Adam.

I snort in reply.

Chris: He needs an update.

Rich: Working on it.

Chris: Cheers! Catch you all later. I need to go to sleep.

I run my hands through my hair, frustrated but not surprised that Emma's ex has, or had London gang connections. While the gang I was in ran south of the river, Lamberth and Southwark, her ex's lot ran some stuff on the north side, Enfield way. I know that Adam's girl was beaten up when she worked the sex trade by a "client" of another gang down Croydon way. The guy in question now needs a stick to walk, and Adam's girl got out of the trade.

I know this much—I'd hate to be Chris Anderson when Adam gets this info. I'm half tempted to get his number from my old phone and message him, telling him I want in on any action that they dish out. After thinking about it, I decided against it, though reluctantly.

A message pops up from Rich in our private chat.

Rich: Do. Not. Contact A. I'll deal.

I sigh. *Chris: Stop reading my damn mind.*

Rich: You cannot *get involved, not like that. Stay your course, we got this.*

Chris: Was tempted to ask.

Rich: Don't.

At its back, one from Craig arrives.

Craig: I will say this once: Do not engage A in any conversation, no matter how tempted you are, son.

Chris: Rich just said the same.

Craig: Listen to us, then, yeah?

Chris: I do.

I run my hands through my hair and put the phone into sleep mode. My uncle, I'll listen to; he's never steered me wrong, only asked that I take responsibility and consider my actions before I do anything. Turning the light off, I sigh and head back to bed. Emma hasn't moved, so I slide in gently so I don't disturb her. My phone is charging on the nightstand and will be in DND mode until tomorrow.

I jolt awake through the night, convinced I have knocked Emma, but I haven't. A few times the nightmares hit and she tries to move her broken arm, but she doesn't manage it, and I calm her by calling to her softly over and over. In the last nightmare, she wakes up partially and calls out for me.

"I'm here," I reply quietly, holding her good hand. She snuggles into me, but I can't hold her as I want to. My simple hand-holding seems to be enough for her and she settles. I follow soon after, exhausted.

I blink and find Emma isn't in bed, though her side is still warm. Then I hear the toilet flush and smile. Rubbing the sleep from my face, I get up to find her and ensure she's okay.

"Mornin', twirl," I say as I leave the bedroom. I don't like creeping up on her, so I try to let her know where I am at all times.

"Morning!" she says, brighter than I've seen her in days. She's holding her toothbrush in her casted hand and putting toothpaste on with the working hand. I watch as she figures out how to get her hands to do as she wants.

"You're determined," I tell her, praising her. She's a fighter and that's another thing about her I love. I'm going to have to start making a list of all her good qualities.

"Need to brush my teeth and do this on my own," she says with a smile.

"Good! I've got today off, but I want to tell you what rotations I'm on so you know where I am and when, okay?"

With her toothbrush poking out of her mouth and toothpaste running down her chin, she nods. It's a sight that makes my insides ache, bringing a smile to my lips.

"I'll put the kettle on," I say, walking away to the kitchen, still grinning at the sight of Emma brushing her teeth.

I fix her some cereal. Pouring milk over the biscuits, I pop some raspberries next to the bowl and make up a mug of tea how she likes it.

She comes out with her bed shirt still on, a pair of bottoms that look like they might be mine, and a pair of fluffy pink slippers. She's running a hand through her hair to tame it.

"Hope you don't mind," she says, pulling at the tracksuit bottoms. I get now why women like men wearing grey jogging bottoms. I'd be happy to pull them off her and devour her.

"Not at all, twirl," I quip back, making a mental note to order a few more pairs or grab some next time I'm clothes shopping.

"They got the machine plumbed in?" she asks and I turn to see the washer is in and so is the drier. There's no dishwasher, but I can get a small countertop one, maybe even a slim one if I can get permission to rearrange the cupboards a little.

"Yeah, looks like. I've set you some breakfast out, twirl," I say, pointing to the small table I'm sure wasn't at her last place.

"Where'd the table come from?" she asks and I shrug as she confirms my suspicions.

"Not sure. It was here yesterday," I tell her and she nods. Then she pulls her phone out of a pocket and texts someone.

"Rosie says that it was on the van…" She frowns as she picks some raspberries to go on top of the now soggy wheat biscuits and begins to eat. Then she texts someone else. The phone vibrates and she smiles.

"Col saw the small table and knew I wouldn't have anywhere to eat, so she nabbed it." Emma texts her back and then she scowls as it vibrates again.

"She won't tell me what it cost," she huffs and I go across, taking the phone from her.

"It doesn't matter, not really. Col did something nice and if she won't take the money from you, we can find a way to pay her back later. Also, focus on eating, twirl, that's not your usual hand," I remind her and she nods.

"Yeah, you're right," she admits and focuses on her breakfast. She struggles to finish two biscuits with fruit, but I know that healing takes a lot of energy—a lot more than people think.

She sips her tea which is now drinkable. Making up my second coffee, I take both drinks to the sofa and turn on the TV, changing it to a movie channel.

"I figure we can chill today. You sleep when you want to; I'll potter about and look after you."

She nods and settles in on the sofa, or tries to. She has to swap ends before she finds a position that doesn't hurt. When she's comfortable, I sit with her feet on my lap. I cover them over with a blanket from the ottoman, stretch my feet out and chill.

We eat when we're hungry, not caring about what time of day it is when we do, at least when she's awake. She dozes here and there, which I expect and encourage.

"Stevo?" I hear my nickname being called and I wake up. Emma's not next to me and her voice calls me again from the bathroom.

"Twirl?" I call back, focusing on her need for me and following the sound of her voice.

"In the bathroom," she calls and I enter to see what she needs. I take a quick stock of what's going on, then help her. "Having one arm is a hindrance," she tells me and I grin.

"We're going to have to work out some way to change the layout in here until you can use that arm," I point out. Everything is set to be on the right, the side that's bruised, broken and currently unusable. I quickly move things around and for the moment, placing such things as wipes and toilet roll on her left. "Does that help?" I ask, knowing I've got to leave her for my shift tomorrow.

"Yes, that does. Thank you," she breathes and I nod as we wash up.

"Sorry, twirl, I was having a nap," I grin, apologising.

"I saw. I tried not to wake you, but then I couldn't..." She goes red, not wanting to admit that she was hindered.

"Yeah, I know. But, it's done now. That change should help and it'll only be for a few more weeks," I remind her. "It ain't a permanent arrangement." She nods, smiling.

I encourage her to sit on the sofa and I bring her some snacks, fresh soft fruit and another tea.

She picks up her phone as we idle and she shifts away from me, a frown on her face. I could demand to see her phone, but I need to trust her. I need that back; for her sake as well as my own.

"You okay, twirl?" I ask, and she snaps out of whatever she was thinking, her confused state slowly going.

"Twirl...Stevo," she says, and I nod as recognition dawns.

"Yeah, that's me, RAF Chris. Remember?" I ask her and she nods at me with a smile. Then, she's relaxing again. She does it again about an hour later, and it's starting to concern me. I am working out in my head how to ask her what's going on when I get a text from Byron and the light goes on.

B: Rosie just declared your new name is Stevo as Emma seems to be getting confused by you and her ex both being called Chris...

C: Yeah...She's been calling me Stevo and I've been answering by that name, today. I'm speaking with Johnson when I get back. She already knows I need a visit.

B: Let me know if there's anything I can do.

C: Roger.

Shaking my head, I fire off a text to Johnson and then look at Emma.

"Byron sent me a text; Rosie's concerned about you," I share, not giving any more details.

"It's all a muddle…" She sighs. "In here." She taps the good side of her head gently. "I'm sorry," she says in a small voice. I put my phone down and turn to her, taking both of her hands in mine.

"You don't need to be. That bastard needs to be sorry. Remember, I'm Stevo, RAF Chris. The guy who stubbornly moved you to a new flat near an RAF base." I grin. "We have guns," I remind her, a reference to the first time she asked me about them and Rosie's flying visit onto the front car park very early one morning.

Emma nods and a light appears in her eyes, along with a smile on her lips.

"Big guns," she whispers, recalling the memory and I nod, chuckling at her, my mind going to the gutter about her innocent comment.

"Yeah, with big guns." I grin again, flexing my arms. "I'm arranging for you to see a counsellor on the base, to help you through the muddle." I watch her as I tell her, noticing the slight frown that appears.

"Why?" she asks and I'm not quite sure what she means.

"Why? Why would I do that?" I ask and she nods. "Because I care about you so fucking much, twirl, more than I have any other before." I look at her, deciding to suck up how I'm feeling and just tell her. "If you don't feel the same, I'll still get you in to see the counsellor, but I'll not come by here if that's what you want."

Emma's eyes go wide and she shakes her head. "It's not what I want," she admits. "But, I get so confused…I know what my ex did to me, but I've got memories of you mixed up in there."

"When I first came to see you, when Byron and Rosie called…" Emma nods and swallows hard. "The cops wouldn't let me in until I proved I wasn't Anderson. My military ID, tags and Byron's statement were needed."

"All I wanted was you." She begins to weep; fat, soft tears begin to roll down her face. "He said you wouldn't want to…"

I stop, wondering what he said to her. I had heard that he'd dared to utter a word in her direction, but not what.

"That I was a way in. That you wouldn't want to fuck me like this," she sobs, her heart breaking.

"Fuck…" I swear. *If I ever get a fucking hold of him…* Then something else tugs at me. "Twirl?" I call out, making Emma look at me. I hand her a tissue and let her dry her eyes. "Will you tell me what he told you? Can you?" I ask, not sure what her powers of recall are like. She sighs and the tears stop.

"He said I was his ticket in…" I nod, understanding what that might be, though I know there's no way on God's green earth that Adam will let him back in after this, not given his girl's background. "And that you wouldn't want to…" She pauses, hefting in a huge gulp of air.

"It's okay, twirl, in your own time, darlin'," I smile at her, gently.

"You wouldn't want to fuck me when I'm broken," she sobs and I pull her to me, hugging her.

"Fuck, twirl, he's a dickhead," I snarl. "I ain't angry at you, twirl, I promise you." I hold her to me, letting her sob. When it starts to lessen, and I think she can now hear me over her own emotions, I tell her what my heart already knows.

"I can't fuck you right now, that's true. Doesn't mean I don't *want* you, or that I will ever stop fucking loving you." She pulls back and I offer her another pile of tissues. "Love ain't just the physical stuff, twirl, though that's pretty damn good with you!" She grins and sobs; trying to laugh and cry isn't easy, but she manages it. I carry on, determined to set this out. "You being here, in this flat, near *my* base, is because *I* love you. If I could end his life and not suffer the consequences of doing it, I would."

"You…love me?" she questions and I nod.

"Yeah, I do. Have for weeks. Been trying to find the right moment to tell you, but it never seemed to be right. But, right here, now? It feels right." I watch as she takes in a huge, calming breath.

"So…you…one day?" I blink, not quite sure what it is she's asking or trying to get me to admit to, but I take a leap and hope to hell I've got it and her sussed right.

"So…what? That one day, I will want to fuck you? Babe, as soon as your ribs are healed, that cast is off, and you're able to go to the toilet by yourself, you bet I'm going to make you scream my name. I want that, just as much as I want to roar yours. I want it all, twirl." I smile at her and she launches into me with more tears cascading down her cheeks, unable to speak.

As we're heading to bed, I get a text from Johnson and smile.

"Twirl, Johnson says she can see you the day after tomorrow. I'll get some time to come walk you to the base via the guest entrance. Johnson says we're going to need a few hours with her to start with. You okay with that?"

I watch as Emma sips the last of her water and nods. "Thank you," she says, hugging me. "Cuddle me?" she requests, her voice small.

"Absolutely," I reply and double-check the flat is locked up before she leads us to bed.

CHAPTER TWENTY-ONE

The Talk & Clarity

EMMA

At night, Stevo holds my hand so I can sleep. He even helps me go to the loo when I have to sleepily make my way to it. Going often is apparently a good sign of healing, or so Stevo tells me.

The morning I'm going to see the trauma counsellor, he writes down his rotations for the next two weeks. I don't have anywhere obvious to pin it and considering getting a corkboard when I'm able to go out. Tearing off the half sheet of paper he's written on, he puts it under a potted plant on my desk that's come with me everywhere. I always seem to find a good spot for that money plant.

"That plant is a little dry," he says and goes to water it.

"Don't! It's a cactus..." Hoping that will tell him all he needs to know. His brow furrows. "It's meant to be that dry most of the time. I'll water everything this coming weekend. I usually do it every six weeks and the last time was just before..." I swallow, hating to admit what happened to me. "Before he grabbed me."

"And assaulted you. Remember, he's a fucking coward," Stevo seethes as he finishes off his coffee. "You've got my number, and the one for the gatehouse, yeah?" he asks and I nod. "And that's my rotation schedule..." He seems to be ticking things off in his head. "I'll be back at thirteen hundred to fetch you and walk you to see Johnson. Remember to eat?" He's always checking what I've eaten; since I fainted that weekend, I've not ignored my food intake.

Gently, he cups my face; my right side is not as swollen as it was only a few days ago. The eating and rest seem to be helping me more than I thought. Then his lips are softly on mine. I can taste the coffee, and I love it.

"My twirl," he whispers and I smile at him. "I'll see you later. Remember to rest up, yeah?" he reminds me, as he did yesterday and I nod. He walks out of the flat and I fling the deadbolts across the top and bottom. When I've slung the second bolt home, I hear Stevo's steps on the metal stairs, and the vibration of the gate closing as the magnetic catch pulls it shut. I sigh, letting out the breath I'd been holding. It's time to chill and plot some more stories.

At exactly thirteen hundred, I hear the access stairs vibrate and there's a fancy set of knocks coming from the door; Stevo's knock. Through the peephole, I spy Stevo in his military fatigues, minus the gun. Smiling, I unbolt the door and let him in.

"I'm glad you waited until you knew it was me. Well done." He looks around and closes the door behind him, but my heart is beating fast. My shoulders are pulled back and I'm standing straighter, wearing a huge smile. I got something right; for him! "Gotta keep that shut, twirl. It's getting colder outside. Let's get you a warm coat and we'll walk to the guest entrance, okay?"

"Won't people comment about...me?" I ask quietly, slipping on some shoes as Stevo finds me a decent coat.

"None of my lot will, but we can't avoid it forever," he says.

"I just don't want to have to explain it to everyone," I sigh, and Stevo nods.

"Ask Johnson when you're there about her coming here if you like?" he suggests. I shake my head; I don't want too many people in this space.

"Not right now. I know I'm being silly," I admit and he smiles.

"No, you're not. You're worrying about things you can't control, trying to head imaginary things off at the pass. I get it." He holds my coat for me and carefully fastens it around me. Once the hood is up, you can't see my face, but we pull the right sleeve inside when we can't find anywhere else to tuck it. It feels funny, but as I look in the mirror, I decide I don't look that bad.

"Are you ready?" he asks and I nod. Stevo opens the door for me, offering to carry the small jute bag I have with a notebook and pen. I shake my head, then he lets me go down to the security gate as he deadlocks the front door.

"I love how many locks are on that door," I admit when he catches up to me and he smiles. Apart from going outside at night to stand in the darkened car park for a little fresh air, this is the first time I've left the flat since he brought me here.

"Colleen said you would appreciate it. One of her guys was good at locks and things in the army, so he sorted it. I'm glad you're happy with it," he shares.

"Did...did it cost much?" I ask, my voice shaky and Stevo shakes his head.

"No. The landlord said he was happy for it to be done as it needed updating, so he paid for the parts."

I smile, grateful that I'm safe and that it didn't cost a lot.

Stevo holds my good hand as we walk around the quiet, picturesque village to the guest entrance of the base. We pass the pub, the clock tower at the junction, and the main corner shop. We walk along a path that passes through a small housing estate until we're there.

I sign in as best I can with my working hand, and he takes me to Johnson's office. The group of buildings are set away from the main complex and has its own little garden.

He holds the door open for me and we enter the warm reception area, which has house plants for décor and people in military uniform walking and sitting around.

"Stevenson," a woman greets him with a smile, her voice happy.

"Johnson." He nods to her, then pulls me to his side, as if showing me off. "This is my girl, Emma. Emma, this is Dr Johnson," he says and I shake the doctor's hand with my good one. Stevo helps me out of the coat, and Johnson smiles. Her blond curls and slight frame make her seem friendly; the smile in her eyes echoes that.

"My office is this way," she tells me and motions for us to follow. For the first time in my life, I enter a psychiatrist's office. It feels like my flat with how the sofa and desks are laid out—homely.

Stevo waits by the door, and Johnson motions for him to come in.

"Okay, let's get the introductions and the basics are taken care of." She pauses and smiles at us both. "As Stevenson said, I'm Dr Michaela Johnson. It's my job to help service personnel and their families over any trauma so that those who serve can focus on what they have to do here." She smiles between us both and I reciprocate the gesture, instantly feeling safe. "I understand you're dating?" she questions, and I nod in reply.

"Yes," Stevo says with a hint of happiness in his tone.

"And your injuries?"

I tense up at her question. "Inflicted by my ex, who is also called Chris," I share and she nods, noting it down in her notebook.

"To start with, I want to have you both talking together, then Stevo can go back on rotation and we can carry on. Is that okay with you, Emma?"

I take a deep breath and nod. "Yes."

"That's great! Stevenson, just listen for now, please. Emma, can you start telling me about your ex?"

I talk about Chris. How it was great at the start, but went downhill after a few months. I can see Stevo's jaw tick in places but I keep my focus on Michaela.

"Okay. Remember, *that* Chris is in the past," she confirms and I nod. I wish it were that easy.

"We've been using my military nickname," Stevo offers when Michaela looks at him. She nods in understanding.

"Since when?" she asks and I sigh.

"Since...after the assault. I get them confused." I look up at her desperately. "That's why I'm here."

She goes wide-eyed for a very brief second. "You're mixing them up?" she confirms gently and I nod. Stevo holds his hands between his open legs and I look at him.

"I'm sorry," I whisper, letting the tears finally fall.

"It's okay, twirl," he calls out, and through blurry vision, I see him holding his hands out. "I'd never hurt you, Emma." He swallows, and his voice is gravelly and emotional. "Never."

"I know." I gulp in some air. "That's not why..." I look at Michaela, and she nods.

"It's time Emma and I carried on our chat. I'll see you when you come to pick her up. When does your shift end?"

"Eighteen hundred," Stevo replies gruffly, and she nods.

"She'll be here until you retrieve her, Corporal." With the use of his rank, he rises and is dismissed.

He leans down to kiss me and I accept it, afraid he'll not come back, and as he walks out of the room, I break. Falling back onto the chair I'm sitting in, I can feel Michaela watching me.

"Okay, so you're getting the two Chrises mixed up," she clarifies when we see Stevo heading towards the front gates. I nod and dry my eyes with some of the tissue she has given me. "That's not unusual. I've checked the base records; he was here on duty," she gently tells me.

"With a big gun," I quip, my anxiety receding and Michaela tilts her head.

"Yes. Is that important?" she asks, and I smile.

"Just…" I sigh, wanting to tell her. "My best friend drove onto the base late one night and Stevo was on duty. That's how his best friend, Byron, was able to find her again," I share.

"Ah! I know of the incident. Go on," she encourages, sitting back in her big chair.

"And when Rosie told me that they had big guns, we made a joke out of it. I shared it with Stevo and now it's…it's silly, I know," I offer but Michaela shakes her head.

"It's not. It's something to note as a difference between the two. So how did you two meet?"

I go through how Stevo came with Byron to Rosie's house, fixed her guttering and took care of her dad's gardens. How we ate pizza and about the incident at the club I worked at.

For hours, Michaela talks me through dates with Stevo, making me remember that what I did with him was nothing like the activities I went through with my ex.

I talk for so long that I want to check the time, but I can't see a clock here. Michaela sees me looking for one.

"There's no time limit here, Emma. You're the only person I have booked for this afternoon. I knew from Stevo's request you'd probably need a good consultation. Here's what I want you to think about for next time, okay?" she asks and I nod. I'm exhausted. "And you can chat with Stevo about this, it's fine."

I lift my head a little straighter.

"Can you consider that the reason you thought about Stevo being there, during the assault, is that you wanted him to intervene? That you *needed* him there?"

I gape and close my mouth. "I did," I reply in a small voice a moment later. Michaela nods.

"I need you to explore why. How does Stevo make you feel?"

I go to answer, but she holds her hands up with a smile and a small shake of her head. "Write them down for me in your notebook for Monday, okay?" she asks and I grin.

I clutch my notebook to me and she smiles at me.

"I'll meet with you after the weekend on Monday," she clarifies, reaffirming the next appointment. "Is that okay with you?" she questions as she rises. I hear a knock at the door; Stevo's knock.

"Fancy knock," she points out, and I smile.

"Stevo's knocking," I reply and she nods.

"Your ex wouldn't have done that, would he? Let you know it was him on the other side before you saw him?"

I shake my head. No, he wouldn't. Only Stevo has told me it's him like that.

"Twirl," he says and Michaela smiles.

"Stevenson, I need ten minutes of your time. Emma, feel free to have a hot drink before you go and brave the weather." She smiles and ushers Stevo out of the room. I know she's telling him about me; I'd be curious if it were him in here too. *How can I help him? What can I do?* Those would be questions I could ask and smile about. I can use that on myself; can't I?

I take my phone out and begin tapping away at ideas as it's easier than writing them down right now, when I hear them come back into the small room.

"Are you ready to go home?" he asks, his voice heavy, and I nod.

"Yes," I breathe out. "Michaela, thank you," I tell her and she smiles.

"I'll see you on Monday, Emma. Take care until then, both of you, okay?" she adds and I nod. Stevo helps me on with my coat, sans my tucked-in sleeve, and then we're walking back to the flat, heads down against the wind, though the rain has eased off. We don't get a chance to talk on the way home.

I love how the gate works on a proximity fob and softly unclicks as we approach. "What did she want with you at the end?" I ask as he locks the door behind us. I cannot believe I was talking for almost five hours. I yawn.

He sighs as he slides the deadbolts home.

"To tell me why you might be confused," he says, removing his fatigue jacket. Outside is damp, but inside, it's dry. "And how to help you out of the fog." He sighs and reaches out to me.

"Twirl. Emma...I'm so sorry I wasn't there. I couldn't be, but that doesn't mean I wish I weren't." His voice is heavy, growly and full of emotion. I reach out to hold his hand and he pulls me to him, being careful of the arm that's still in a sling.

"I'm sorry, babe, I really am!" I close my eyes as he hugs me as tightly as he dares; something I told Michaela he hadn't done a lot of. "I didn't think that you'd be up for me holding you." He sighs into my hair and kisses me on the temple. "I didn't want to hurt you," he croaks and I squeeze him as best I can with my good arm. "Wish you'd told me that you needed them," he adds in a small voice.

"I do. I need you," I whisper between tears. He's all I need right now.

He pulls back and lifts my chin so I have to look at him. "Promise me, you'll tell me if you need a hug, or anything else, and I've not been forthcoming, yeah?" He waits for me to nod, and then he's holding me again and I lose track of time.

"We need to eat and I need a shower. Want a cup of tea first?" he asks, and I shake my head. "What do you need?"

"Don't blame yourself," I tell him, taking a half-step back to look up at him. He's easily six foot tall, strapping. I can tell that whatever Johnson told him is affecting him. I'm ashamed that I'm a part of why. "I didn't know I had to tell you," I admit and one corner of his mouth lifts. "Or how to."

He sighs, his mouth doing a goldfish impression for a moment, and then he makes up his mind about what to say to me. "Twirl, you can tell me you want me anytime you like," he says, trying to hide a smile.

"What?" I ask, letting my brow furrow.

"I was just thinking of an old TV advert, not sure if you've seen it. *The Martini* ad? Anytime, anyplace, anywhere?" he asks and I gasp, then giggle.

"So you're my *Martini* man?" I tease, trying to find a way to make it up to him. I've made him feel bad and I hate that I did that.

"Twirl, I'll be your damn everything," he growls and kisses me like he's never kissed me before.

"You are," I admit when we stop. "I want you in my life. I need you, even though I got angry at you for moving me here. You've done everything to make me feel safe." I play back some of the things Johnson made me explain to her. "I have homework to do for Monday's session," I share and he nods. "To write down how you make me feel." The side of his mouth turns up, hiding a smirk.

"Johnson said you did. I'll make you a mug of tea and let you chill out while I shower. What do you fancy to eat?" he asks as he removes his fatigues. He hangs his military jacket over the heater; I guess drying that can take a bit of time.

We agree on chicken ramen and he reads the instructions on the packet before going for a shower. As he cleans up, I work on how he makes me feel—has made me feel—since we've been together.

As he cooks dinner, I look across and watch him. He's got his grey jogging bottoms back on, and he's wearing a loose-fitting t-shirt. I feel safe, knowing he's here and I add that word to the list that's forming.

Other words get added and I go back through my texts with Rosie and Ruby. The ones with Ruby are mostly about my books and her suggestions on the edits. But it gives me more words as he believed in me and found a way to support me. By the time we've eaten the chicken ramen and we're getting ready for bed, I've filled up a page.

"Stevo...can I show you?" I ask. I feel a need for him to see this.

"Sure, hang on," he says, drying his hands. He comes and joins me on the sofa and I hand him the open notebook.

He takes it from me with a puzzled look, then sits back and reads it, mouthing some of the words out but not making a sound.

"Twirl," he whispers many minutes later. "Oh, my twirl," he says, and I'm in tears watching him understand that I know exactly what he's done for me. Never before have I told anyone what I'm feeling, least of all a man. A man I want in all ways; if he's even willing. Sharing how he makes me feel, that I need him, is scaring me.

He's known what I've needed and provided it, even if I have been a brat about it. He did it anyway.

"Come here, twirl," he says, holding out his hands for me. I reach across and he pulls me to him. "Let me take you to bed," he tells me and I nod. I'm not above begging, far from it, but I realise I don't need to. I just need to let Stevo know I need him. And I did.

He saw the very bottom statement: *I need you.*

Chapter Twenty-Two

The First Day

Chris

'*I need you,*' is scrolled beautifully on the last part of Emma's page of homework, and I'm choked to see it written down. My military nickname is at the top, surrounded by swirls and other pretty patterns. I'm stunned by her admission.

'Safe', 'secure', and 'loved' are other words she's written down. The '*sexy*' is a surprise, but when I think back, it shouldn't be. The same with the other words, '*desirable*', '*seductive*', '*irresistible*' and '*attractive - at last!*' make me stall.

Reading through every word and small phrase makes my heart swell. She doesn't just *want* me, she *needs* me to bring all this to her daily. Putting the book down, I offer to take her to bed. She might think she's broken, but so are crayons and they can still make bright pictures.

In the bedroom, I flip on the side light and close the curtains, then I turn to her. She's biting her lip and looking at the floor. Her hair is in a ponytail that I'm getting better at doing for her. Closing the space between us, I reach behind her to gently tug it lose. Fanning it out makes me realise that she could benefit from a haircut; another thing I can get organised on base to happen on Monday.

"Tell me what you need, twirl. Let me make it happen," I whisper as I softly kiss her jaw.

She moans at my feather-soft kisses and I'm careful not to knock her arm. I slowly run my arm down her good side and she shudders and writhes at my touch. Smirking, I run my hand down to the bottoms that she's once again borrowed from me, but I don't care.

Sliding my fingers into the band, I gently tug them down off her hips. The bruising is colourful, showing us that her body is getting better. This is for her, her mind, her soul. *Us.*

I follow the bottoms down and gently brush my fingers up both of her legs.

"You're fucking amazing, twirl, you know that?" I ask, looking up at her. Her pupils are wide and she's still gnawing at her lip. She shakes her head in reply. "You are," I repeat, tracing her legs to tend to her knickers. They're the soft sporty ones she loves to wear, even if she can't stand doing anything more than walking.

"You're finding you and you're letting me come along for the ride," I admit.

"I'm not letting you," she says and I stop and look up. "I want you with me on this. I can't do this without you," she whispers as tears form.

"I want to be along for this ride, twirl, and everything else after. You understand?" I lift the nightshirt and plant a small caress on her stomach. She smells of exotic fruits and sucks in a breath as I lay gentle kisses on her bruised softness.

"Yes," she breathes as I sprinkle light, feathery kisses across her stomach and up to the bruised ribs. Her knees threaten to give out and I place my hands on her hips as I go down.

"Lie on the edge of the bed, twirl," I command and like a good girl, she does. Her legs fall over the side as she lays herself down gently. "Enjoy," I tell her and go back to kissing her thighs, rising towards her sex with every light touch and lick I bestow.

Hooking my fingers into the sides of her knickers, I gently pull them down her legs and discard them, kissing down the inner thigh and calf of one leg, then back up the other, more bruised side.

"Stevo..." she moans my name, her chest heaves and her hand is in my hair, tugging, encouraging.

"Enjoy, twirl. I got you," I say just loud enough to be heard as my mouth finds her sex and her clit. I suck gently; I have no idea how bruised or sore she might be here, but bringing her pleasure is something I need to do. Getting her off is a necessity.

"Oh!" I hear her cry out and her only working hand grabs more of my hair as her thighs try to close. I firmly place my arms up to stop her and let my tongue delve deep into her, licking and sucking. Bringing a hand down, I gently thrust a finger into her. I grin as she tries to clamp down on it, but it's not thick enough. I add another, firmly using both. Not satisfied with that, I turn my hand and beckon with them inside her, making her moan. In seconds, she's climaxing, writhing this way and that, chasing her orgasm and letting out the most beautiful groan.

I slow down to help her through it and flick again as she nears the end, making her arch up and cry out again. Her insides clench my fingers so I cannot move my hand. The juices flow and she's as sweet as honey. I enjoy sucking and licking her, watching her reactions.

"Please," she begs, her good hand trying to find me, rubbing against my hard-on in my joggers as I stand. "Please?" she repeats, and I smile, stripping and standing before her at the edge of the bed.

"You're sure?" I ask and she nods.

"Please, Stevo, I need..." With that, I push gently into her until I'm balls deep. "You...oh...yesss..." I lean forward, intending to kiss her. She runs her hand along my chest and wraps her legs around me, wanting me, trapping me.

Slowly, I glide in and out of her, taking care to not grab or touch her in bruised places. My hands drop to either side of her shoulders and I reach down to kiss her, claim her as I make love with her.

She lifts her hips to meet me thrust for thrust and it's the sexiest thing I've ever encountered.

This is it.

What I've been waiting for my whole damn life.

Her.

This.

Us.

Her breathing gets erratic and I drop my head to her good side, kissing her jaw as she comes. Her soft moans and writhing take me over the edge and together we find bliss.

Eventually, I lift my head, arms shaking from the effort to not collapse onto her bruised body, but I do need to hold her.

"Dear God!" She grins and I can't help but smile back, grabbing another deep, tongue-twisting kiss.

"I did get blessed with parts to use." I grin and she laughs. It's the first time I've heard it in weeks.

"You didn't wrap up though," she tells me and I freeze.

"Fuck…twirl, I'm sorry! I hadn't…shit!" I gently pull out, but any consequence is done with.

"I am on the pill, but with the other drugs and the week I took off it because of…"

I kneel before her, kicking myself. "Twirl, if we did just make another human, I'm there. The whole way. You, and any potential it, are mine. Got it?" I didn't want to go there, not yet, but if we have, we have. I resign and embrace myself to that fact now.

She nods, and strokes the side of my jaw, running her hand into my hair and I turn my head to place it gently against her.

"I know. You'll make a great dad," she tells me and I close my eyes.

"You'll be a fantastic mum," I say, holding her close before I tuck us both into bed and hold her as best I can for the rest of the night.

We chill on Saturday; I'm not on rotation again until Sunday evening. I mention to Em she can use all the facilities on base, including the hairdressers and she smiles saying she'd love a haircut. I call in and the lady who runs it, Sam, tells me that there's a space at three for a cut and blow-dry. Getting the nod from Emma as I relay the information, we book it and at three, we're at the salon in a wing of the main building. Usually, it's the wives of serving personnel in attendance; there are a few guys there that I nod and acknowledge.

"What happened?" one guy asks me, nodding towards Emma.

"Her deranged ex found her in Milton. They've got him in custody," I tell him, being honest.

"Saw something about that in the newspaper. Bus depo, wasn't it?" another mentions and I nod.

"Yeah. A friend of hers went hunting for him when he ran like the coward he is. She found him, pulled the cops down on him."

The first guy growls. "He comes anywhere near here…" he promises and I grin. Different divisions, but all families. *I love the military for that.*

"Only if he's able to get out of the remand prison he's in, or away from the cops on transfer," I state. "Which, I doubt."

"Let's hope not, yeah?" says the first, whose name suddenly comes to me: Andy Hodgeson. Their wives or girlfriends have engaged Emma in a conversation and one of them comes up to us.

"We'll look after her. You guys can head to the mess hall," she instructs. I know who she is now; her hubby's a squadron leader and the man who I think is her hubby stands up.

"You do that, love. See you in a bit, but don't take all afternoon, gotta fetch the kids, remember?" Andy says.

She rolls her eyes and nods. They exchange a quick kiss and I check in with Emma.

"You okay staying here with the ladies, twirl?" I ask and she beams at me.

"Yeah...they asked," she tells me, motioning to her arm and I nod.

"I know. Truth, yeah?" I remind her and she nods. Then Johnson walks in and beams at us both.

"Stevenson! Emma! It's so good to see you out and about!"

"We're trying to persuade these guys to head to the mess hall or the bar," says Mrs Hodgeson and Johnson smiles.

"Great idea!" I smile at Emma in the mirror's reflection.

I lean down to whisper into her ear. "See you soon, twirl." I kiss her gently on the side of the head before Andy and the others drag me to the bar for what turns out to be several pints.

As we wait for the girls, we chat. I've never really spoken with the flying crew before, not like this—Byron would though. Byron's not around; he's down with Rosie, a fact they comment about.

"So, a girl has turned his head," they tease and I shrug.

"We ain't getting any younger," I remind them. "You lot have kids, wives and careers. We're just a bit late in catching onto the whole family thing," I reply.

"And how did you meet her?" Andy asks.

"She's Byron's girl's best friend."

Andy nods. "And the issue with her ex?" he asks as another half appears before me.

"He's a fuck-wit. Narcissistic arsehole from what I can work out. Happy to gas-light and beat up women."

Another—Nigel—snorts. "Probably can't take it from another bloke," he states and I shrug, indifferent.

"Probably. No idea. Just aware of what is going to happen if I ever meet him." The guys look at me then nod.

"Yell if you do," Andy says and I smile with a nod in thanks.

"My lot are aware of what he looks like, his name." I go on to tell them how he incapacitated her car outside her work and that when her arm is better, she'll be looking for a new job.

"There's an on-base café opening up after Christmas," Nigel tells me. "The wife's sorting it out, reusing one of the old cabins near the guest entrance."

I nod. "Been seeing lots of wood being transported to it. Knew it was being done up, but hadn't heard why," I confirm. We talk about what it needs, the re-wiring, plumbing and kitting out.

"Just can't get a hold of a plumber," Nigel says and I wink.

"I can pop in early tomorrow, and see what's needed if you guys like?" I offer. They gape at me. "My uncle runs a property improvement business, so I went out on jobs with him before I signed up. I get collared for the harder repairs when I'm home, which are a three-man job." I grin, recalling the boiler replacement that went south one winter and took nine hours to replace.

"We'd appreciate that, mate."

With a few nods and confirmation of the times, we agree to meet tomorrow a few hours before my shift. Andy looks up and grins and I turn to see Emma in the middle of a group of RAF wives, smiling and joking. She looked bloody gorgeous and pretty before, but now...hot damn. Today was just what we both needed.

Sunday morning has Emma's voice calling out for me in alarm, and I bash my shins on a side unit trying to get to her as I am still half asleep. When I do, I notice why. Guess we're not going to be parents soon.

"Oh, twirl! Tell me what to do." She goes through what to make up for her and how to clean her up. With only one hand, she can't do it herself.

"I'm sorry," she sobs and I just hold her.

"It's okay, twirl. It wasn't meant to be right now, but if you want to, come off the pill, yeah?" She sniffs.

"You...want a child with me?" she asks and I nod, smiling.

"Yes, I do, twirl. I told you, I want the whole thing."

She smirks but doesn't tell me what she's thinking. I cock my head to the side and wait; will she tell me or do I have to tell her to tell me? She folds her lips in onto themselves.

"Twirl?" I caution, making her sigh.

"I want to do it the right way, first, please." She looks at me with such trust and love. She can have whatever she wants.

"If that's what you want, twirl, we'll do it that way. But, not while I'm in the service. After I get out, okay?"

She nods slowly, then asks, "Why?"

I sigh, and then I perch on the side of the bath so I can think. When I look at her, her face is full of concern, worry and love. *How the hell did I get so damn lucky?*

"I'm so close to getting out, leaving this kind of life behind. I've done my time, twirl. When we marry, you'll get all the benefits I had with the pension. But I just wanna see this gone first. I promised myself I'd never make a loved one doubt if I were ever coming home. I've seen grown men break like little girls when they've lost their service partners. I've seen grown-assed women nearly kill themselves because their partners died on tour, or kids go off the rails because a parent met their maker. I ain't putting you through that, babe, not a fucking chance in hell."

She comes over and cuddles me to her, stroking my hair as I wrap my arms around her. Maybe I'll put in for that garden leave duty sooner rather than later.

"You were born to be in a dangerous position, to do what is right. Your job, no matter what it is, I think will always have that risk. I doubt you'll be happy doing what your uncle does, not for the long term."

I begin to think of arguing against her, but she's right. And I tell her so.

"So, you do you. If you want to get married, away from the RAF, that'll be fine by me. In the RAF, also fine. I just want..." She places her hand over my clasped one and her pupils expand. "Need...you."

I stand up quickly, walking her back to the bathroom door, which shuts with a click.

"And you've got me," I tell her. The bulb must be playing up as there's a small rainbow of light hitting her across her neckline. I pay it no mind as I ravage her mouth, pulling her to me. She winces and I kick myself.

"Sorry, twirl. I didn't mean to knock it," I sigh, regretful that I've hurt her.

"I'll be glad when the pins get taken out, I tell you!"

She won't be the only one.

I explain where I'm going and why I'm leaving for work earlier than normal. She smiles and nods.

"Nic explained it to me. I was wondering," she begins and I grin.

"A job for after Christmas?" I finish airing her thought as I shove my feet into the uniform boots. Emma nods.

"If you think..." she hesitates.

"Twirl, you can do anything you want to. If you wanna work at the on-base cafe, that's fine by me. If you want to work in a pub again, or in the village, that's fine with me. I like this talking stuff; very useful." I grin, making her smirk.

"I'll let you know what I decide, once the doctor has taken these pins out and we have dates on when I can start using it."

I stand up and shake my uniform down my legs as I grab my waterproof fatigue.

"That'll be great, twirl! Lock up behind me, yeah?" I ask, grabbing my fob and stealing a kiss.

"Always," she breathes, and I ensure that she's bolted the door and the gate is secure before I head off to the base via the guest entrance so I can talk with Nigel and Nic.

What they needed, I can do in about half a day. The hot water tank needs replacing, making what Nic wanted to do with the counter placement a shed load easier. I agree with the half-day I can spare if Nigel can grab me some waste pipes and other things. I make a list and Nic nods, agreeing to have it for me. Then I call Emma before I go to muster.

"Hey, twirl! I need to spend about half a day with Nigel and Nic to sort out the plumbing. Fancy coming with me on Tuesday to do it?" I ask.

"I can't help much," she says.

"Babe, have you ever not helped someone fix something? Even chatting with someone can help loads! Say you'll come with me?" I'm not making it an offer. "Nic is looking forward to the chat," I add and then hear her sigh.

"Okay. It'll be good to get out again," she agrees, and I grin.

"Great! I will call you again when I'm on a break, but I'll tell Nic she can expect you too. Catch you later on, twirl!"

"Bye, you," she whispers and then I let her go. Grinning like a Cheshire cat, I go to get organised for the night.

My break isn't until nearly midnight, and I hope my twirl is in bed. I text her and she texts me right back.

"I am in bed," she admits, "but I didn't want to sleep until I had spoken with you." She yawns, though she tries to keep it quiet.

"That's sweet of you, twirl. Hey, I've been thinking..." I begin, and she chuckles.

"Isn't that dangerous? Go on," she teases. *Minx.*

"Haha! That sounds like something Byron would say!" I pause for a second, letting my words form how I want to say them. "How about I move into the flat with you?" I ask, testing the waters.

"Permanently?" she clarifies.

"Yeah," I respond, unsure of how else I could mean that.

"I'd love that!" she tells me and I grin.

"I can move my stuff in after each shift, bring stuff back. We might need another wardrobe," I comment and she yawns again.

"I'm sure we can make room," she tells me.

"The furniture in the room has to stay on base, so it's clothes, mostly. A couple of kit bags worth and that's it." Considering I've lived out of my kit bag for over a decade, I think I've done well to have a few possessions.

"Sounds great! What time are you due back?" she questions.

"Seven hundred," I confirm and she chuckles.

"I'll set an alarm so I can come and unbolt the door," she tells me.

"Not a problem, twirl. You go and sleep. I'll see you in the morning." I turn to make sure I'm alone. "Love you," I whisper to her.

"Love you too, Stevo. Night!"

I hang up with a grin still on my face, finish my break and head back on duty.

CHAPTER TWENTY-THREE

Rosie's Bombshell

EMMA

October gives way to November and I do my routine check-in with Rosie. Today is the day of her dad's MRI; something that I know has been worrying her as Dave's been so quiet and not moaning as he usually does. She sends me a text to tell me he's just gone down for the procedure, but that she'll text again when he's back on the ward.

I know Stevo finishes his rotation at ten am. They work weird, irregular patterns to make up the hours that they do; I guess it's a security thing. I glance at my phone when Stevo comes home and he asks why. When I explain, he nods, hugs me and then he's off for a shower. I'm left with the overwhelming feeling that I am in the wrong place.

He's moved in permanently now and I love having another human to talk with. It helps that Stevo discusses story plots with me and supports what I hope will be a writing career. Usually, I settle when he's back, knowing he's safe. Not today.

By two pm, I'm unable to be still. Rosie doesn't answer my texts and that worries me far more than anything. If she's been told something bad, she won't contact anyone; I don't think she'd be able to. Stevo sends Byron a text, then checks in with the base asking where Byron might be. He's out on a repair flight and my eyes go wide. Something feels very, very wrong.

The phone rings and I scream a little; it suddenly comes to life with an incoming call from a Milton Keynes number has me freezing in a panic. Stevo grabs it and answers.

"Who is calling?" he asks and his face goes from defensive to military hard in a second, and then his look softens. "Hang on. Milton Keynes General, oncology department," he says, handing me my phone. My heart sinks.

"Hello, Emma Blackthorne," I state as Stevo strides off.

"Miss Blackthorne, I've been asked to call you by Dr Simons. He says he'd like you here to support Mr and Miss Mallard," the voice explains.

"We're on our way. It'll take me about ninety minutes to get to you." I look across to Stevo who already has his jacket on, he's grabbed the car keys and he's nodding at me. "Oncology department, yes?" I confirm as Stevo hands me some shoes I can get on one-handed.

"Yes. Please come to the reception desk. Thank you," the lady's clipped voice instructs and ends the call.

"Let's get you ready, then we'll go find Rosie," Stevo says as he begins to lock up the flat.

I watch my phone and Stevo's the entire way down to Milton Keynes. Stevo asked a favour from the base ground crew: call him when Byron's on approach. He's also told Byron via text that oncology has called us and we're on our way to find Rosie.

I watch the scenery fly by as it slowly darkens outside; the phones stay quiet, indicating Byron's not back. That he used to do this run just to see me takes my breath away. His dedication, even then, is beyond anything I could have hoped for.

On entering the hospital car park, I spot Rosie's car, and Stevo parks next to it. The receptionist said to head to the oncology department. Having spent a little too much time in this particular hospital, I know where to go.

"Hi!" I breeze up to the lady behind the oncology reception desk. "I'm Emma Blackthorn. I'm here to see Dave or Rosie Mallard."

I put on my sweet, dumb voice and the receptionist shakes her head.

"I'm sorry," the woman states and it's obvious that she's not the same woman I spoke with on the phone. "Are you family?" she asks and I shake my head.

"The man raised me, but I'm not a biological daughter. I just want to know where they are so I can support my friend, that's all."

Stevo comes up behind me, which makes me jump.

"Sorry, twirl." He grins, and I smile back. When I turn back to the receptionist, she was calling someone. The way she's looking at me, I roll my eyes.

"He didn't do this to me, and I'm not a threat. Look, you called me," I say and fold my arms over my chest as best I can, thinking of all sorts of wonderful names for this *helpful* receptionist.

"I'm here," Rosie's voice calls out to my left, and I run to my best friend, hugging her as tightly as I can. She sobs into my good side and I try my best to reassure her, though I think I've just lied.

"It's not good," she tells us as we sit on the awful plastic waiting room chairs. Stevo is on the phone by the window, but he doesn't look happy.

"Can't get a signal," he states, marching over to us. "I'll be back when I've made this call. You two stay here, okay?" he says to us, and we nod. When he's satisfied we understand, he kisses me and marches off.

"Where's he going?" Rosie asks, her face scrunching up.

"To contact Byron," I tell her, thinking that was perhaps obvious.

"Oh God!" she cries out, running her hands through her now dishevelled hair. She begins to fish around in her huge handbag, but panic has set in and she can't find what she's looking for. I guess it's her phone. "Oh, Christ!" She sobs and I hug my best friend. Somehow, minutes later, Stevo is back—with Byron.

We head up to where Dave's being kept for the night. Rosie and Byron head into his room, and Stevo and I settle into the waiting room chairs as best we can. He lets me cuddle into him. Rosie told us the coffee and tea here were bloody horrid, so we've not bothered with anything to drink.

"How did he get here so fast?" I ask, unsure of how hot on our tail Byron was.

Stevo sighs. "He got my text and hightailed it down here like a bat outta hell. He told Welshy he'd call me, but he didn't put his hands-free kit on. He noticed my car and Rosie's when he arrived," he mutters and I nod.

Much later, as hunger begins to kick in, Byron comes out of the oncologist's office supporting Rosie. Even Byron looks like he's been crying and I begin to cry too. Rosie's in a daze, but somehow we manage to get back to hers. Rosie drives her car, followed by Byron, then us.

When we're at Rosie's, I watch as my friend collapses onto the sofa in a ball and through heartbreaking sobs, she tells us that Dave wants to give her away; she's marrying Byron at her dad's request.

In Rosie's room upstairs a little later, we munch on a sandwich. We can still hear Rosie shuffling about sniffling, Byron's low tones comforting her and I sigh.

"Shit...it means he won't be able to give me away," I quietly state. "He was as near to a parent as I was ever going to get and now..." I hate that I break down, worrying about what *I* won't have when my friend is losing her father to cancer. The pain for me is real, too.

Stevo comes and holds me. "Who gives you away doesn't matter; that's a tradition we don't have to follow. I know that you're hurting too; he raised you." He kisses my head and holds me. Quietly, he continues what he was saying. "What we do, will be for us and I'm sure he'll be there in spirit when we say our vows, Em," he continues, his voice is low like Byron's.

"To do that, though...to make them?" I question, but I know Dave. Something's worrying him and he's doing this to deal with it; he likes to head things off, and sort them out. He's never been one for loose ends.

I hear the backdoor open, Byron's voice mumbles low, but I can't hear what he's saying, or to whom. The conversation doesn't last long and the backdoor opens and closes one more time before sleep takes me under.

The following morning, I hear a voice; Byron's. Just his, not Rosie's or anyone else's.

"Making calls," Stevo quietly tells me and I nod. Stevo helps me dress and we head downstairs to see what we can do to help. If anything.

"Thank you, Chaplain Graeme," Byron says as we enter the kitchen, Stevo letting me enter first. The two men nod to each other in that kind of military way the three of them have. "Stevo's here, so we have another serving witness. We'll see you soon." After a goodbye from him, Byron turns to us, hanging up the call.

Rosie is at the kitchen table and she smiles at me when she realises we're here. "We can go looking for a dress tomorrow," I suggest and Rosie pulls up her phone.

"I was thinking this," she says, handing her phone to me. I love where her ideas are taking her and this can be here in a few days thanks to express delivery.

"Order it," I tell her, sitting down. Stevo has taken charge of making breakfast and Byron goes over to him. I reach out for Rosie's hand, offering some physical form of support.

"Stevo," Byron says, his voice somehow holding true and not choking. "Will you be my best man?"

Stevo nods. "Like you'd want anyone else by your side, mate," he replies and I smile when I realise he expected the request.

"Who will be your maid of honour?" Byron asks Rosie, who smiles at me, though it doesn't reach her eyes. *How can it?*

Rosie grips my good hand, squeezing it gently. "We decided when we were ten, we'd be each other's maid of honour," Rosie shares and I nod in confirmation. Stevo and I have our work cut out.

The chaplain arrives at two minutes past ten. He might be dressed in military fatigues, but he's got a dog collar on, which I find somewhat strange but reassuring. Byron greets him and we head into the formal sitting room.

Byron's serving up tea and coffee with a plate of biscuits. The chaplain goes through how this is a commitment and Rosie explains her father's cancer. I listen as she explains how it's progressed; an update she wasn't able to give us yesterday and quietly, my heart breaks. Dave's known about this for some time and kept it from her, and me.

"I'd like to chat with the ladies, please," he tells the guys and the look he gives them indicates that he's not going to accept any arguments. Stevo and Byron nod, then leave.

"I have to ask," the chaplain begins and looks at me. "Was that done by Stevenson?"

I shake my head. "No. My ex did this, not Stevo. The only reason I'm healing as well as I am is because of Stevo. You can check in with Johnson and Mrs Hodgeson on the base," I tell him and he nods with a soft smile.

"It's good that you're talking with Johnson. Now, Rosie, are you *sure* you want to go through with this?"

Rosie pulls in a huge breath and sighs. "Being honest, Chaplain, we were heading that way anyway, just not right at this moment. Byron spoke with his parents very late last night and very early this morning. I heard the conversations, at least from Byron's side." She smiles about something but doesn't elaborate. "We were just taking our sweet time with it. Dad simply doesn't have that long."

"Let me get the boys back in here," he says and goes to the doorway, calling for Byron and Stevo in a voice I'm sure even God would listen to.

"Chaplain." Byron nods as they come back into the room.

"Grievson, Stevo. I'm happy that things are in order, that these ladies aren't being coerced into this...well, not by either of you." He smiles at me, then at Rosie.

"I'm glad you're being vigilant, Chaplain," Byron says, kindly.

"I'm glad you think so. Now...I have to impress upon you all, this is a lifetime deal here. You're doing this because you love each other, am I correct?"

Byron and Rosie nod.

"Yes...the circumstances could be a hell of a lot better," Rosie ventures. "But, where can we hold it?" She looks at the chaplain, then Byron. "The event, I mean. The ceremony?"

"That would be on base," the chaplain confirms. "Can your father travel up for the day?" he asks. "Milton Keynes doesn't have a formal church on site, but Waddington does as it's a bigger base."

"We'll need to check what support he's sent home with," Byron answers softly, looking at Rosie. "But, we need that licence. The rest, we'll work out today and tomorrow."

The chaplain rises and nods, shaking hands with us girls, then the guys.

"Gentlemen, I'll speak with you both soon. Ladies." He smiles at us, then he heads out quietly.

Dave comes home with a nurse at around three on patient transport. We said we'd stay until he was home and saw what provisions if any, he was sent home with. Rosie and Byron are sitting with Dave and the nurse in the front room and though we've not been invited in, we can hear what's going on as the doors are open. I haven't had a chance to hug him yet.

"Live-in nurse?" I gasp; this is the final road for Dave if he's got that in place. I like the sound of the nurse though; she has a soft Yorkshire accent and she's already not taking nonsense from Dave.

Stevo nods, his lips thin. He reaches a hand out for me and I take it. Squeezing his hand, I want that connection and reassurance.

"There's a lot to do for them," he says, indicating to the front room and I nod.

"I know." And there's not a lot of time to do it all.

We head off once we've met the nurse and I've hugged Dave, heading straight onto the base. Stevo signs me in. He finds who he needs, enlisting their help. In the mess hall, I meet up with Nic, who knows the kitchen crew.

I also meet Josie for the first time and between her and Nic, engage the kitchen crew to do the catering for the hastily prepared nuptials. With the promise of a donation to the RAFA, which I learn is their support charity for ex and serving personnel, we part ways. I spot Stevo talking with Vicky's husband, Andy Hodgeson. They shake hands and then Stevo finds me.

"You ready for some kip, twirl?" he asks and I nod.

"Very," I reply, trying to keep it together for a few more minutes. Stevo offers me his hand then we head to the flat.

As I take off my boots, I sigh and let my tears finally fall. We walked back from the base, leaving the car secure as it's a short distance and we'll be back there tomorrow. Walking is the only exercise I'm getting.

Poor Rosie! That's two parents she'll have lost to cancer in the time I've known her. Stevo comes and hugs me, not saying anything. There are no words, not for this. Well, not unless you're going to swear at the sky.

"Come on, twirl, we can deal with more tomorrow. Let's rest," he says and I agree, letting him take me to bed. In moments, I'm asleep.

The following morning, Stevo wakes me up with a mug of tea in bed and I can't help but feel loved.

"Thank you," I say softly. He moves the pillows for me, helping me up so I can go to the bathroom. I come back and enjoy my tea under the still-warm quilt. We chat and make a list of what still needs doing. As our stomachs rumble, Stevo heads off to cook breakfast and I get dressed into a grey hoodie and some matching ladies' sweats Stevo ordered for me.

"Have you ordered yourself a dress, twirl? I'll be in uniform," he reminds me and I shake my head. Knowing what kind of look Rosie is going for helps. I find one that's not overly expensive that I like. I show it to Stevo, and he cocks his head.

"Twirl, you sure?" he asks and I nod. "I think we can find you something a bit more up-market," he adds, and we hunt for an alternative.

"I like that one." I defend the dress and he smiles.

"Yeah, I know. But, you're not ugly. Their wedding day ain't a day to hide behind your gorgeous looks, twirl," he says and I sigh.

"I like hiding," I state and he laughs.

"Twirl, if I'm going to be showing off the uniform and looking my best, I want you to join me." He wants me to raise my look and step away from the frumpiness I've been using as a shield. Johnson said the same last week and I sigh. I was holding out on that, but it looks like I don't get a choice. I decide it's about time anyway. I hid in the dumpy clothes because of Chris. Stevo wants to show me off and like a peacock, I want to show off my true colours.

Stevo picks out a few options, and I choose one. In seconds he's ordering it for me.

"Let me," I begin and he shushes me with a deep kiss.

"No, twirl, let me. You can wear it on Christmas Day at the family dinner, yeah?" He smiles.

"The what?" I ask and he winks.

"The family dinner. I've put in for a week's leave at Christmastime so we can travel to London and you can meet Jean, Craig, Ruby and the others." He motions to the dress order that's still on the screen. "And you can double up by wearing that. We always dress up on Christmas Day," he informs me.

I sigh, then resign myself to the fact that Christmas is not that far away.

"What about Rosie and her dad?" I ask, aware that I'll be missing any time with them.

"This might be their last Christmas together. Byron will be with them, as will the nurse. Figured it would be best to give them that space, don't you?" he asks. I hadn't thought of it like that, but I nod.

"I was hoping to be there too. I usually am," I tell him and he stops.

"Of course, you were. Shit. Let's see how it plays out then, yeah?" he checks, and I nod, smiling.

Byron pops by in the early afternoon before he heads back to Rosie's.

"Hey, you two," he calls out in greeting as Stevo lets him in.

"Hey, how's Rosie?" I ask as he closes the front door behind him. Then Stevo asks him to bolt it. I watch as he sends his friend a curious glance, but there's a quick nod of acknowledgement. I offer him tea how he likes it, and my shoulders relax.

"Still in shock, she says. She's been crying on and off; I'm glad that nurse is there, though I can't wait to get to her tonight," he tells us.

"She's not had a chance to think," I observe. I know I haven't either, not really.

Byron shakes his head. "No...we'd be planning this better if we had more time, but the truth is, we simply don't know how long Dave has. No one does."

"But, you'd have asked her to marry you anyway?" I ask, hoping that they do love each other at least. Byron nods in answer.

"I called my father up at one am his time to talk it through; as I was explaining to him why I hadn't asked her, I realised I was always going to. Just...not quite like this." He smiles, though I can tell it's forced.

"But you love her?" I demand and it looks like he's seeing me for the first time.

"Yes," he replies and I hold my gaze with him for a few moments before he nods.

"Good," I say, smiling as I curl my legs up underneath me. I'm happy with how Byron replied, not just what he replied with.

"Do you have a dress?" he asks as he sits down with his tea and I nod.

"Already sorted; it's on the way," I reply. He doesn't need to know Stevo had a hand in it.

"And the wedding dress?" he asks, hesitantly, as if Rosie's going to walk down the aisle in a bin bag.

"Sorted," I respond, happy that I know something he doesn't.

"We just need our dress uniforms sorted, mate," Chris tells him. I watch as Byron nods, then blinks, as if the realisation is just setting in!

We go through our list and two items are left: stag and hen do.

"What can we do for either?" Stevo asks.

"Bring Byron over here and chill with the man? Or organise something on base with some of his crew?" I offer. Stevo grins.

"Just here will be good. I'm going to need to go to the off-license though. We don't have much in to get him drunk with."

"You can't get him too drunk, he needs to make it to the altar," I state and his jaw drops. "Chris, please, don't," I plead. "This is too important to Dave and Rosie," I remind him. Stevo backs up; partly I think because I called him Chris for the first time since I was attacked and secondly, I used Dave's name. "Giving him a hangover is fair, but don't give him such a bad one that he'll not be at the altar. I might let Rosie castrate you if you do!"

I fold my arms over myself, determined to set *some* boundaries on the booze, more for Rosie's sake than anyone else's.

"You're right, twirl," he says as he comes over and hugs me. "Thanks for the reminder." He kisses me before he disappears out of the front door, wallet and coat in hand.

Chapter Twenty-Four
The Stag & The Night Before

Chris

Emma's plea to not get Byron *too* drunk doesn't go unheeded; neither does the threat of Rosie castrating me. The poor girl has enough on her plate right now with her dad, not to mention this situation.

Getting Byron to visit us isn't hard. A text inviting him over for a few hours is all it took. As soon as he's in the flat, I hand him a beer, starting off lightly. Emma enjoys a beer too and I realise, I've never seen her drink before. Until now. I make a mental note to find out what that's all about another time. Byron downs the beer and accepts the whisky Emma offers him. She hands one to me too and I thank her.

I'd loosened off all the bottles so she could help pour. I notice she doesn't hit the hard stuff, but helps herself to a second beer that's going down very slowly.

"We're lucky," I tell Byron later. I'm not sure how much Emma's plied us with, but I know she's keeping count, as good barmaids do. "We've got our girls." The alcohol loosens my tongue.

"Never thought I'd find her again. Or that I'd get to apologise," he says.

"What *did* happen on that flight?" Emma asks, taking the smallest sip of her beer. She's with it, much more so than Byron or me, but I know I'm nearing my limit. I look at the drinks area and some of the bottles are missing. She's hidden them from us, just in case—smart move.

"I proclaimed loudly that she wanted me. We'd been making jokes, the innuendos were getting lower and dirtier, and I didn't lower my voice. I should have. Should have done a lot of things." He sighs and leans back on the sofa, glass in hand.

"Did that make you grow up?" Emma asks, leaning forward from the single chair.

Byron nods. "Aye, but too late. She'd gone when I came to my senses; transferred out. Where did she go?" he asks Emma and she smiles.

"Halton," Emma says clearly. "Dave had started to show signs of arthritis, so she wanted to be nearer to him and as far away from you as possible."

Emma puts her beer down on the coffee table and calls for Byron to look at her.

"Do not hurt her," she says to him. I wish she'd demonstrate this level of tenacity for herself, but I get why she doesn't. Not yet. It is something to suggest that Johnson work with her on. Emma probably thinks she's not worth it, thanks to her useless twat of an ex.

"I won't," he says, drinking some more. "No more *deficiente*," he adds, and Emma nods.

"I'll see you two in the morning." She nods to the blankets we pulled out earlier.

"Night!" Byron calls and goes to leave.

"Naw, stay for another," I encourage, pouring him another one. We sit in comfortable silence as Emma gets ready for bed. When I hear the door close gently, I turn to my friend. "I want what you're about to do, but with Em. When she's ready," I tell him as I hand him another vodka with just a splash of cola. "Just want you there," I say, nodding.

"You two are well suited." He slurs his words as he speaks. "And sure, I'll be there. Payback's going to be *una cagna*," he tells me. Even I know just enough Italian to know he said *a bitch*. Let's see if he remembers how much I got him to drink when he wakes up.

The following morning, I walk in and grin as I see what state Byron is in. I snap a photo; there's no way he's going to be allowed to forget last night!

He stirs as I move about, clearing up. Emma doesn't need to be mothering either of us and frankly, she doesn't need the grief. I take her a tea and come back to find Byron's untangling himself from the heavier blanket.

"You're a sight," I tell him straight, almost chuckling.

He tries to stand, then sits back down and I can't help but chuckle. Finding the pain killers, the 'morning after alcohol cures', I pop two from the packet and fill a glass of water.

"Get that down your neck, mate," I instruct and watch as he starts to drink it, his face contorting as the tablet catches in his throat. He's lucky I was behaving well last night; his eyebrows are intact. Getting the coffee machine going, Byron turns to me with a grimace.

"What the hell?" he asks and I can only laugh, which comes out as more of a cackle.

"We got you drunk, mate, nothing more," I share. "You needed to loosen up."

"You both got me drunk?" he asks as he shakes his head.

"Em wouldn't join in for more after about ten; she hid some of the neater, stronger stuff. Apparently 'giving you a hangover was fair, but not to give you such a bad one that you'd not be at the altar.' That," I say with a grin, "would've gotten me castrated." I don't tell him it would have been by his fiancée.

"So you two are on good terms?" he confirms and I nod with one almighty smirk playing on my lips.

"Yeah...there's good days, bad days. We just take it as it comes," I explain as the coffee finishes brewing the first cup. I fetch it and have to call his name out to get him to focus on me. He really needed that session last night; so did I.

"There ya go," I say as I hand him his coffee, and then I go to make mine.

"What the hell did we consume?" he asks me and I look across to the booze table.

"Well, we did have rum; that's gone. There's not much beer, vodka or Jägermeister left either." I chuckle at the memory of him downing a few shots of that beast. "I forgot you could drink most of us under the table." He laughs as he sits down and sips his brew.

"Guess we'd better go get ready," he says when he's finished his coffee, glancing at the clock. I nod in reply and follow suit.

"Emma's meeting Rosie at the guest house you booked, then they're being brought in the car."

"What car?" he asks and I laugh at the state of him.

"The fruit's, ye numpty! Did the chaplain not explain?" I ask and he shakes his head.

"His own personal, base one?" Byron questions, and I nod.

"We, however, better get our arses over there. You," I say as I throw his fleece at him, which he manages to catch, "need a bloody good shower."

I quickly say bye to Emma, giving her a kiss.

"Make sure he's there!" she orders me as I leave the bedroom.

"He's hungover, but not as badly as I first thought. Some grub, more coffee and a shower will sort him out. We'll be there. Are you going to be okay to meet the fruit's car at the front gate?" I ask and she nods.

"I've got this, go sort him out," she instructs me with a grin. "And Stevo?" she calls and I pop my head back around the door. "Love you." I bloody wish it were us marrying today.

"Love ya too, twirl!" I reply before I drag Byron back to base.

The mess hall is a hub of people organising it for the wedding. We're the last ones to grab breakfast, thanks to us having a run to clear our heads. I don't know about Byron, but I feel better about it. We get what's left and it could feed us and the girls if we were having lunch. I doubt we will. Byron's nerves kick in and he doesn't finish his food. For him, that's unheard of. It makes me realise he's taking this very seriously.

"Hey, she'll come," I whisper to him. He nods.

"I know. But...fuck, Stevo. I'm getting *married*!" he says as his eyes go wide and his pupils expand. I chuckle.

"Yep, you are! Just as well I pressed our dress uniform, isn't it?"

"Thank you," he states as he finishes his coffee.

"Come on you, shower time, Romeo!" I tease.

Byron tells me to fuck off under his breath, but I enjoy ribbing him, knowing I'll get it back when it's my turn.

We dress and head over to the chapel. Byron's sister and her 'men' as he called them, arrived yesterday and now I get to meet them. Rosie's not due for another hour, so Byron and I mingle.

"Ricardo!" a loud, large Italian man shouts across at him from the other side of the courtyard and he's hushed by a striking woman next to him.

"Papa! Mama!" Byron calls and I grin. There are a few others around them too and I recognise them from the TV footage from months ago. "Sis!"

"Mind the shoulder, ye numpty!" she scolds, but embraces her brother.

"Papa, Mama, meet Chris 'Stevo' Stevenson, the best man." He introduces me and I shake everyone's hand.

"Snowflake?" Blythe asks me as she glances at the dress uniform and I nod.

"Yeah," I confess and she grins.

"I was the same. We can talk later; Byron says you're getting out just before him next year?" I nod in response. One of her men is taller than Byron and broader too. The other has more of a boho look about him but he makes me more nervous than the bigger guy.

"Ade, Marc, this is Stevo. He's getting out next year," she says, eliciting an eye response from them, as if that's code for something.

"Oh, are ye? What do ye plan to do when ye get out?" the one called Marc asks me.

"Being honest, I ain't thought that far ahead," I say. "Depends on what happens with the twirl," I state, and he gives me a weird look. "Girlfriend," I clarify and he nods.

"Byron says she's the maid of honour?" Adrian asks and I nod.

"Yeah...about that..." I begin and Byron buts in.

"What about it? Has something happened?" he asks in alarm and I laugh.

"Jeez, mate! No, I was just going to mention her ex assaulting her," I explain, and Marc holds his hand up.

"We know already. We were informed yesterday," he says, nodding towards Byron. Of course, he gave them a heads-up. "If you want information on him," Marc offers. I nod.

"Maybe another time? If we need it." This time he nods. He doesn't need to know I'm ahead of the game on that front.

I excuse myself and ensure that other things are in place. The photographer, Andy, is setting up, getting a small 'scene' he called it set so that the couple and respective parties can have their photograph taken under the RAF Crest. To be honest, it's more than I thought of, and I thank him.

Checking that the food is being organised, that I have the rings, the chaplain is awake and with us, takes me longer than I'd like. My phone buzzes in my pocket and I see a text message from the gatehouse. She's here.

I nod to Adrian, who organises the arch for me. None of this lot served with him, but all he does is ask in that way of his and they fall into place. I nudge Byron when Adrian gives me the nod and the music begins. It's showtime.

"She's here. Ready?" I whisper. He nods as he licks his lips and rubs his hands against his dress trousers. He turns to watch Rosie walk up the aisle. While he's watching her, I watch Emma and my heart is in my throat. I know what I said to her the other day, but I'd go through the vows now. I just need to plan when to ask her.

I notice Byron's gobsmacked stare and lean into him. "Close your mouth, mate." He shuts it with a snap.

I watch as Dave hands Rosie's hands off to Byron and the nurse is there to help him to his chair, though he makes it there with the aid of his cane. When Dave's sitting, we turn to the chaplain and he gets the ceremony underway.

"Are we ready?" the chaplain asks but Byron is so lost looking at Rosie, he doesn't answer.

I nudge him and he goes red.

"Are we ready?" the chaplain asks again while trying to suppress a laugh. Byron nods this time, and I can hear his family and some of the congregation chuckle.

They exchange vows, and then I get asked about the rings. I nod and produce them, deciding that 'losing' them isn't worth trying. Emma raises her eyebrows at me and I wink as I retrieve them from my dress pocket.

As they exchange rings, they tell each other why they're here. Then their union is blessed before they're pronounced man and wife. When they kiss, I look at Emma, wishing it were us.

When we leave, I search for Emma's good arm and escort her out of the chapel. She has a shawl covering her arms and she's wearing a white medical sling that she didn't have on this morning. I'll ask her about that when I get a moment. Hodgeson takes over everyone with the photography, the chapel entrance and armed salute photographs. I know he said he didn't want paying, but the man does us proud and saved my bacon.

Convincing him to do this was a whole different kettle of fish. I nod to his wife and she winks at me, a knowing look passing between us both. I know exactly how Andy is being paid back for this.

When Andy's finished with people's photographs, I corral them into the mess hall to await the bride and groom while handing Byron a drink. Emma is following suit, and Rosie gulps the wine down in nearly one go.

"Careful!" Emma chides her and Rosie sticks her tongue out, making Emma laugh. "You needed that," she states and Rosie's smile broadens.

"Too right...I still can't believe it," Rosie says, before she's snaffled by Andy for larger group shots.

When I get a nod from Andy, I raise my voice and ask that everyone enters the mess hall. The thirty people that are around head in, aware that it's time to welcome the bride and groom to their reception.

Emma gives me a nod and then I announce their 'arrival' to the assembled mass, grateful for the pint Emma hands me as they're greeted by cheers, confetti and hugs.

Emma and I are tucked away in the mess hall. People come and go as the evening wears on. Before Dave goes, he shuffles over to us and motions for a hug from Emma.

"I can't do two," he says and smiles at her. He turns his gaze to me and there's something in the air, so I blink.

"You look after her. And if that scumbag…"

"Now, Dave," Claire begins and he raises his hands.

"I'm dying, leave me be, woman!" he barks and she backs off, but she's trying not to laugh. "Now, if that scumbag comes near her, you finish him off," he instructs me. I nod in agreement and hope that the justice system takes care of him, so I can focus on taking care of Emma.

"They've still got a lot to sort out," he says as he begins to turn in his walker to go wherever he wants to. Everyone helped him, bringing him drinks and food. The kids loved him and one even told him his daughter was a princess.

"They'll get there, Dave," Emma says and plants a huge kiss on his cheek. "Thank you, for everything," she says and it's only when he vanishes behind the doors leading outside that Emma slowly lets the tears fall.

"There you are," says a broad Italian voice from behind someone else later on. Byron is about to leave with Rosie, leaving Emma and me to either help tidy up or get back to the flat.

"Mr Mancini." I smile, holding out my hand for him. "You've got quite a son," I tell him. The older man's laughter booms out.

"How much did he pay you to say that to me, eh?" he asks; his accent is thick Italian but spoken with good knowledge of English.

"Lorenzo!" the woman scolds him as he continues to laugh at Byron's expense.

"Not enough! Seriously, he's a hell of a man. I'm grateful he's my friend."

"Dinnae listen to him, Papa," a woman's voice suddenly answers. "Byron has Stevo here in his pocket. I saw a hundred be paid for him to say that," she says, winking at me and I laugh. The Mancinis do like to wind each other up.

"Blythe, honestly," the older woman admonishes. "I'm Ava," she says, introducing herself. "And thank you for kind words about my boy. My daughter," she says, throwing Blythe a look she laughs off. Emma and I laugh in return.

"I see you've been in the wars," Ava says, motioning to Emma's cast. Emma nods and sighs.

"Did he tell you?" she asks and Ava nods.

"He did. When you're able and you have some leave, we'd love to have you come to our place in Italy for a few weeks. Even in the winter, our little corner of Italy is stunning."

"We'd like that, Mrs Mancini," I begin, answering for us both when Emma's eyes turn to mine, a smile emerging from within.

"Please, call me Ava. Mrs Mancini was Lorenzo's mama," she says and I chuckle.

"We'd like that, Ava," Emma enforces, squeezing my hand before Ava pulls her into a hug.

"Good! Now, here's my number." She gives us her mobile and the number in Italy. I note them in my phone, as does Emma. Seconds later, Emma texts Ava so that they've swapped numbers. I follow suit.

"Now, let me grab you for a drink," Lorenzo says and I'm dragged away, leaving Emma with Ava and Blythe.

At the other end of the bar, Lorenzo shoves a drink into my hands and I grin, sipping the whisky he's generously paid for. Adrian and Marcus find us and I nod to the brothers.

"Now, Byron told us what happened," he says, his voice lower. "Do you need anything to happen to him?" I shake my head.

"He's on remand. I'm still serving so I need to play this by the book," I reply, looking between Lorenzo, Adrian and Marcus.

"You do, aye," Adrian says, his voice just audible. "We don't."

I blink. "He's got London gang connections, nothing I can't sort out, or utilise against him," I explain. Adrian pats me on the back.

"Good man. Holler if ye need us," he says, shoving a business card into my hand. I tuck it away. "Could use a man of your resources, if yer up for it."

"Have you offered the same to Byron?" I ask and he winces.

"No yet, no. Not checked in with Blythe that she'd be alright with that." He smirks, a dangerous light dancing in his eyes before it vanishes.

"You hated him; why the change of heart?" I ask. Lorenzo laughs again and slaps Adrian on the arm.

"He's got you there, *lo uomo*," Lorenzo says and I hold Adrian's gaze. After a few seconds, he backs down. Not something I expected.

"He's going to be my brother-in-law, at some point. He's just married Duckie, I mean, Rosie. And family look after each other, even if we don't always get along," he says, glancing at Lorenzo.

"Give him what he needs," Lorenzo chuckles heartily. "A swift kick when he needs it." He finishes off his whisky.

"I'll check out your company," I tell him and he nods. Marcus inclines his head across to something and we turn. Emma and Blythe are talking about something, finding common ground in using one arm.

"What happened to Blythe?" I ask, confused.

"Dislocated shoulder and repair surgery. Popping it out seven times will mess with your body, so she finally agreed to have it operated on," Marcus explains, watching her closely. I can't tell who is with her; both stare intently at Byron's sister as if she's an angel. Emma leans in and whispers something to their little huddle, making Ava and Blythe laugh. I love hearing Emma enjoying herself.

"Seven times?" I ask, wincing at the thought of dislocating the joint once.

"Yeah, twice by the same guy," Adrian growls and Lorenzo joins him. "Last time, it made it to the news," he says.

I sigh and shake my head. "Yeah, I saw that as it was being broadcast. I was with Byron when he found out. That was a fun evening," I tell them and recount what happened from my point of view, including the incident which brought Rosie onto his radar. All three listen intently.

"So that's how he knew she was in the area," Adrian huffs when I finish, before taking a large swallow of whisky.

"Yeah, sorry! I had no idea," I admit and he laughs.

"Que sera, sera," he says, waving his hands.

CHAPTER TWENTY-FIVE

Whatever Will Be, Will Be

EMMA

I watch as Blythe and Rosie emerge from the ladies, smiling at each other. Stevo comes over to me as Ava and Lorenzo mingle with their son and new daughter-in-law. It's a sight that makes me happy; Rosie deserves this.

"Penny for them?" Stevo asks me softly. He's nursing a drink, something with cola in a shot glass and I nod as I flex my bad arm as best I can. It hurts more tonight.

"I want that," I whisper, "one day."

"Until today, I was kinda wanting to take my time with you, twirl, thinking you needed it. But damn, I'd have married you today if we had the licence," he confesses, his voice low and husky.

"You said when you were out," I remind him and he shrugs nonchalantly, his amber eyes sparkling. I think the alcohol has gone to his head.

"A man is allowed to change his mind and up his game, twirl," he says, winking at me.

"Seriously? You'd change your mind...because of this?" I ask, my heart soaring, and he nods.

"When you walked up the aisle with Rosie, I did wish it was us," he confesses. We hear Byron's voice saying goodbye to his parents, and we join them in waving him and Rosie off, the Commander's car having returned from taking Rosie's father and carer back to their hotel for the night.

"Right," the tallest guy with us exclaims, his Scottish accent strong and proud. "Let's help ye all tidy up, aye?" He leaves us with no doubt that we're all helping.

An hour later, with everyone's help, the mess hall is cleared and we're all heading home. Big Mac, Marc and Blythe have left for their hotel in a taxi that came to the guest entrance. Another cab takes Ava and Lorenzo back to where they're staying and when they pull away, we begin a slow walk back to the flat.

Stevo has me tucked up against him, a borrowed long coat covers my light blue bridesmaid's dress and the rain has eased so my feet won't get too wet walking back. I'm comfortable tucked away under his arm, safe. Stevo pulls open the security gate to the stairs after clearing out our post-box and I head up first, unlocking the door as normal.

The flat is warm and I know it'll get warmer with both of us here. We remove our coats and Stevo focuses on the mail he's picked up for us both. Since the attack, he's been filtering all my mail, just on the off chance.

"Em? There's a letter from the hospital here," he says, holding it out to me. I take it from him, nervous about what it contains, though I'm guessing it's the appointment about when to go and get these pins removed. I smile and tuck it under a glass to read again tomorrow.

"My appointment," I confirm to him with a smile. "We can sort it out in the morning. Whenever we wake up." I grin, and Stevo nods, undoing his uniform belt. "I have to say, you look as sexy as hell in that uniform," I admit, which makes him stop taking it off.

"Always an officer," he tells me as he eyes me up and down, making me grin.

"And a gentleman," I praise him, which he huffs at.

"I'm a dirty gentleman," he growls. He comes up to me, walking me back to the fridge before kissing me senselessly. His body pins mine, but he's not threatening with it; he'd stop if I asked or my body told him. The kiss stops for a moment as he bends to let his hand touch my knee and slowly, he rises, bringing the skirt of the cocktail dress up with him. I know he felt the top of the stockings I have on beneath.

His eyes search mine when he gets to full height and his lips are millimetres away from mine. There's an intensity in those amber eyes that I've not seen before.

"Tell me you want me, twirl," he whispers, his voice all husky and deep.

"I want you," I whimper back and then he's kissing me softly, one arm boxes me in on the side, his legs scissor mine as he pins me up against the fridge.

I want more than this though. I need more, even if I can feel him against me. I wrap my hand around his head, tugging on his hair, running my fingers through it, not wanting this to stop.

The hot, sweet kisses move along my jaw. I want to turn into them, but that will make them end. I turn away from them, arching up, feeling his uniformed body against mine, the heat pouring off him.

I open my eyes when the kisses stop; Stevo's holding out a hand for me. I take it and he walks me through the flat, securing the door and turning off the lights before escorting me to the bedroom.

Stevo closes the curtains as I turn on a small lamp. I grin as my officer turns to stand before me, beckoning.

I manage to walk to him, though his hungry look has me weak at the knees. No one has ever made me feel this alive, engaged, wanted or adored before. I doubt anyone else can.

His hands cup my face and my one hand tries to work the dress belt, but I can't manage it. He stops kissing me and with a cheeky grin, undoes it for me. Then he slowly undoes the dress jacket, one gold button at a time. I go to reach out, but he pulls back.

"Watch," he says with a mischievous wink and I take a few steps back to sit on the bed. Slowly, he begins a strip tease for me. The jacket comes off, thrown onto the bedroom chair. His hands make slow work of the blue button shirt and gradually, he reveals his chest and abs to me. The tattoos I've seen before look different tonight, though I don't know why.

The shirt comes off and I stare at his large tribal tattoo and lick my lips.

"You like this?" he asks and I nod. He reaches for his trouser belt and undoes it, whipping the leather out before slowly undoing the button and releasing the trousers. They're pressed neatly, so that the fold is at the front. The flaps are pulled open and Stevo saunters across to me, before lowering himself so he's inches above my lap.

Dancing to music only he can hear, he begins to gyrate and thrust, making me bite my lip. I want to reach out, to stop him, take him out and play. All I can do is watch, drool and fantasise. I glance up at his eyes, hooded with lust and my hand reaches up to touch him. The cheeky man flexes his pecs and tightens his six-pack, popping even more muscles, and I groan at the sight.

"Go on, twirl," he whispers and I lick my lips before scratching my nails down his torso, switching to my fingertips as I near his V. The light chest hair he has in the middle is enticing, but so is the mound right next to my prize. I grab it firmly and remove it from the confines of the briefs and dress trousers, which he shakes off.

I grin before taking him in my mouth, swirling and enticing, a drive to please Stevo spurring me on. I swirl my tongue around him, gently licking the slit, tasting him. As he hits the back of my throat, I gag, making him hiss and grab my hair.

"Twirl, you're so damn good...do that again," he says, his voice breathy and I do, knowing that it adds to his enjoyment. I swallow him again, sucking him back and forth before he pulls out of my mouth and grins.

"Your turn," he says and offers his hand to help me up. He's totally naked; I'm not. A fact I'm sure he'll rectify any moment. Trapping me in his arms, he undoes the back of the dress and helps me out of it and the sling. The strapless bra I have on is removed in moments and tossed aside. Pleasurable noises emerge from Stevo as he takes one breast into his mouth and fondles the other.

I can't arch against him as he switches his attention; his arms are holding me firmly in place. I shiver, both in response to being semi-naked and to Stevo's dedicated attention to my body.

"So bloody gorgeous," he murmurs and I bring my focus back to him, what he's doing to me. The need I have right now is driving me towards madness; I need a release.

"Stevo," I whimper as he eases me onto the bed.

"Gotcha, twirl." He grins at me in the low light. "Lay down for me." His fingertips trace my body all the way down to the suspenders; a favour to Rosie. "You...are bloody amazing, girl," he tells me as he first kisses my stomach. Then, he blows, sucks and licks my tummy.

I bring my only working hand across my wobbly tummy so he can't fully see it.

"Ah, no...no covering yourself up. You're perfect," he says as he gently removes my hand, kissing the palm before he tucks my good hand under my bum, holding it there. His hot kisses reach my sex and I have no room to do more than writhe against his electrifying mouth. I feel my knickers being removed slowly. The touch of them as they slide down my stockinged legs sends goosebumps over every inch of me. Then his kisses are on my sex, his tongue swirling and licking my clit in a way I've not felt before.

What Stevo does to me makes me feel so dirty, but so good at the same time. My hand is free and I snake it to find his hair, running my fingers through it as Stevo's tongue swirls. His fingers come to play and soon, I'm panting; then he stops.

I focus on him to find he's above me, placing his wonderful cock at my entrance. I lift my hips, wanting him inside me. A small, satisfied groan escapes my lips as he buries himself in me and holds me there. His mouth finds mine, making me taste myself and slowly, he begins to move. He's considerate of my arm. My legs wrap around him, lifting me to him, trapping him to me, making me take him as deep as he can go.

His thrusting quickens, my breathing turns to panting and I pull him down for a kiss as the fire within me builds. I can hear our flesh slapping and the sound drives me upwards into him. I fall off the edge and seconds later, Stevo follows.

Panting, Stevo holds himself up over me and kisses me as I turn my head to look at him. He nips my bottom lip, making me hiss and draw in a breath, and then he's kissing it better.

I feel empty and bereft as he pulls out and helps me up so we can finish getting ready for bed. As he helps me remove the garter belt and the stockings, his grin becomes wolfish.

"You're a hidden kitten, aren't you, twirl?" he teases. The room becomes a little hot and I notice that the bedroom door is open. "Hey, you're amazing, twirl. I wish I could make you see what I see," he says, helping me get the nightshirt.

"I'm getting there," I confess and he smiles at me; his amber eyes are darker, but that could be the light.

"One day at a time, twirl," he confirms as he pulls on some boxers, before pulling back the covers for me to climb in. He tucks me in and then sorts the flat out, turning off the light in the hallway and closing the door tightly.

"Come here, gorgeous," he calls out from the other side of the bed, his voice just audible. I reach out and he holds my hand, but tonight, his legs entwine mine as he faces me. "You can cuddle up on this side, if you want?" he suggests and we shift so I can snuggle up to him. His arm is around my shoulders, holding me to him firmly.

He kisses me on the head and soon, I'm sleepy and warm.

It's quite late for us when we finally stir the following morning. Stevo stretches, then rubs his eyes and yawns.

"Morning, twirl," he says, turning to me. I don't think I've changed positions since we fell asleep.

"Morning." I smile at him, sighing as I stretch out.

"Fancy some breakfast and tea?" he asks as he reaches across and kisses me. Goodness knows what we drank or ate last night; I'm not impressed with my morning breath.

"Sounds like a great idea," I reply, covering my mouth.

"I'll make you something," he tells me but doesn't move to go and do it. I give him a quizzical look, but it makes him smile at me even more.

"What?" I ask, squinting at him, which makes him smile.

He reaches across, pecking my nose before wrapping a hand around my head and pulling me in for a kiss.

"You are," he pulls back, "bloody amazing. Brave, strong, courageous," he whispers, huskily. I look into his eyes as they dart around, taking in what I think are my features. Then his eyes rest on mine. The grip on the back of my head isn't threatening or controlling; it's firm and reassuring. "I'm so looking forward to proposing to you," he continues as if it's a guilty secret.

He kisses my nose again, then quickly leaves the bed, throwing on some jogging bottoms and a t-shirt that shows off his build. When I hear the coffee machine start-up, I make my way out of bed and head to the bathroom, confused about his change of plans, but wanting what he's promising. It's something I never thought I'd get to have.

I get dressed, still in a daze that's maybe down to alcohol and I decide that's what Stevo is suffering from. He's still drunk. He has to be.

Grabbing the diary that I've been keeping with questions, I write down the latest one: 'Why does Stevo want to propose?' I slide the pen away and close the book, ready to take it with me when I see Johnson tomorrow. Today is Sunday and I remember my appointment. Finding the letter, I note down when my appointment is, looking at Stevo as he sips some coffee.

"My appointment is a week on Monday," I say, sipping the tea. Stevo's gotten very good at making food that I can eat with just one hand.

"That's good," he says, pulling his phone out and grinning. "I'm off that day. What time?" he asks and I check.

"I'm to be there from eight am with nothing to eat and drink from ten pm the previous evening," I read out. "They're going to knock me out?" I ask and he shrugs.

"Twirl, I can imagine it'll hurt like hell removing the pins. I wouldn't want to be awake for that." He shivers, making a horrid noise as he does so.

"I hadn't thought—you're right," I admit and sigh, accepting that this is just how it's going to be. Only one more week of this discomfort though.

"How does your arm feel?" he asks as he finishes his coffee.

"Itchy, from the bones outwards. I want to scratch, claw at it, but I can't get near it." I grin at my broken arm. "And I'll bet the smell from it will be just as bad when the cast is removed," I tease, holding the offending arm out to him. He touches it gently, then he gets up and starts searching the odds-and-sods drawer, coming back with a marker pen.

With a wide grin, he holds it out and motions to my arm. "Can I?" he asks and I nod. No one else has signed it; I never thought to ask people to do that. On the arm, he writes: 'Will You Marry Me?'

I read it in the mirror, taking my time to read it in the reflective form before I can work out what it says.

I turn to him, to find him on one knee before me and using a small keyring loop as the ring.

"Let's go pick a ring, twirl. Just please tell me you'll be with me for whatever life throws at us? Marry me?" he asks, his voice thick and breaking. I could think of a thousand reasons to say no yesterday, but none of them come to mind now.

"Yes," I whisper, unable to say anything else and feeling something I had never felt before this very moment. What I suddenly felt wasn't a place or thing. It was him. Christopher Michael Stevenson is home.

Once Stevo put me down from all the hugs and kisses, we dress and I text Rosie. Stevo takes a picture of the cast message and moments later, the phone rings.

"Hi!" I answer Rosie's call, putting it on loudspeaker, still elated by Stevo's proposal.

"Please, tell me how it happened?" Rosie demands, the happiness evident in her high tone.

"This morning. Stevo noticed my cast hadn't been signed and grabbed a pen before asking to sign it. You saw what he wrote," I begin, before I burst into tears of happiness. "I'm so happy! I never expected this." I pause, the clenching in my stomach still evident. "I don't deserve it," I utter, not realising I said it aloud, until everyone exclaims as one:

"Nonsense!"

"You *do* deserve it, twirl," Stevo tells me, holding my hand as he wipes away tears with the other. "But, it'll be after Christmas. Gotta introduce twirl here to my lot," he says, his voice light and happy.

"Gives us a chance to get over ours," Rosie says, which makes Stevo and I laugh.

"You do deserve this, Em. You both do," Rosie confirms and I break out in more sobs but try to laugh. It doesn't work.

"We're off to get a ring, so we'll send a picture when we've got it. See you guys later!" Stevo calls out and after a few goodbyes, we hang up.

"Speak to Johnson about why you think you don't deserve this, twirl, because," he says, pulling me to him and holding me close, "you bloody do." He plants a kiss on my temple that stays there for longer than normal. I breathe in his scent before I let more tears fall and when I'm all cried out, he helps me clean up before we change into better clothes and head off to Lincoln city centre.

Before we leave, Stevo sends me a link to a website about how to overcome why I don't think I deserve love and as he drives, I read. One point on it sticks out and triggers me. *'If I can't love myself, how can anyone else?'* It goes on to suggest ways of overcoming this. I put the phone down on my lap with a heavy sigh, almost slamming it into me as the words hit home.

"Something triggered you?" Stevo asks as he drives. I nod, then sigh as I reply.

"Yeah..." I admit. I'm fed up with crying and wonder how I can turn this around. I re-read the bottom part of this website, about removing people and situations that undermine my self-worth, happiness and practising mindfulness.

"Listen, twirl," he says, and I look across. "This life has so much to give us both. I want that journey to include you. Seeing you at their wedding made me realise that. I don't want temporary; I don't *want* an alternative."

He turns to me at a set of lights and reaches out for my good hand, briefly squeezing it before letting go so he can drive.

"I'm choosing love and happiness, twirl, because life's too short for anything else. I've seen Byron be twisted up, avoid other women because they weren't Rosie. I didn't know who the hell she was until the night she drove onto the base and I told him what happened. It's been fun watching him find himself through her." He pauses a moment as he watches the traffic and we begin to merge for the car park. "I told him to wake up and smell the coffee and," he says as he pulls up at the multi-story in Lincoln, "I'm taking my own advice."

"It's scary that you want me," I admit and when he's parked up, he reaches across and pulls me to him for a kiss.

"It's scary that you want me, twirl—the bad-boy from the gangs in London." He smirks.

"You're not a bad boy," I tell him and he grins.

"See? You have a different opinion of me than I have of myself. You see me so differently from how I do."

I nod, understanding what he's saying, at least I think I do.

"So, I'm to trust that you see a much better version of me than I do?" I ask as he comes to help me out of the car.

"Just as you do with me, twirl." He winks at me, locking the car, before cuddling me under his arm and walking me to the jewellery place he's got in mind.

"What am I allowed to go for?" I ask as we come out of the car park, unsure of either his budget or his style.

"A fair bit. There's a jewellery-making place just around here," he explains, as we head down a little side street. There are a few businesses that specialise in custom jewellery, such as wedding bands and engagement rings.

"Wow," I whisper, seeing the window displays.

"If there's nothing here you like, I know Birmingham has a huge jewellery quarter and there are places in London I know," he says as my eyes take in all the displays.

"I'm sure we can find something here," I assure him. "Did you want me to wear something traditional?" I ask and he chuckles.

"Twirl, this is what *you* want, yeah? If you want traditional, we can do that. If you want something more modern," he says, pointing to a different tray about halfway up the display, "we can do that too."

"I have no idea," I begin as the sunlight breaks through the clouds, catching a few and there's one that catches the light just right. Stevo follows my gaze and smiles.

"Let's have a closer look," he says and taking my hand, he leads me inside.

An hour later, we're having a hot drink as the ring I've picked out needs adjusting down to two sizes. Other than that, it is perfect. I've opted for a hot chocolate and a piece of biscotti cake, Stevo is having his usual black coffee. I don't know how he stomachs it.

"I could get addicted to this," I say, pointing at the biscotti cheesecake with my fork. He laughs and takes the piece I've offered him. His eyes widen and he nods.

"Yeah, I could. In fact..." He stands, returning moments later with two slices. He gives me the smaller one and has the larger one for himself.

"You've had a slice already, twirl." He grins and I chuckle before claiming my second piece. Moments later, the waitress comes over with more tea and coffee and I wiggle back into my comfortable seat as we wait for another half an hour.

We head back to the jewellery shop when Stevo gets a text to say that the ring is ready. We're greeted by a very smiley man, the proprietor and jeweller, who shows us the ring.

It's perfect. Oval in shape with little diamonds on the side of the double shoulder, set off in white gold. The jeweller holds the ring out to Stevo, who takes it.

"I'd like for the lady to try it on, to ensure it fits," he says and we do. When the jeweller has checked it, I take it off and hand it back to Stevo, who winks at me before placing it in the box. He tucks it into his inside coat pocket and we head back to the car, wrapped up in each other.

Back at the flat, Stevo recreates the scene from this morning, asking me to marry him, but this time he presents the ring. I'm in tears again and then send a picture of it to Rosie. We have a quick video chat and they congratulate us again, chatting about potential dates. Stevo didn't want to do this while he was still in the RAF, though he might have changed his mind on that too.

Our stomachs rumble when evening time comes around. Despite the cakes and hot drinks, I am now properly hungry. My stomach growls, Stevo's joins in and together, we decide what we're having.

One chicken noodle Waggamama later, we're snuggled up on the sofa, watching a movie when Stevo gets a call.

"Oh, finally," he mutters as he accepts the video call and an older man stares back at me. I have no idea who he is, but Stevo seems quite comfortable sitting next to me with his arm around me.

"Craig," he says and I know instantly who this is. "Is Jean there too?" he asks and then a woman is next to Craig.

"Oh, is this the lady that you've been telling us about?" she asks, smiling. Her eyes dance and Stevo nods.

"Yeah, and we've got something to share," he says. He looks across at me and my engagement finger, nodding to it. I hold it up and Jean's squeals deafen us.

"Oh my goodness! My boy, congratulations!" she cries out. "When are you coming home so we can meet you?" she asks, turning to face me more than Stevo.

"Congratulations, Chris!" Craig praises.

"Hi, I'm Emma." I wave at them both and Jean laughs.

"It's nice to meet you," she tells us. "Chris, you didn't mention anything!" she scolds and he shrugs.

"Got the idea at Byron's wedding. Wished it was us, but I want more than four days to plan ours," he says, laughing. Craig nods and Jean laughs at the joke, but I am glad I don't have to do it in four days. "So, I took the chance this morning," he says, telling them how he asked me.

"We want to be there," Jean says and Stevo nods.

"I wouldn't do it without any of you there. You've raised me. Just, don't tell the donors. Not that they'd care," he adds, his voice sad.

"They'd only be along for the free party," Craig scoffs and Stevo nods.

"Yeah, ain't wanting them there for this. They didn't put the effort in when I needed them, they're not getting any reward from us," he states, making Craig nod as his lips go thin.

Stevo catches up about his sibling-cousins, and Ruby appears behind her parents. We wave when she sees us and I hold up the ring for her to see. She covers her mouth, then does jazz hands as her mouth opens, as if to scream, but we know she can't. Her eyes are watering and she moves her hands to clutch over her heart before she signs something to Stevo.

"Ruby sends huge congratulations to us both," he tells me.

"Thanks, Ruby! And to you, Jean and Craig. You've raised one heck of a man," I admit, snuggling into his shoulder.

"Oh, I like this one," Jean says and Ruby signs something to her. Jean signs back and Ruby sticks her tongue out in response.

"Oi, Ruby, don't be a brat," Stevo chides her. She sends him a scowl and signs something. Stevo turns to me and translates. "Ruby says she'll see us soon."

"Yeah, gotta work out when we're coming down," he tells them as he turns back to the phone, and Ruby gives us a thumbs up. "Emma has the hospital next week to get the pins out, so it depends on when they want her back, along with my leave," he says.

"Keep us informed," Jean instructs, and we sign off. I snuggle into him again and he kisses my head.

"What did Ruby say to Jean?" I ask as he goes to resume the movie.

"Ruby said that I was bribing you somehow, because of your compliment. Jean told her to behave, that I'd not do that. Ruby said she was just teasing."

"Oh. I've so much to learn," I sigh, making Stevo pull me closer.

"Slowly, twirl, slowly. You've got lots of time to learn."

Chapter Twenty-Six

The Holidays

Chris

News of my engagement travels around the base fast. I'm quick to reassure everyone there's no improper reason why, other than I realised I wanted to marry her at Byron's wedding.

It makes some of the girls 'ahh' in response when they learn how I asked her, as well as when I worked it out. Emma spent a full morning with Johnson, and she seems a lot happier, as well as more contented and focused when she joins me for lunch. Usually, I eat in the mess hall with Byron when I'm on rotation, but not today. He's not due back until tomorrow and I'm on shift in a few hours.

I've been helping Nic with the rest of the plumbing. An additional sink was needed and I connected the waste pipes up, creating the necessary stud work for the sink to hang onto when the plastering is done while Emma was in her session.

Walking back home, holding hands with Emma, we pop into the butchers, eyeing up the pork pies and pasties, settling on a few treats for us to share. At the flat, over the small kitchen table, we get to chat about her morning.

"I really like Johnson," Emma says with a small voice. "She's given me a lot to think about and tricks to undo all this brainwashing." She reaches across with her good hand and I take it, rubbing my thumb over her soft knuckles. "She offered to put in a statement on my behalf if it shows how my ex mistreated me. She says I might exhibit...what was it? PTSD? Symptoms for some things and I was to tell you about it."

I nod, already aware that she might. I know anything to do with her hands and arms is one thing, especially the arm that's currently broken. Or reaching out to touch her when she's not expecting it.

"Do you need to talk about it now, or have you had enough for today?" I ask, aware that the chat with Johnson would have covered anything Emma needed for now.

"I've had enough," she tells me, laughing nervously, "but I'd like your help from time to time, when I wobble."

I grin, fingering the engagement ring as we hold hands. "This," I say as I twirl the ring, "isn't just a symbol to others that you're taken, loved and looked after. It's a message to you as well, that I'm here for you. Always; however you need me." She sucks in a breath while holding back a tear or two. "I'll try to preempt it, help you navigate around it. But, twirl, you'll have to tell me if you wobble, especially if that wobble is all up in that pretty head of yours."

Emma nods, whispers a thank you to me and stands, beginning to clear the plates away. I watch as she gets on with life with one arm. I've stopped doing a lot of things for her, not because I want to, but because Johnson advised me that Emma needs to find her independence.

I'm also aware Emma's not written any of her stories since she moved into this flat, so I go across and boot up her laptop, pulling out the notebook I know she has ideas penned down in.

"I'm on shift until twenty-two," I tell her and she nods. She's finally understanding the time references we use. "I thought you might like to plot," I point out, smiling softly at her. She doesn't say anything, but comes and hugs me.

"Thank you," she whispers, as if this is some secret that only she and I share. *Maybe it is?* I'm not sure. I'm sure Rosie knows about her writing, as does Ruby.

I kiss her on the temple and hold her close. "You're mine, twirl, always," I remind her, before I lightly kiss her on the mouth and head out to the base for my shift.

We get back into our routine and encouraging Emma to write helps make her calmer. She's also doing a lot more for herself, not just physically, but in other ways too.

I come back from a night shift to find a bag of clothes at the front door. The stuff she wore before she and I got together; the stuff she'd wear when she was with him, to hide.

"Had a clear out?" I ask as I sip a decaf coffee and eat some breakfast before I crash out. This is the first of four-night shifts, the last ending Sunday morning, giving me Monday to be with her at the hospital.

I see she's made us both the same: wheat biscuits and thawed raspberries for breakfast.

"Yeah, it's time to say goodbye. I have been carting them around and I don't need them: I don't wear them anymore. When we go to Lincoln General on Monday, can we swing by a charity shop and drop it in?" she asks as we eat and I nod.

"Would Women's Aid want them?" I ask and she drops her mouth open, her eyes widening.

"I never thought of them," she says and looks up their number. "I'll call and ask." I listen as I drink my coffee and continue to mentally unwind. Emma beams at me a few moments later. "They'll come to collect them tomorrow. All I need to do is leave it at the bottom of the staircase," she says as she comes to sit at the table with me.

That's one thing I love about her; she's not talking to me from another place in the flat, she makes the effort to sit next to me, stand next to me, be near me. She knew when I'd be home and had breakfast with decaf coffee ready for me. I love her looking after me.

"Great stuff!" I yawn, aware that sleep is catching me. "Make sure you eat something for lunch," I remind her and she smiles.

"I will, I promise," she says as her eyes follow me.

"I'm going to go and shower before I get my head down." She lets me cup her face for a kiss before I do exactly that.

We stick to our routine until my last shift on Sunday, when I sleep for four or five hours. It's a perfect Sunday afternoon and we catch up with Rosie and Byron via video call. They share that Dave's going in for another MRI in a few weeks. Emma reaches out for my hand as we're told the details and I see her make a note of it so she can put it on her phone calendar later. We end the call with our friends, happy they're as best they can be right now.

We finish eating at eight, our last 'drink' is at nine and though Emma was told she was "Nill By Mouth" from ten pm, I'm doing this with her so she has that support. Rosie and Byron have sent their good wishes to her, which cheered her up but increased her anxiety a little.

"You'll be fine," I tell her. "This is just them removing the pins while you're asleep so that you don't flinch when they do it. I'll be right there as soon as they let me," I assure her. She nods and we head to bed, though sleep for Em is elusive. I can tell she's been awake for part of the night; she's rigid when she's awake so she doesn't disturb me.

"Try to rest, twirl. This time tomorrow you'll have a whole new cast on your arm and you can start doing things with it," I tell her. "Come on, hold my hand," I offer, but she doesn't just hold my hand. She snuggles into me, curling herself up so she's small.

Sighing, aware she's anxious about tomorrow, I hold her and finally, she falls asleep around two am.

This morning, coffee is my best friend, right above Byron. The mere five hours of broken sleep I got because of Emma's anxiety demands it. We were the first ones here, which wasn't hard since we got up at six. Lincoln General has decent coffee facilities and I find a quiet corner in the waiting room once she's booked in.

The nurses ask me to look after her engagement ring, and for a while I twiddle it in my fingers, shining the light this way and that, making it cast rainbows across the waiting room. It occupies my mind, seeing the colours bounce this way and that.

When I'm finally bored and have tucked the ring away, I lay my head back and snooze. I get maybe an hour before a nurse gently wakes me.

"Mr Stephenson? Your fiancée is out of surgery," she says, and I come to in seconds.

"How did it go?" I ask as I wipe the sleep from my eyes and cover my mouth as I yawn.

"It went well. She's in recovery; we'll bring her up in about half an hour. I thought you might want to go and get something to eat, you've been here for ages," she tells me.

"Thanks. I think I will. Is she allowed to eat now?" I question, and the nurse smiles.

"Yes, we'll give her a light lunch. As soon as she's seen the surgeon and physio, she can go home."

"How long might that take?" I enquire as I stand and stretch.

"They're due for their rounds after two. She's one of the first post-op patients on the list," the smiley nurse explains, and I grin before thanking her. She nods and heads off, leaving me to find food and more coffee.

I smile at Emma as she turns her head to me. Her arm isn't in a soft cast, which I expected. I was escorted through to her bedside as soon as they were happy she was awake.

"Hey, twirl," I call out, making her smile.

"Hey," she croaks and I pour her some water. Once she's had a drink, she lifts her arm and turns it this way and that, as if she's never seen it before. The skin is blotchy and there are two plasters on it where the pins once were. Other than that, you can't tell her arm was ever badly broken.

We sit and chat, small talk taking over for a time once she's eaten. She's ravenous and I produce her favourite chocolate bar out of the cupboard.

"When did you get that?" she asks, her voice almost yelping in glee at the sight of the bar.

"When you were in recovery and I went to eat."

Her shoulders drop and she gives me a funny smile, then reaches out the hand I've not been able to hold for nearly two months. "Thank you," she whispers and I smile.

The doctor and physio do the rounds just after half past two. They go through things with Emma, what exercices to do and how often, emphasising that this is just as important a step for her recovery as the pinning of it was. Overall, the operation was simple.

"We could put you back into a cast, but being honest, the bones have healed up. There's no strength there," the surgeon says as the physio makes Rosie do simple tasks with that arm and hand, "at the moment, but that's expected. Do the exercises and we'll see you after Christmas for another assessment."

"Have a good one!" they tell us and a nurse comes in fifteen minutes later, advising us that Emma can get dressed and we can go.

"My ring?" Emma asks and I hold it out to her before gently sliding it back onto her finger with a kiss. Grinning, I watch as she slowly gets herself dressed, but I help her with certain items as her arm can't quite twist that way right now.

The following morning, I'm on the early shift and Rum calls me over. Boomer is with him and there's a mischievous look on both their faces.

"What?" I ask, expecting the worst. The chaplain is around, which is unusual, but he hangs back and Boomer gives him a nod.

"We had a team vote," Rum tells me and I frown, wondering what about.

"Go on," I say, tempting fate. *With Boomer involved, anything is possible.*

"About Christmas shifts," Boomer tells me. "You get it off, to take Emma down to your family in *Landon*." She says London in a bad accent, but it makes me smirk.

"Seriously?" I ask, looking between the pair of them. Boomer nods.

"Yeah, I'm staying here this Christmas," she tells me and her eyes dart to the chaplain. Rum grins and I join him. *She's got a thing for our chaplain? I didn't see that coming!*

"Okay..." I nod at Rum and Boomer slaps me on the arm, then she heads off, the chaplain falling into step beside her as they walk away. "She got it going on with the chaplain?" I ask and Rum nods.

"Have been for a few months discreetly," he tells me, before addressing me directly. "They both get out soon," Rum adds. "So, you've ten days over Christmas. Everyone's pulled in to let you have this off as you've covered for them all over the years. You've never had Christmas with your lot."

"Wasn't aware you had paid attention," I reply, genuinely floored that he's noticed.

"I had. The others had too and Boomer..." He glances at the way she's just walked. "She needs Chaplain Graeme right now," he shares. "And he'll be here."

"Anything we can do?" I ask, unsure about how to help but he shakes his head.

"You know she's going through a divorce; she caught her hubby screwing a local woman in their bed and house." I wince and swear; that's a nasty situation. And it explains the situation months before too. No wonder she's leaning on someone dependable like Graeme. "Nothing we can do but be there and right now, *home* ain't where she wants to be," Rum explains.

Here was me thinking Boomer had it all going on, roses and everything. Turns out, I was wrong. Thankfully, there are no kids involved.

"Understood. I'll tell her thanks when I see her away from the chaplain," I say, heading back to the rest of the squad.

I catch up with Boomer, giving her my heartfelt condolences on her situation. She shrugs, but it's clear that she's putting a brave face on it.

"Don't waste the time, Stevo, please?" she asks and I nod.

"Don't intend to. You do the same, yeah?"

She winks at me, this time the smile reaches her eyes.

When I tell Emma, she's elated and starts asking questions about what gifts to get, what to take, and how long we're away for. I laugh at her.

"Let's video call them," I say and Jean responds as Emma did. Craig looks happy, and Ruby's telling me in sign language that she's happy. I sign back that she has to be gentle with Emma, she's not learned a lot of sign language yet.

"We can text," Ruby signs to me and I laugh, telling her that yeah, they can. "And I'll teach her some new words and phrases too, like when we were kids," Ruby adds.

I repeat it for Emma's benefit, and she signs a thank you to Ruby. Then we begin to plan.

"Stevo!" Boomer's voice rings out across the space between me and the gatehouse one night. Yesterday was Dave's MRI and it wasn't good news. It's nearly five am and for Boomer to hail me like this fills my stomach with dread. I wave as I head up to my colleague.

"Byron called. Asked that you call him ASAP," she tells me. I nod and head into the break area, pulling my phone out to call my best friend. I can only guess what's going on.

"Hey," I say when he answers.

"It's bad," he tells me, his voice low. "He slipped into a coma a little while ago. Thought you'd want to know," he tells me.

"Have you called Emma?" I ask, pouring myself some coffee. "I can get off shift now." There's nothing more I can do other than take Emma to be with Byron and Rosie.

"Neither of us has, but there's no sense in rushing down, aye? We're at the hospital and they'll likely move him to hospice." He sighs. "Not sure how long it's going to take."

"Emma will want to see him, to say goodbye," I remind him and he agrees. "We'll head down when you have details," I confirm, and then I let him go to be with Rosie. Turning, I see Boomer at the door, leaning against it, her face sad.

"Not good news?" she asks softly and I shake my head.

"Rosie's dad has gone into a coma. I think this is it," I state and she sighs, then nods, but even she is trying to hold back the tears.

When I get back to the flat, Emma's up and unaware of what's happened. As soon as she sees me, she knows something's wrong.

"What's happened?" she asks, concern etched onto her beautiful face. Her lovely brown eyes are wide, searching.

"Dave slipped into a coma around five am," I state and she bursts into tears. I reach out to hold her as she breaks, her hand covering her mouth in an attempt to stifle her cries.

"Rosie," she gulps, sucking in some air at some point.

"I know. They're at the hospital now, just waiting for the final act. He'll tell me when hospice hours are, so you can go and say goodbye," I explain to her. She nods and looks at the food she's prepared for us both, as always.

"Twirl, I need to eat first. So do you. We can't help them if we're not fueled up, yeah?" I coax and she nods. We eat in silence, both of us lost in our own thoughts. I reach across and hold her hand, twirling the ring.

Byron texts us hours later with the hospice that Dave's been transferred to, and the visiting times.

"I'll go pack," she says, putting her dishes into the sink.

"You do that. I'll clear this down and be ready in a few. Won't take me long." I kiss her on the forehead as she goes to pack for a few days. Once I've cleared the dishes, I get us ready and then we hit the road, hot drinks in hand as the rain lashes down.

Byron texts me to say they're at the hospice with Dave. When we arrive, both girls cry buckets of tears when they see each other. No one bothers us, but the box of tissues does get replaced when the girls have used them all up.

Two days later, I get the call via the gatehouse that we'd been expecting and dreading. Dave's passed on. Rum lets me finish my shift early so I can go and inform Emma. When I enter the flat, I can see she's been told.

She's curled up on the sofa, the curtains are drawn, and the room is in darkness. Only faint sobs come from the sofa and I switch on the light by the door after securing it tightly, pulling the draught curtain over it to help keep in the warmth.

"I'm so sorry, twirl," I whisper to her, making her react and sit up. I sit next to her, offering her a hug and that's how we stay for most of the night.

I hate being on shift when she's hurting. Byron at least has grief leave, but I've got an odd shift that she insists I honour, then we can head down to Rosie's. I agree, letting Byron know via text what time we'll be down.

When we arrive, Byron has tea set up in the kitchen. The foldaway bed the nurse was using has been taken away, and the formal front room that Dave loved was back to 'normal' and doesn't look like it had ever been touched or moved around.

We have some tea, do the small talk thing and then Rosie and Emma head off to make up Dave's bed, where we'll be sleeping. Emma's come down to help clear away some of Dave's things on Rosie's request. It's going to be hard on Emma, but for Rosie, she would literally go through hell.

We're chatting in the kitchen when Emma's voice carries through, high, screeching and demanding both of us. I reach the girls first, to find Rosie almost collapsed onto Emma, who with her arm can only just hold her friend up.

I reach for Rosie and she clamps onto me like a limpet, barely able to breathe. Byron curses as she starts to hyperventilate and collapse. We all hug her, trying to reassure her, but she's grieving—being in this room must have triggered her somehow. Byron and I know enough to spot that this might be PTSD, and we remove her from the room. Emma apologises as if it's her fault.

"Not your fault, twirl, it'll be okay. Remember when Johnson said about PTSD being physical?" She nods. "This is what it can look like," I tell her and she nods again, crying silently.

"She'll get through it, we'll help her, that's what family do," I remind her and she sucks in some breath, wipes her eyes and I help her finish making the bed. Byron comes downstairs, without Rosie.

"She's zonked out," he tells us, rubbing a hand over his face and through his hair.

"You need a hug," Emma says and goes to hug him. He embraces her like a friend and then he sits down heavily on the kitchen chair, his head in his hands with his elbows on the table.

"So that's what PTSD looks like?" Emma questions, and I nod.

"It can do. I think being in her dad's room and talking about him just double-wham-mied her," I say, watching Byron. He lifts his head up and sighs, then he spews something in Italian. I don't speak the language, but it doesn't sound kind.

"I don't know what to do," he says and pulls his phone out. He's reading something, and then he sighs. "She needs to let this out, shout, scream...anything!" he says and we nod. "Somewhere high or a sea-front," he adds, grasping at faint ideas.

Emma hums then looks at Byron. "Dave used to take us to Clacton-On-Sea when we first became friends, just after her mum had passed from cancer. Dave bought this house as his old one reminded him of Lynn too much. Anyway, he'd pay for a static caravan with three beds. Rosie and I always got the room with the twin beds in it, but we didn't care. We were hardly around, unless we were hungry or it was getting dark; he gave us the freedom to just be kids. Maybe take her there?"

Byron nods, a contemplative look on his face.

"There's a good fish-and-chip shop near the pier, and there's an ice-cream parlour next door too," Emma continues, and his eyes light up as she grins.

"If her mood doesn't improve..." he says and I can see him starting up Google.

"When did you last eat?" I ask him and he shrugs. "I'll cook us three something. You can't help her if you're weak and underfed, mate," I explain and he nods, giving me a weak smile in thanks.

Sometime later, after I found a pie in the freezer, he heads up to be with Rosie.

We use the ensuite and curl up in bed. "I've said I'll start getting rid of some of his things. There's a Men's Aid charity and homeless shelter that will take them; we just need to bag them up," Emma tells me softly in the quiet dark.

"Good idea, twirl. I'll help," I offer as she snuggles into me and finally we rest.

The following morning, lashing rain wakes us and all the yard work we did months ago pays off. I can see the river being dumped on the bungalows opposite and it must be the same for us. The new guttering Rosie replaced, and we finished, is helping with the deluge. I listen for Byron or Rosie, but I don't hear anything for ages. We check the perishables and find that they're mostly out of date. The bread is mouldy, and the milk is off. With resolve, Emma and I head out and Byron texts me when we're at the corner shop, saying he's taking Rosie to Clacton.

I show Emma and she sighs, but nods, and then she puts back a particular box of cereal. I pick it up and wink at her. It's not one she eats, so I'm guessing it's for Rosie.

"She'll appreciate the gesture," I say and Emma smiles. We head back and get the heavy-duty black bags we just bought out. While Byron helps Rosie, we get on with clearing out Dave's clothes as per Rosie's instructions, splitting things up so that all the charities we drop these into will benefit from a range of items.

It's dark when I text Byron about pizza. It's the easiest thing to order and I grin at the memory of Dave ordering those huge ones when we first all met.

He texts back with where to get it from and an ETA, so I time it for their arrival and it's here a few minutes before they return.

"Did you get much done?" Rosie asks as we eat and Emma nods.

"We did. There's more to do, but the bulk of it is done as you asked. The rest can be done when you're ready," Emma answers.

"Thank you," Rosie says softly to Emma, who blushes as she throws her friend a warm smile.

"You've been there for me. I'm here for you. Just like we promised," Emma reminds her as she reaches out to hold Rosie's hand. Rosie simply nods, squeezing her hand and eats some pizza.

The following morning, Rosie's galvanised and determined. Emma finds out why and says the death certificate came through late last night. All the tasks that Rosie has been wanting to do can now be done.

Like a whirlwind, Rosie has the final details of the funeral confirmed, the wake semi-organised, and a call into the probate lawyer, who she arranges to meet at fifteen hundred today.

"Come with us?" Rosie asks, looking around all of us. "Please?" Emma nods. Byron, of course, is going to be there and as we set off in my car, I pull Byron aside. I don't need to actually be in the meeting; I doubt I'm mentioned, but I am sure Emma will be, so I offer to wait in the reception area. Byron agrees and we head off, letting me do what I need to mentally for Emma.

The receptionist makes me a coffee and for about half an hour, I sit in the reception area, browsing glossy magazines. The Baz Lurman song comes into my head; they are designed to make anyone feel ugly, even fit military guys like me. I throw it down in disgust and pick up my phone, browsing social media to pass the time.

Eventually, they come out and Rosie looks ready to explode again. *What has happened now?*

Outside, she screams until she can't anymore, then declares that she needs to walk back. *March back more likely.* Byron offers to walk with her and he tosses me the house keys. I take Emma's hand and escort her back to the car. She's quiet.

"He's left me a sum of money," she says when we're in the car. "I get it in ninety days. The rest, Rosie and Byron don't get for a year, but she's got to move out in ninety days. She's not allowed to live in the house. It's to be sold and the money held in trust unless they find a plot of land to build her dream home on." My eyes go wide; Rosie's frustrations and anger are now understandable.

"Why did he do that?" I ask, bewildered. I wish I'd gone in now.

"To ensure that they stick it out. They've not had a chance to talk about what family they want, what they want in careers, where to live...he took all that away from them, so now he's giving it back to them."

I nod, but it doesn't feel right that he's done this. I have no say, he's already done it, but Byron and Rosie have to work it.

"So, what's their game plan?" I ask her, thinking she might have an idea.

"Finding some land to build on is going to be the issue. It isn't easy to find." She pulls out her phone and starts searching, though for what, I don't know.

"Where?" I ask and Emma turns to me. "Where are they looking to build?" I ask, clarifying my scatty thoughts.

Emma shrugs. "No idea, but we can offer to help look, can't we?" she asks and I nod. We can.

Chapter Twenty-Seven

Family

Emma

It breaks me to see Rosie as she is, but she decides that she'll spend her last Christmas in her dad's house while packing it up. We chat and I offer to stay, but she insists that I go to meet Chris's family.

So the day before Christmas Eve, that's what we do. Catching the train from Lincoln to Kings Cross, we change at Newark before the longer part down to London. We could have driven down to Milton Keynes, but I have no intentions of going near that town again and the taxi ride to Lincoln was better for us. Chris's car is secure at the base, which makes me breathe easier.

We snuggle up, chatting between ourselves, with Chris telling me stories about his family from when they were little. He enjoys fetching drinks and snacks for us, as if we didn't bring enough from home. The gifts are wrapped, the weather is colder and my arm is much better. We play on our phones and Chris seems excited as a text message lands.

"We're going to meet someone on the tube, twirl," he tells me quietly. "I don't want you to get alarmed. I've asked for this meeting—the tube is neutral territory, okay?"

I gasp. "That scares me," I admit to him and Chris nods. "Who is it with? And why?"

"Your ex's old gang leader," he says and I feel my jaw slacken. "I know, twirl," he replies in a soothing voice. "I've learned he's still making threats to find you while he's inside. He's deranged. I want to see what the lay of the land is with his old gang, and why he did what he did. This is an update, nothing will happen." He pulls me to him, kissing my head and hugging me tightly. "Trust me, okay?"

It's not like I have a choice.

I think back to all that's happened since Dave passed. The police filed a case with the CPS days after my attack and Anderson pleaded not guilty at the hearing that was scheduled. His request for bail was denied too, thank goodness. The judge decided that if he broke a non-molestation order so violently, he'd break bail. I'm on tenterhooks waiting for a trial date, watching over my shoulder, thinking Anderson's going to get out. Chris was livid and marched me to the base when we learned of this, depositing me with Nic at the cafe as it was being kitted out.

I should start working with her after Christmas, as well as two evenings every other week at the local pub. It'll be good to be around people again.

When Chris found me hours later, he had worked up a sweat. I asked him where he'd gone and he said to the gym. It was either that or find Anderson himself. I simply nodded, grateful that he found a way to release the tension in him that did not involve taking it out on me, as Anderson was known to do.

"I needed to know you'd be safe, twirl," he said at the time. I was not sure what he meant by that—it seemed double-edged somehow, and the look in his eyes suggested more.

In London, Chris navigates us out of Kings Cross to an underground line. It's not too busy when we travel and someone nods to him from across the compartment. When Stevo nods back, the guy comes closer.

Stevo leans into me and quietly says, "Let me do the talkin' here, twirl, okay?" He winks at me and I feel my eyes going wide. *Is this the contact?*

The other guy stands close to us, and Chris offers him a cigarette. He's as large as Chris, and I grab a hold of my fiancé's hand and arm while I try to keep my snacks from decorating the compartment floor.

"Stevenson," the other man nods.

"Smithy. Talk to me," Chris instructs and receives a wide smile.

"He's still inside, like he should be. He wasn't one of us when he beat up that woman." Smithy looks at me, then at Chris. "This her?" he asks and Chris nods. The man tilts his buzz-cut head, thinking as he looks me over. I shiver at the stare from his ice-blue eyes, and then he nods, as if agreeing to something with someone, but I can't see an earpiece. He looks back to Chris. "He was trying to get in with the London mob as an enforcer," he continues as if he didn't just pause to assess me. "He was told to sort something out for them, get payment back for something, but he didn't. He went up and did what he did."

He rubs his hands over his eyes and turns away from us to look out of the window, the same as Chris.

"They said they won't go after him while he's inside," Chris states. I look at him, not quite sure I'm hearing what I am. "Unless there's due cause to do so."

Smithy leans into the support pole. "He still makes statements about how he's going to sort out his *old lady, even if she is somewhere with a blue rat'* and thinks he's gotten back in with us."

Chris sighs heavily. "I don't want him coming after us, or her, at all. Ever." I gasp and turn my head to hide my face from this other man. I scrunch my eyes closed, wishing I could do the same with my ears. Stevo leans down to me. "Twirl, look at me, please?" he encourages, and I do, silently pleading to not do this. "He still wants to do you harm, twirl. I ain't havin' it."

"You'll have him killed?" I ask quietly, hoping that I don't throw up. Chris shakes his head, his eyes soft.

"No. Though I want him to understand, he'll be dead if he tries," he says, looking at the other man. "Can you get that message through his thick skull?"

Smithy nods. "We can. Mob lot have cut him loose, told him he's not wanted, not what they need. So, he's on his own," he confirms slowly. "We've made him think he's back in with us. Far from the bloody truth."

Chris sighs. "Do what you gotta, but as my twirl says..."

Smithy nods and backs away. At the next stop, he hops off. *Did Chris just speak to a gang and arrange to have my ex beaten up?*

I'm still stunned by the time we get to Southwark station. Craig is waiting for us, as are Jean and Ruby. They're excited to see us and hug us. I try to play along, but I'm unable to engage with them. Ruby notices something and taps Stevo, then signs to him very fast. He sighs and signs something back, and then she slaps him on the shoulder, pushing him. She grabs me and marches off, dragging me behind her.

"Ruby, wait," I say, but she shakes her head. She darts under a canopy, then pulls open the door and ushers me inside. It's a café, and the aroma of coffee, cake, paninis and people hits me.

She points to a table and motions for me to sit, then holds up her hand, asking me to wait. I nod. She signs her order at the staff, who clearly knows her as they sign back to her, then she's back with me. From her bag, she pulls out a small whiteboard and a pen.

I grin; she knows I don't sign very well and is catering for me. A waitress comes over with two slices of a layered cake, tea, coffee and a pile of napkins. Ruby and the waitress sign something, then she smiles, tells me to enjoy and goes on with her job.

Ruby taps me and points to the board.

"I know who he talked to," she writes.

I lean into her, so I can reply quietly, knowing she can hear me.

"I don't like that he's just asked someone to beat up my ex," I say and Ruby clears the board to write her reply.

"Would you rather he comes after you again?"

I gape. No, I don't want that, so I shake my head. I watch as Ruby clears the board again; knowing she'll do that with each reply, I begin to ignore her doing it.

"Stevo doesn't want you having to look over your shoulder. You deserve to be free."

I can't reply to that—I have no idea how deranged my ex is. Ruby nudges me and carries on with her essay.

"Some guys only take the hint when you beat it into them. Your ex is one of them. The guy you met—Smithy—his girl was beaten up by a client when she worked the sex trade. He found her dumped, helped her get better, and got her out of the trade. He takes a very dim view of what your ex did."

She holds the board so that I can see it and I nod. Then she carries on. "If Chris didn't ask, Smithy would have done it anyway. We've been talking about your situation for weeks down here. Chris got out of the gangs, we did too, Dad made sure of it. Smithy makes sure we're left alone, as does our old gang. This..." She makes sure I've read with a nod. "If he did come after you, Chris would go after him; Smithy's lot and our old gang would back him up because that's what they do. Gang equals family, even if we don't talk. We don't need the tension, neither does Smithy."

I sigh and take a sip of tea, letting her carry on telling me what she wants to. "This is heading it off at the pass, preventing an escalation, okay?" She smiles, then hugs me before writing out her next statement. "He'd go to war over you. He's never done that for anyone before," she writes, before drawing a heart on the whiteboard.

I twizzle the engagement ring, then I nod in understanding.

"I didn't want this," I whisper to her and she smiles.

"No one does," she writes. Then she wipes the board and pulls out a red dry wipe pen, before drawing hearts all over the board. "He loves you," she writes in a corner. I grin, still unsure.

"I'm glad you're a part of the family," she adds while giving me a huge smile. Then, she picks up her fork and begins eating the cake, encouraging me with gestures to do the same.

An hour later, we're at her family home. Jean comes to greet us and drags Ruby off when Chris appears, hugging me fiercely.

"Are you okay, twirl?" he asks, his voice shaky.

"I am now I've spoken with Ruby," I admit, handing Chris my wet coat. "I didn't like witnessing that." Suddenly, I'm in his arms being held.

"I know, twirl, but I needed you to see that I don't want him hurt either, but that I will take measures to ensure you're safe, yeah?" He rubs my back as he holds me. "Did Ruby tell you what'll happen if he comes after you? I wanted to tell you, but she dragged you away so fast." He half chuckles and I smile as I nod against his hard chest.

"Yes, she told me." I pull back so I can look at his amber eyes. "Would you really start a gang war over me?" I ask and he nods. Now I feel like Helen of Troy. "I would never have asked that of you," I state and he smiles.

"You didn't need to. What happens to Anderson now is on his head. It depends on what he does and says to his old gang now, remember? Nothing to do with us." He leans down. "But I do have to ask...if the cops come asking, he asked for some fags, then left and we didn't speak beyond me handing him a few, okay?" he clarifies.

I gasp, but nod, praying in my mind that we don't get the police visiting us here, or back home, over my ex.

Chris kisses me on the temple, then Jean comes up to us.

"Put her down, Christopher," she scolds and Chris sighs, rolling his eyes. It makes me giggle how he obeys the lady that raised him and as the evening wears on, I understand why he does. She does remind me of some of Chris's colleagues on the base.

"I'm sorry about all the theatrics," she says later, smiling at me when it's just us girls.

"I hope that's the last of it," I say and Jean agrees.

"Me too. I'd like a quiet alleyway chat with your ex myself, but the lads won't hear of it." She smirks, motioning to the living room.

I can hear the TV, but it's not loud.

"You'll get to meet Maxine on Christmas Eve, but come on in, let's have a chat," she says. Ruby appears and smiles, asking me how I am. I sign back shakily that I'm okay and thank her for the talk.

Ruby smiles broadly and tells me that I'm welcome, before signing something quickly to Jean, who nods.

"Be back for 6? I'd like to at least have one meal with you this week," she instructs. Ruby rolls her eyes and waves, then puts on her coat and vanishes.

I glance at Jean, then back to the front door as it clicks shut.

"She's got a guy that gets her," she says, her smile happy. "It's nice to see all the kids settling down."

"Especially Chris?" I ask as I catch her looking towards the living room where Chris and Craig are, and Jean nods.

"Given his parents, he was our biggest concern, especially when he went into the RAF. But it's all paid off." She smiles, touching me on the arm.

"Can I help you with anything?" I ask as she sorts something out on the cooker.

"Could you ready the green beans?" she asks and I nod. Jean passes me the knife and chopping board and I get on with destringing the beans and chopping them up roughly for the saucepan.

"I hope what happened earlier didn't scare you," she tells me, "though I guess it did."

"Yeah, it did. Chatting with Ruby helped," I reply as I cut the beans. "I've...no one has done that for me before. Not even my own parents," I confess.

"Wanna tell me about them?" Jean questions, smiling. She reminds me of Dave with her caring nature, the need to provide and protect, and welcoming me into the family as if I've always been here.

"Not really," I quietly reply. "They won't be at my wedding and I'm not going to find and tell them." There's a laugh from the doorway and Chris is there with Craig.

"I wouldn't want them there either," Chris says, grinning at me before he comes up to me and hugs me.

"What else needs doing, Jean?" Chris asks and she instructs him to set the table for six people. Though it's just past four o'clock now, there's a lot to get ready.

Much later, after I've met Richard and he's taken the mickey out of Chris for finding someone quieter than Ruby to join their noisy family, Jean drags me off as the men clear up. Ruby joins us, bringing her whiteboard with her.

We chat about how I met Chris and what our plans were for the future. Maxine arrives with her two kids and her partner, sharing that they're engaged now too, much to Jean and Craig's delight. We get talking about what kind of weddings we want and I confess that I loved Rosie's RAF wedding. Maxine and John are organising a registry office wedding and she shows me pictures of the old Victorian building where they met for another friend's wedding. It's very picturesque and atmospheric.

That night, huddled into Chris in the double bed, we talk quietly.

"Would you really want a military wedding, twirl?" he asks and I sigh, afraid that I bought up Rosie and Byron's. "Emma?" Chris asks, shifting so that he's above me but not threatening.

"It's a part of you," I confess. "I loved the men in uniform, seeing you all dressed up like that, the sword arch...the party atmosphere from everyone, even your Wing Commander."

I feel, rather than see, his reaction; the soft huff of his breath on my face makes me think he's smiling. The next words he says make me realise he was smiling.

"If that's what you want, twirl," he tells me, his voice light before he kisses me. "Byron gets to find out just how much work you and I did for him." He chuckles, pulls me close and holds me until the morning.

It's Christmas Eve and not even dawn when I hear footsteps running down the hall and Chris laughs.

"Ruby," he whispers as I stir. "It's not Christmas until tomorrow," he teases. Then we hear the front door being knocked and Chris is up and off to see what's going on, half-dressed in boxers and checked pyjama bottoms. He comes back a few moments later and throws on a pyjama top.

"Ruby's fella's here and I hear Jean and Craig are awake." He grins. I smile and get up to meet the newest member of this ever-growing family.

In the kitchen, Ruby has tears streaming down her face and she seems very happy. When she shows Jean her engagement finger, I get why. It's a rectangular engagement ring and Chris slaps the guy on the shoulder.

"Three next year! You two are going to be busy," Chris tells Craig and Jean, switching on the bean-to-cup machine that takes up a corner. I swear his family live on freshly brewed coffee.

"Yeah, it is going to be busy!" Jean agrees and we get introduced to Gary, a policeman with the Met. Ruby doesn't leave his side and answers Craig and Jean as they sign her questions.

Chris translates and Gary responds verbally, signing questions only meant for Ruby.

"She's not decided what kind of wedding she wants," he tells us all after some frantic hand gestures. He leans down and suggests something to her quietly, and then she's darting off and I can hear her feet thud up the stairs, making the guys laugh.

"I think you've just made her Christmas," Craig tells him, smiling.

"I think I may have. It's been hard, not asking her before now." Gary grins. "I think you're Emma?" he says and I nod, offering my hand in greeting. He smirks, taking it. "Ruby's told me all about you and your books. They've kept her busy," he adds, and I tilt my head at him. "She's loved editing them, reading them and re-reading them. She's even designed some covers for you. She's had fun." His smile is warm and his eyes dance.

"I'm glad," I tell him. Then, he leans across and lowers his voice.

"I'd love to gift her printed, physical copies. Let me know when and I'll pay you for them," he says. I blink; I wasn't expecting that!

"You...would?" I reply, doubting his sincerity and he nods.

"I would," he says and stands up as Ruby comes in freshly dressed, signing something to him. As he signs back, he says the same words.

"Just talking to my new sister-in-law about her books, nothing more." He smiles at her and she signs back something, making him laugh. "Did you think I'd learn all this, for just anyone?" he asks as his hands move quickly. Ruby shakes her head and jumps at him, then comes and hugs me, tells me she loves me and grabs her fiancé. Chris comes over at that point and when Ruby's out of earshot, I quietly tell him what Gary said to me.

"Are you going to publish them?" he asks, his voice is tight and I shrug.

"I wasn't writing them for that, but after all this work, it would be a mistake not to, wouldn't it?" He winks at me as he pops some snacks into his mouth that Jean is just putting out. She slaps his hand as he reaches across for more.

"Christopher, you can help set it all out," she scolds him. Chris rolls his eyes, but he has a cheeky grin on his face. I smirk and offer to help make breakfast as the rest of the house wakes to the news of another engagement.

Ruby and Gary head off after breakfast, promising to be back on Christmas morning for the presents. They're going to Gary's parents to tell them and they're nearer to Ealing. They're wished a safe journey and I help Jean prepare tomorrow's huge dinner, as well as today's snack-a-thon. Craig and Rich make a huge pile of toasted sandwiches for lunch later in the afternoon, and even though it doesn't look like much, I can't eat anymore come early evening.

We laugh at TV shows, watch movies and generally just chill out. Chris gets a text message that he responds to and he promises to tell me about it later. At bedtime, I ask him about it again, but he says he'll tell me about it when he's ready. I nod, trusting him.

Christmas morning and Ruby's feet thump across the landing, then back to her room at six am. We groan and stay in bed, which we think she's doing. We're just dozing back off, half an hour later, when Ruby starts thumping on the bedroom doors and Gary's voice rings out with her knocks.

"It's Christmas!" He imitates the Slade song. Chris and I groan, but we wrap ourselves up in dressing gowns and head down.

"I should have warned you," he moans and heads straight for the kitchen and the coffee machine first. I laugh but put the kettle on, finding that Gary also prefers tea to coffee. He comments that at least he won't be alone if there are large gatherings.

Once everyone has a drink, we begin opening the gifts and there are a few under the tree for me. I wasn't expecting anything and I'm glad that we have some for everyone, well, except Gary, but he waves us off, saying being here is enough. He pulls Ruby to him and kisses her temple, which makes her smile and wiggle further into his embrace.

A new jumper, jeans, boots and a necklace later, I feel loved. Everyone has new clothes, snacks or vouchers for stores. Maxine arrives with her fiancé and their kids, with more presents and before long it's time to eat. I hadn't noticed Jean wasn't with us, but she says she has it all under control and winks at me. Goodness knows how she's done it.

We sit and eat as one huge family, except for the kids who are at a table by themselves with their new toys and under Maxine's watchful eyes. The family laughs and jokes, sprinkled with Ruby signing something and Chris translating for me. Everyone voices their responses back and Gary spends most of his time replying to Ruby, though, at one point, I think what she said and what he voiced were two different answers. Then he points to the kids and she rolls her eyes but nods. *My soon-to-be sister-in-law seems to have a potty mouth.*

Everyone helps clear up the wrappings, the dinner, and the mess. Even the kids clear their own little table down which impresses me. They've been polite and mindful all day, lost in their own little world with their new toys and gadgets. As soon as Craig and Jean sit down, they're on their grandparents' laps for cuddles and it's not long before almost everyone is snoozing.

I cuddle up to Chris as we chill, whiling the hours away. We watch the Queen's speech, the first time ever for me and I'm entranced by Her Majesty. *How is the lady still working at her age?* Chris and Gary watch and when it's over, they begin discussing some of the points made. I roll my eyes and let them get on with it, deciding to help Jean in the kitchen with more drinks.

"Oh, it's been a lovely day!" she tells me and she looks happy. "You're good for him. You let me know if he does something daft, okay?"

I blink. "Will he?" I ask, getting nervous.

Jean laughs. "He's a guy, sweetie, he will!"

Chapter Twenty-Eight

Epilogue

Chris

The time spent with the family isn't long enough. Ruby getting engaged on Christmas Eve, Maxine telling us she was engaged the day before and the many, many discussions about weddings mean I'm glad to get back to work. On the way back, I share an update about her ex with Emma. Smithy's lot delivered a dire message to him from Smithy himself.

When he was asked about it, I'm told that Anderson says he didn't know who jumped him. I don't tell Emma just how extensive the injuries to Anderson were, but a car crash might have been kinder. Gary was aware of the situation and discreetly found out, not that we asked him. The single text from Smithy was simple: *He's been told*.

When I tell Emma, we're on the train back home, having left London; she just sighs and goes quiet on me for a short while. In the silence, I think of my family: Ruby's moving out to be with Gary and out of Southwark, Rich was contemplating asking his girl to marry him, but wouldn't be drawn on more details.

"What did they do to him?" she asks me about twenty minutes later and I feign ignorance.

"No idea, twirl. Best we don't know, eh?" I encourage and she nods. I hate lying, but if she didn't like the chat with Smithy on the way down, she sure won't like the results of it.

We get back to Lincoln and a short cab ride later, we're at the flat. It doesn't take too long for the heating to warm up the place and for us to unpack.

Months later, I sigh as I pull at my dress jacket again, the hangover from the stag night pushed away thanks to some decent painkillers.

"Shoe is on the other foot," Byron sniggers at me and I discreetly give him the middle finger. My family are here, every one of them. Ruby and Gary married at the registry office as soon as they could on January 21st. It's nearly May now and Ruby's already sporting a nice, round bump, much to Jean's delight. Richard proposed on Valentine's Day and they're sat together. Helen is certainly the quieter of the girls, though with Maxine and Ruby, that ain't so hard.

Andy Hodgeson is doing the photography again and Nigel volunteered to give Emma away as she's gotten close to Nic at the café, until Byron told me that Lorenzo and Ava were coming. Nigel was happy to let Byron's dad take that honour; it seems his parents have adopted us as extra children as much as mine have taken to Emma.

We've taken our time to get things organised this time, much to Chaplain Graeme's delight. Boomer is on Emma's side of the chapel, as is Nic and Johnson and I'm grateful for that. I nod to the women with a tight smile, pulling at my jacket and checking the time. *She's running late. Is she not coming? What's happened?* I wipe my hands on my dress trousers and swallow hard. Boomer winks at me and I see Ava scoot to the bridal side and take her seat. *She's here, she made it!*

The music starts and I breathe a sigh of relief. Everyone stands as Emma slowly walks down the aisle with Lorenzo. Before her is Rosie and Dave's nurse, Claire. I wasn't expecting the nurse, maybe that's why Emma was running late?

When Claire steps out of the way as the 'flower' girl, I get to see my bride and I'm speechless. Byron nudges me.

"Fly-trap, close yer mouth," he chuckles at me in a soft Scottish accent. Git gets me back for his wedding.

Our first dance is something Byron and Rosie helped me pick—'Hero' by Enrique Iglesias. Given Emma's success with her books, it was rather fitting as she's had great reviews about them, especially her Alpha Heroes. Each dedication is to me, Rosie, Byron, my family and their love for her. She sends a special message up for Dave too. In every book, she buries something he's said to her within it, a nugget of wisdom.

"Twirl, I've booked a honeymoon for after I leave the service. I hope you're okay to wait?" I ask as I twirl her around the dance floor, silently thanking Johnson for the lessons.

"Sure. Where to?" she asks and I grin.

"Italy," I explain. "A week with Ava and Lorenzo, they're insisting. Then a few days in Venice and down to Napoli, before heading back to be with Ava."

"You've got it all planned," she tells me, her voice light and carefree. I nod, before kissing her as the song stops.

"I hope so, Mrs Stevenson," I smirk and she laughs at me, making our evening together light and happy.

Emma

Chris is out of the RAF. Byron will follow suit in a few short weeks, long enough for us to have our honeymoon at his parents, a few days in Venice, Napoli then back to Bologna, before we return home and head to Edinburgh.

When we land, Ava and Lorenzo are waiting for us. The sun is shining and it's warm, sticky, and close as if a thunderstorm is brewing.

"Come on, let's get back to the air con," Ava instructs and we let them boss us around. As Lorenzo drives, Ava tells us how happy she is that we are married and that they were there.

The money from Dave's will has been put into a bank account, and sat there doing nothing more than accruing interest for me—us—when we build our own.

At the Mancini's, we get to chill out and we learn quickly to rest in the heat of the day and explore in the coolness of the evening. At night, the village lights up. Small lanterns in the open windows of the shops are lit, and the lights inside are on low. I enjoy exploring the small bookshops on the colourful cobbled streets. We indulge in sweets from the bakeries and cake shops. I over-indulge the first night and the following day, I can't eat anything Ava offers to me. Chris pokes fun at me but I learn to cut back. It's a full day before I feel hungry enough to actually eat.

In Venice, we enjoy boat rides. Lorenzo has lent us a small family-owned house that's literally two up, two down. A kitchen and bathroom downstairs, a bedroom and sitting room upstairs. The sitting room overlooks the best waterways, the bedroom hasn't quite got the same spectacular view. Following his advice, we operate the shutters and veils, which makes the place much cooler when we need it the most: siesta time.

Napoli is different again and we explore hand in hand. We're given gifts when people learn we're on our honeymoon, so much so that we stop telling shopkeepers and street vendors. I still can't drink coffee; the taste doesn't agree with me and the smell has gotten to me too.

On return to Bologna, Lorenzo and Ava ensure that we experience the quieter side of Italy, the real Italy as Lorenzo calls it. We're nearing the end of our stay here and I'm sad to leave, but it's time to go back. We've jobs to apply for, a house to build and it seems that the McGowans have learned of a plot of land that might suit our plans. We just need to return to Edinburgh.

"Is this the right place?" Chris asks the cab driver and he nods.

"Aye, this is the address ye gave me," he says as he gets out and takes our cases out of the boot.

This house is huge; it can't be the house I agreed to rent. It's like a mansion, set back and behind a gate. Chris presses the buzzer and there's a cackle, and then we hear Byron's voice.

"There ye are! I'll come to help you with the cases," he tells us and there's a 'ping' as the gate releases. The cabbie shouts out a hearty goodbye and leaves. I look at Chris, wide-eyed, wondering what we've gotten ourselves into now.

Resources:

Website for 5 False Reasons

(https://www.aconsciousrethink.com/14528/i-dont-deserve-love/)

This was a good source for Emma's beliefs. If what she's gone through resonates, I hope this helps.

My Other Works

Dutch Bound Trilogy

Gone Dutch - books2read.com/gonedutch

Going Forward - books2read.com/goingforward

Gone Strong - books2read.com/gonestrong

Tango Down Duology

Dionadair - books2read.com/ourdefender

Trodaiche - books2read.com/myfighter

Standalone

The Storyteller - books2read.com/thestorytellerlm

Relight My Fire - Firehouse 49, Book 6 - books2read.com/relightmyfire

Let's Be Friends

COME AND STALK ME WITH APPRECIATION;

Follow me on

Instagram

@louisemurchieauthor

Facebook

https://www.facebook.com/louisemurchieauthor

Tik Tok

https://www.tiktok.com/@louisemurchieauthor

Visit my website and subscribe to my newsletter!

https://louisemurchie.com/newsletter

About The Author

Louise lives in the West Midlands with her husband and children. Scottish born and bred alas, she doesn't live in Scotland any more. Her heart though always will be in the mist-covered mountains.

She writes for the more mature characters, often in a #sweetwithheat setting and for the over 35s; because as she says, she's no 21 anymore!

Not all of them are Scottish, though there's going to be a connection to that place, somehow!